SANCTUARY

It was an ancient privilege the dying man seemed to claim: fleeing to a church for sanctuary. Yet who was he? And why had he come to so distant a hamlet as Chipping Cleghorn?

He was dead on the chancel steps before he could explain.

The only clue was a ticket sewn into his shabby jacket. The vicar's wife took it to her godmother, Miss Marple, and together they set out to trace its owner's dread secret—a secret others wanted, and were prepared to kill for . . . again and again!

AGATHA CHRISTIE

13

CLUES
FOR
MISS
MARPLE

A DELL BOOK

Published by
Dell Publishing Co., Inc.
1 Dag Hammarskjold Plaza
New York, New York 10017

PRESENTING MISS MARPLE

For many years Jane Marple has lived next door to the rectory in the little town of St. Mary Mead, not far from London. In some ways she is quite unusual; she can be sweet-faced, sharp-eyed and vinegar-tongued all at the same time. Otherwise she is busy with the commonplaces of marketing and knitting and the usual social diversions of a small town. Actually she is a charter member of the famous Tuesday Night Club whose membership, composed of local celebrities—a popular actress, a widely read novelist, a former commissioner of Scotland Yard and others—meets weekly. Each member in turn propounds a problem of which he knows the answer and invites the others present to solve the mystery.

In working out these mysteries, Miss Marple is most successful. Although most of the incidents happened in the world outside little St. Mary Mead, she maintains that people are much the same everywhere. Very painful and distressing things happen in villages sometimes, she insists. And once the mystery puzzle is explained in all its details, her swift mind goes straight to the truth, like a homing pigeon.

This book contains thirteen mystery stories in each of which the solution is brought about by a clue discovered by Miss Marple. It is a pleasure to present one of the most engaging characters ever to appear in the literature of crime stories, in print or on the screen.

R. T. B.

CONTENTS

TAPE-MEASURE MURDER

Miss Politt took hold of the knocker and rapped politely on the cottage door. After a discreet interval she knocked again. The parcel under her left arm shifted a little as she did so, and she readjusted it. Inside the parcel was Mrs. Spenlow's new green winter dress, ready for fitting. From Miss Politt's left hand dangled a bag of black silk, containing a tape measure, a pincushion, and a large, practical pair of scissors.

Miss Politt was tall and gaunt, with a sharp nose, pursed lips, and meager iron-grey hair. She hesitated before using the knocker for the third time. Glancing down the street, she saw a figure rapidly approaching. Miss Hartnell, jolly, weather-beaten, fifty-five, shouted out in her usual loud bass voice, "Good afternoon, Miss Politt!"

The dressmaker answered, "Good afternoon, Miss Hartnell." Her voice was excessively thin and genteel in its accents. She had started life as a lady's maid. "Excuse me," she went on, "but do you happen to know if by any chance Mrs. Spenlow isn't at home?"

"Not the least idea," said Miss Hartnell.

"It's rather awkward, you see. I was to fit on Mrs. Spenlow's new dress this afternoon. Three-thirty, she said."

Miss Hartnell consulted her wrist watch. "It's a little past the half-hour now."

"Yes. I have knocked three times, but there doesn't seem to be any answer, so I was wondering if perhaps Mrs. Spenlow might have gone out and forgotten. She doesn't forget appointments as a rule, and she wants the dress to wear the day after tomorrow."

Miss Hartnell entered the gate and walked up the path to

join Miss Politt outside the door of Laburnam Cottage.

"Why doesn't Gladys answer the door?" she demanded. "Oh, no, of course, it's Thursday—Gladys's day out. I expect Mrs. Spenlow has fallen asleep. I don't expect you've made enough noise with this thing."

Seizing the knocker, she executed a deafening *rat-a-tat-tat* and, in addition, thumped upon the panels of the door. She also called out in a stentorian voice: "What ho, within there!"

There was no response.

Miss Politt murmured, "Oh, I think Mrs. Spenlow must have forgotten and gone out. I'll call round some other time." She began edging away down the path.

"Nonsense," said Miss Hartnell firmly. "She can't have gone out. I'd have met her. I'll just take a look through the windows and see if I can find any signs of life."

She laughed in her usual hearty manner, to indicate that it was a joke, and applied a perfunctory glance to the nearest windowpane—perfunctory because she knew quite well that the front room was seldom used, Mr. and Mrs. Spenlow preferring the small back sitting room.

Perfunctory as it was, though, it succeeded in its object. Miss Hartnell, it is true, saw no signs of life. On the contrary, she saw, through the window, Mrs. Spenlow lying on the hearthrug—dead.

"Of course," said Miss Hartnell, telling the story afterward, "I managed to keep my head. That Politt creature wouldn't have had the least idea of what to do. 'Got to keep our heads,' I said to her. 'You stay here and I'll go for Constable Palk.' She said something about not wanting to be left, but I paid no attention at all. One has to be firm with that sort of person. I've always found they enjoy making a fuss. So I was just going off when, at that very moment, Mr. Spenlow came round the corner of the house."

Here Miss Hartnell made a significant pause. It enabled her audience to ask breathlessly, "Tell me, how did he look?"

Miss Hartnell would then go on: "Frankly, I suspected something at once! He was far too calm. He didn't seem surprised in the least. And you may say what you like, it isn't natural for a man to hear that his wife is dead and display no emotion whatever."

Everybody agreed with this statement.

The police agreed with it too. So suspicious did they consider Mr. Spenlow's detachment that they lost no time in ascertaining how that gentleman was situated as a result of his wife's death. When they discovered that Mrs. Spenlow had been the moneyed partner, and that her money went to her husband under a will made soon after their marriage, they were more suspicious than ever.

Miss Marple, that sweet-faced (and some said vinegar-tongued) elderly spinster who lived in the house next to the rectory, was interviewed very early—within half an hour of the discovery of the crime. She was approached by Police Constable Palk, importantly thumbing a notebook. "If you don't mind, ma'am, I've a few questions to ask you."

Miss Marple said, "In connection with the murder of Mrs. Spenlow?"

Palk was startled. "May I ask, madam, how you got to know of it?"

"The fish," said Miss Marple.

The reply was perfectly intelligible to Constable Palk. He assumed correctly that the fishmonger's boy had brought it, together with Miss Marple's evening meal.

Miss Marple continued gently, "Lying on the floor in the sitting room, strangled—possibly by a very narrow belt. But whatever it was, it was taken away."

Palk's face was wrathful. "How that young Fred gets to know everything—"

Miss Marple cut him short adroitly. She said, "There's a pin in your tunic."

Constable Palk looked down, startled. He said, "They do say: 'See a pin and pick it up, all the day you'll have good luck.' "

"I hope that will come true. Now what is it you want me to tell you?"

Constable Palk cleared his throat, looked important, and consulted his notebook. "Statement was made to me by Mr. Arthur Spenlow, husband of the deceased. Mr. Spenlow says that at two-thirty, as far as he can say, he was rung up by Miss Marple and asked if he would come over at a quarter past three, as she was anxious to consult him about something. Now, ma'am, is that true?"

"Certainly not," said Miss Marple.

"You did not ring up Mr. Spenlow at two-thirty?"

"Neither at two-thirty nor any other time."

"Ah," said Constable Palk, and sucked his moustache with a good deal of satisfaction.

"What else did Mr. Spenlow say?"

"Mr. Spenlow's statement was that he came over here as requested, leaving his own house at ten minutes past three; that on arrival here he was informed by the maidservant that Miss Marple was 'not at 'ome.' "

"That part of it is true," said Miss Marple. "He did come here, but I was at a meeting at the Women's Institute."

"Ah," said Constable Palk again.

Miss Marple exclaimed, "Do tell me, Constable, do you suspect Mr. Spenlow?"

"It's not for me to say at this stage, but it looks to me as though somebody, naming no names, had been trying to be artful."

Miss Marple said thoughtfully, "Mr. Spenlow?"

She liked Mr. Spenlow. He was a small, spare man, stiff and conventional in speech, the acme of respectability. It seemed odd that he should have come to live in the country; he had so clearly lived in towns all his life. To Miss Marple he confided the reason. He said, "I have always intended, ever since I was a small boy, to live in the country someday and have a garden of my own. I have always been very much attached to flowers. My wife, you know, kept a flower shop. That's where I saw her first."

A dry statement, but it opened up a vista of romance. A younger, prettier Mrs. Spenlow, seen against a background of flowers.

Mr. Spenlow, however, really knew nothing about flowers. He had no idea of seeds, of cuttings, of bedding out, of annuals or perennials. He had only a vision—a vision of a small cottage garden thickly planted with sweet-smelling, brightly coloured blossoms. He had asked, almost pathetically, for instruction and had noted down Miss Marple's replies to questions in a little book.

He was a man of quiet method. It was, perhaps, because of this trait that the police were interested in him when his wife was found murdered. With patience and perseverance they learned a good deal about the late Mrs. Spenlow—and soon all St. Mary Mead knew it too.

The late Mrs. Spenlow had begun life as a betweenmaid in a large house. She had left that position to marry the second gardener and with him had started a flower shop in London. The shop had prospered. Not so the gardener, who before long had sickened and died.

His widow had carried on the shop and enlarged it in an ambitious way. She had continued to prosper. Then she had sold the business at a handsome price and embarked upon matrimony for the second time—with Mr. Spenlow, a middle-aged jeweler who had inherited a small and struggling business. Not long afterward they had sold the business and come down to St. Mary Mead.

Mrs. Spenlow was a well-to-do woman. The profits from her florist's establishment she had invested—"under spirit guidance," as she explained to all and sundry. The spirits had advised her with unexpected acumen.

All her investments had prospered, some in quite a sensational fashion. Instead, however, of this increasing her belief in spiritualism, Mrs. Spenlow basely deserted mediums and sittings and made a brief but wholehearted plunge into an obscure religion with Indian affinities which was based on various forms of deep breathing. When, however, she arrived at St. Mary Mead, she had relapsed into a period of orthodox Church-of-England beliefs. She was a good deal at the Vicarage and attended church services with assiduity. She patronized the village shops, took an interest in the local happenings, and played village bridge.

A humdrum, everyday life. And—suddenly—murder.

Colonel Melchett, the chief constable, had summoned Inspector Slack.

Slack was a positive type of man. When he made up his mind, he was sure. He was quite sure now. "Husband did it, sir," he said.

"You think so?"

"Quite sure of it. You've only got to look at him. Never showed a sign of grief or emotion. He came back to the house knowing she was dead."

"Wouldn't he at least have tried to act the part of the distracted husband?"

"Not him, sir. Too pleased with himself. Some gentle-men can't act. Too stiff. As I see it, he was just fed up with his wife. She'd got the money and, I should say, was a trying woman to live with—always taking up some 'ism' or other. He cold-bloodedly decided to do away with her and live comfortably on his own."

"Yes, that could be the case, I suppose."

"Depend upon it, that was it. Made his plans careful. Pretended to get a phone call—"

Melchett interrupted him: "No call been traced?"

"No, sir. That means either that he lied or that the call was put through from a public telephone booth. The only two public phones in the village are at the station and the post office. Post office it certainly wasn't. Mrs. Blade sees everyone who comes in. Station it might be. Train arrives at two twenty-seven and there's a bit of bustle then. But the main thing is he says it was Miss Marple who called him up, and that certainly isn't true. The call didn't come from her house, and she herself was away at the Institute."

"You're not overlooking the possibility that the husband was deliberately got out of the way—by someone who wanted to murder Mrs. Spenlow?"

"You're thinking of young Ted Gerard, aren't you, sir? I've been working on him—what we're up against there is lack of motive. He doesn't stand to gain anything."

"He's an undesirable character, though. Quite a pretty little spot of embezzlement to his credit."

"I'm not saying he isn't a wrong 'un. Still, he did go to his boss and own up to that embezzlement. And his em-ployers weren't wise to it."

"An Oxford Grouper," said Melchett.

"Yes, sir. Became a convert and went off to do the straight thing and own up to having pinched money. I'm not saying, mind you, that it mayn't have been astuteness —he may have thought he was suspected and decided to gamble on honest repentance."

"You have a skeptical mind, Slack," said Colonel Mel-chett. "By the way, have you talked to Miss Marple at all?"

"What's she got to do with it, sir?"

"Oh, nothing. But she hears things, you know. Why don't you go and have a chat with her? She's a very sharp old lady."

Slack changed the subject. "One thing I've been meaning to ask you, sir: That domestic-service job where the deceased started her career—Sir Robert Abercrombie's place. That's where that jewel robbery was—emeralds—worth a packet. Never got them. I've been looking it up—must have happened when the Spenlow woman was there, though she'd have been quite a girl at the time. Don't think she was mixed up in in it, do you, sir? Spenlow, you know, was one of those little tuppenny-ha'penny jewelers—just the chap for a fence."

Melchett shook his head. "Don't think there's anything in that. She didn't even know Spenlow at the time. I remember the case. Opinion in police circles was that a son of the house was mixed up in it—Jim Abercrombie—awful young waster. Had a pile of debts, and just after the robbery they were all paid off—some rich woman, so they said, but I don't know—old Abercrombie hedged a bit about the case—tried to call the police off."

"It was just an idea, sir," said Slack.

Miss Marple received Inspector Slack with gratification, especially when she heard that he had been sent by Colonel Melchett.

"Now, really, that is very kind of Colonel Melchett. I didn't know he remembered me."

"He remembers you, all right. Told me that what you didn't know of what goes on in St. Mary Mead isn't worth knowing."

"Too kind of him, but really I don't know anything at all. About this murder, I mean."

"You know what the talk about it is."

"Of course—but it wouldn't do, would it, to repeat just idle talk?"

Slack said, with an attempt at geniality, "This isn't an official conversation, you know. It's in confidence, so to speak."

"You mean you really want to know what people are saying? Whether there's any truth in it or not?"

"That's the idea."

"Well, of course, there's been a great deal of talk and speculation. And there are really two distinct camps, if you understand me. To begin with, there are the people who think that the husband did it. A husband or a wife is, in a way, the natural person to suspect, don't you think so?"

"Maybe," said the inspector cautiously.

"Such close quarters, you know. Then, so often, the money angle. I hear that it was Mrs. Spenlow who had the money and therefore Mr. Spenlow does benefit by her death. In this wicked world I'm afraid the most uncharitable assumptions are often justified."

"He comes into a tidy sum, all right."

"Just so. It would seem quite plausible, wouldn't it, for him to strangle her, leave the house by the back, come across the fields to my house, ask for me and pretend he'd had a telephone call from me, then go back and find his wife murdered in his absence—hoping, of course, that the crime would be put down to some tramp or burglar."

The inspector nodded. "What with the money angle—and if they'd been on bad terms lately—"

But Miss Marple interrupted him: "Oh, but they hadn't."

"You know that for a fact?"

"Everyone would have known if they'd quarrelled! The maid, Gladys Brent—she'd have soon spread it round the village."

The inspector said feebly, "She mightn't have known," and received a pitying smile in reply.

Miss Marple went on: "And then there's the other school of thought. Ted Gerard. A good-looking young man. I'm afraid, you know, that good looks are inclined to influence one more than they should. Our last curate but one—quite a magical effect! All the girls came to church—evening service as well as morning. And many older women became unusually active in parish work—and the slippers and scarves that were made for him! Quite embarrassing for the poor young man.

"But let me see, where was I? Oh yes, this young man, Ted Gerard. Of course, there has been talk about him. He's come down to see her so often. Though Mrs. Spenlow told me herself that he was a member of what I think they call the Oxford Group. A religious movement. They are quite sincere and very earnest, I believe, and Mrs. Spenlow was impressed by it all."

Miss Marple took a breath and went on: "And I'm sure

there was no reason to believe that there was anything more in it than that, but you know what people are. Quite a lot of people are convinced that Mrs. Spenlow was infatuated with the young man and that she'd lent him quite a lot of money. And it's perfectly true that he was actually seen at the station that day. In the train—the two twenty-seven down train. But of course it would be quite easy, wouldn't it, to slip out of the other side of the train and go through the cutting and over the fence and round by the hedge and never come out of the station entrance at all? So that he need not have been seen going to the cottage. And of course people do think that what Mrs. Spenlow was wearing was rather peculiar."

"Peculiar?"

"A kimono. Not a dress." Miss Marple blushed. "That sort of thing, you know, is, perhaps, rather suggestive to some people."

"You think it was suggestive?"

"Oh no, I don't think so. I think it was perfectly natural."

"You think it was natural?"

"Under the circumstances, yes." Miss Marple's glance was cool and reflective.

Inspector Slack said, "It might give us another motive for the husband. Jealousy."

"Oh no, Mr. Spenlow would never be jealous. He's not the sort of man who notices things. If his wife had gone away and left a note on the pincushion, it would be the first he'd know of anything of that kind."

Inspector Slack was puzzled by the intent way she was looking at him. He had an idea that all her conversation was intended to hint at something he didn't understand. She said now, with some emphasis, "Didn't you find any clues, Inspector—on the spot?"

"People don't leave fingerprints and cigarette ash nowadays, Miss Marple."

"But this, I think," she suggested, "was an old-fashioned crime—"

Slack said sharply, "Now what do you mean by that?"

Miss Marple remarked slowly, "I think, you know, that Constable Palk could help you. He was the first person on the—on the 'scene of the crime,' as they say."

Mr. Spenlow was sitting in a deck chair. He looked bewildered. He said, in his thin, precise voice, "I may, of course, be imagining what occurred. My hearing is not as good as it was. But I distinctly think I heard a small boy call after me, 'Yah, who's a Crippen?' It—it conveyed the impression to me that he was of the opinion that I had—had killed my dear wife."

Miss Marple, gently snipping off a dead rose head, said, "That was the impression he meant to convey, no doubt."

"But what could possibly have put such an idea into a child's head?"

Miss Marple coughed. "Listening, no doubt, to the opinions of his elders."

"You—you really mean that other people think that also?"

"Quite half the people in St. Mary Mead."

"But, my dear lady, what can possibly have given rise to such an idea? I was sincerely attached to my wife. She did not, alas, take to living in the country as much as I had hoped she would do, but perfect agreement on every subject is an impossible ideal. I assure you I feel her loss very keenly."

"Probably. But if you will excuse my saying so, you don't sound as though you do."

Mr. Spenlow drew his meager frame up to its full height. "My dear lady, many years ago I read of a certain Chinese philosopher who, when his dearly loved wife was taken from him, continued calmly to beat a gong in the street—a customary Chinese pastime, I presume—exactly as usual. The people of the city were much impressed by his fortitude."

"But," said Miss Marple, "the people of St. Mary Mead react rather differently. Chinese philosophy does not appeal to them."

"But you understand?"

Miss Marple nodded. "My uncle Henry," she explained, "was a man of unusual self-control. His motto was 'Never display emotion.' He, too, was very fond of flowers."

"I was thinking," said Mr. Spenlow with something like eagerness, "that I might, perhaps, have a pergola on the west side of the cottage. Pink roses and, perhaps, wisteria.

And there is a white starry flower, whose name for the moment escapes me—"

In the tone in which she spoke to her grandnephew, aged three, Miss Marple said, "I have a very nice catalogue here, with pictures. Perhaps you would like to look through it— I have to go up to the village."

Leaving Mr. Spenlow sitting happily in the garden with his catalogue, Miss Marple went up to her room, hastily rolled up a dress in a piece of brown paper, and, leaving the house, walked briskly up to the post office. Miss Politt, the dressmaker, lived in rooms over the post office.

But Miss Marple did not at once go through the door and up the stairs. It was just two-thirty, and, a minute late, the Much Benham bus drew up outside the post-office door. It was one of the events of the day in St. Mary Mead. The post-mistress hurried out with parcels, parcels connected with the shop side of her business, for the post office also dealt in sweets, cheap books, and children's toys.

For some four minutes Miss Marple was alone in the post office.

Not till the postmistress returned to her post did Miss Marple go upstairs and explain to Miss Politt that she wanted her own grey crepe altered and made more fashionable if that were possible. Miss Politt promised to see what she could do.

The chief constable was rather astonished when Miss Marple's name was brought to him. She came in with many apologies. "So sorry—so very sorry to disturb you. You are so busy, I know, but then you have always been so very kind, Colonel Melchett, and I felt I would rather come to you instead of to Inspector Slack. For one thing, you know, I should hate Constable Palk to get into any trouble. Strictly speaking, I suppose he shouldn't have touched anything at all."

Colonel Melchett was slightly bewildered. He said, "Palk? That's the St. Mary Mead constable, isn't it? What has he been doing?"

"He picked up a pin, you know. It was in his tunic. And it occurred to me at the time that it was quite probable he had actually picked it up in Mrs. Spenlow's house."

"Quite, quite. But, after all, you know, what's a pin? Matter of fact, he did pick the pin up just by Mrs. Spenlow's body. Came and told Slack about it yesterday—you put him up to that, I gather? Oughtn't to have touched anything, of course, but, as I said, what's a pin? It was only a common pin. Sort of thing any woman might use."

"Oh no, Colonel Melchett, that's where you're wrong. To a man's eye, perhaps, it looked like an ordinary pin, but it wasn't. It was a special pin, a very thin pin, the kind you buy by the box, the kind used mostly by dressmakers."

Melchett stared at her, a faint light of comprehension breaking in on him. Miss Marple nodded her head several times eagerly.

"Yes, of course. It seems to me so obvious. She was in her kimono because she was going to try on her new dress, and she went into the front room, and Miss Politt just said something about measurements and put the tape measure round her neck—and then all she'd have to do was to cross it and pull—quite easy, so I've heard. And then of course she'd go outside and pull the door to and stand there knocking as though she'd just arrived. But the pin shows she'd already been in the house."

"And it was Miss Politt who telephoned to Spenlow?"

"Yes. From the post office at two-thirty—just when the bus comes and the post office would be empty."

Colonel Melchett said, "But, my dear Miss Marple, why? In heaven's name, why? You can't have a murder without a motive."

"Well, I think, you know, Colonel Melchett, from all I've heard, that the crime dates from a long time back. It reminds me, you know, of my two cousins, Antony and Gordon. Whatever Antony did always went right for him, and with poor Gordon it was just the other way about; race horses went lame, and stocks went down, and property depreciated. . . . As I see it, the two women were in it together."

"In what?"

"The robbery. Long ago. Very valuable emeralds, so I've heard. The lady's maid and the tweeny. Because one thing hasn't been explained—how, when the tweeny married the gardener, did they have enough money to set up a flower shop?

"The answer is, it was her share of the—the swag, I think is the right expression. Everything she did turned out well. Money made money. But the other one, the lady's maid, must have been unlucky. She came down to being just a village dressmaker. Then they met again. Quite all right at first, I expect, until Mr. Ted Gerard came on the scene.

"Mrs. Spenlow, you see, was already suffering from conscience and was inclined to be emotionally religious. This young man no doubt urged her to 'face up' and to 'come clean,' and I daresay she was strung up to do so. But Miss Politt didn't see it that way. All she saw was that she might go to prison for a robbery she had committed years ago. So she made up her mind to put a stop to it all. I'm afraid, you know, that she was always rather a wicked woman. I don't believe she'd have turned a hair if that nice, stupid Mr. Spenlow had been hanged."

Colonel Melchett said slowly, "We can—er—verify your theory—up to a point. The identity of the Politt woman with the lady's maid at the Abercrombies', but—"

Miss Marple reassured him.

"It will be all quite easy. She's the kind of woman who will break down at once when she's taxed with the truth. And then, you see, I've got her tape measure. I—er—abstracted it yesterday when I was trying on. When she misses it and thinks the police have got it—well, she's quite an ignorant woman and she'll think it will prove the case against her in some way."

She smiled at him encouragingly. "You'll have no trouble, I can assure you." It was the tone in which his favourite aunt had once assured him that he could not fail to pass his entrance examination into Sandhurst.

And he had passed.

STRANGE JEST

"And this," said Jane Helier, completing her introductions, "is Miss Marple!"

Being an actress, she was able to make her point. It was clearly the climax, the triumphant finale! Her tone was equally compounded of reverent awe and triumph.

The odd part of it was that the object thus proudly proclaimed was merely a gentle elderly spinster. In the eyes of the two young people who had just, by Jane's good offices, made her acquaintance, there showed incredulity and a tinge of dismay. They were nice-looking people—the girl, Charmian Stroud, slim and dark; the man, Edward Rossiter, a fair-haired, amiable young giant.

Charmian said, a little breathlessly, "Oh, we're awfully pleased to meet you." But there was doubt in her eyes. She flung a quick, questioning glance at Jane Helier.

"Darling," said Jane, answering the glance, "she's absolutely marvellous. Leave it to her. I told you I'd get her here and I have." She added to Miss Marple; "You'll fix it for them, I know. It will be easy for you."

Miss Marple turned her placid, china-blue eyes toward Mr. Rossiter. "Won't you tell me," she said, "what all this is about?"

"Jane's a friend of ours," Charmian broke in impatiently. "Edward and I are in rather a fix. Jane said if we would come to her party, she'd introduce us to someone who was —who would—who could—"

Edward came to the rescue. "Jane tells us you're the last word in sleuths, Miss Marple!"

The old lady's eyes twinkled, but she protested modestly: "Oh no, no! Nothing of the kind. It's just that living in a village as I do, one gets to know so much about human nature. But really you have made me quite curious. Do tell me your problem."

"I'm afraid it's terribly hackneyed—just buried treasure," said Edward.

"Indeed? But that sounds most exciting!"

"I know. Like Treasure Island. But our problem lacks the usual romantic touches. No point on a chart indicated by a skull and crossbones, no directions like 'four paces to the left, west by north.' It's horribly prosaic—just where we ought to dig."

"Have you tried at all?"

"I should say we'd dug about two solid acres! The whole place is ready to be turned into a market garden. We're just discussing whether to grow vegetable marrows or potatoes."

Charmian said, rather abruptly, "May we really tell you all about it?"

"But, of course, my dear."

"Then let's find a peaceful spot. Come on, Edward." She led the way out of the overcrowded and smoke-laden room, and they went up the stairs, to a small sitting room on the second floor.

When they were seated, Charmian began abruptly: "Well, here goes! The story starts with Uncle Mathew, uncle—or rather, great-great-uncle—to both of us. He was incredibly ancient. Edward and I were his only relations. He was fond of us and always declared that when he died he would leave his money between us. Well, he died last March and left everything he had to be divided equally between Edward and myself. What I've just said sounds rather callous—I don't mean that it was right that he died—actually we were very fond of him. But he'd been ill for some time.

"The point is that the 'everything' he left turned out to be practically nothing at all. And that, frankly, was a bit of a blow to us both, wasn't it, Edward?"

The amiable Edward agreed. "You see," he said, "we'd counted on it a bit. I mean, when you know a good bit of money is coming to you, you don't—well—buckle down and try to make it yourself. I'm in the Army—not got anything to speak of outside my pay—and Charmian herself hasn't got a bean. She works as a stage manager in a repertory theater—quite interesting and she enjoys it—but no money in it. We'd counted on getting married but weren't worried about the money side of it because we both knew we'd be jolly well off some day."

"And now, you see, we're not!" said Charmian. "What's more, Ansteys—that's the family place, and Edward and I both love it—will probably have to be sold. And Edward and I feel we just can't bear that! But if we don't find Uncle Mathew's money, we shall have to sell."

Edward said, "You know, Charmian, we still haven't come to the vital point."

"Well, you talk then."

Edward turned to Miss Marple. "It's like this, you see. As Uncle Mathew grew older, he got more and more suspicious. He didn't trust anybody."

"Very wise of him," said Miss Marple. "The depravity of human nature is unbelievable."

"Well, you may be right. Anyway, Uncle Mathew thought so. He had a friend who lost his money in a bank and another friend who was ruined by an absconding solicitor, and he lost some money himself in a fraudulent company. He got so that he used to hold forth at great length that the only safe and sane thing to do was to convert your money into solid bullion and bury it."

"Ah," said Miss Marple. "I begin to see."

"Yes. Friends argued with him, pointed out that he'd get no interest that way, but he held that that didn't really matter. The bulk of your money, he said, should be 'kept in a box under the bed or buried in the garden.' Those were his words."

Charmian went on: "And when he died, he left hardly anything at all in securities, though he was very rich. So we think that that's what he must have done."

Edward explained: "We found that he had sold securities and drawn out large sums of money from time to time, and nobody knows what he did with them. But it seems probable that he lived up to his principles and that he did buy gold and bury it."

"He didn't say anything before he died? Leave any paper? No letter?"

"That's the maddening part of it. He didn't. He'd been

unconscious for some days, but he rallied before he died. He looked at us both and chuckled—a faint, weak little chuckle. He said, 'You'll be all right, my pretty pair of doves.' And then he tapped his eye—his right eye—and winked at us. And then—he died. . . . Poor old Uncle Mathew."

"He tapped his eye," said Miss Marple thoughtfully.

Edward said eagerly, "Does that convey anything to you? It made me think of an Arsène Lupin story where there was something hidden in a man's glass eye. But Uncle Mathew didn't have a glass eye."

Miss Marple shook her head. "No—I can't think of anything at the moment."

Charmian said, disappointedly, "Jane told us you'd say at once where to dig!"

Miss Marple smiled. "I'm not quite a conjurer, you know. I didn't know your uncle, or what sort of man he was, and I don't know the house or the grounds."

Charmian said, "If you did know them?"

"Well, it must be quite simple really, mustn't it?" said Miss Marple.

"Simple!" said Charmian. "You come down to Ansteys and see if it's simple!"

It is possible that she did not mean the invitation to be taken seriously, but Miss Marple said briskly, "Well, really, my dear, that's very kind of you. I've always wanted to have the chance of looking for buried treasure. And," she added, looking at them with a beaming, late-Victorian smile, "with a love interest too!"

"You see!" said Charmian, gesturing dramatically.

They had just completed a grand tour of Ansteys. They had been round the kitchen garden—heavily trenched. They had been through the little woods, where every important tree had been dug round, and had gazed sadly on the pitted surface of the once smooth lawn. They had been up to the attic, where old trunks and chests had been rifled of their contents. They had been down to the cellars, where flagstones had been heaved unwillingly from their sockets. They had measured and tapped walls, and Miss Marple had been shown every antique piece of furniture that contained or could be suspected of containing a secret drawer.

On a table in the morning room there was a heap of papers—all the papers that the late Mathew Stroud had left. Not one had been destroyed, and Charmian and Edward were wont to return to them again and again, earnestly perusing bills, invitations, and business correspondence in the hope of spotting a hitherto unnoticed clue.

"Can you think of anywhere we haven't looked?" demanded Charmian hopefully.

Miss Marple shook her head. "You seem to have been very thorough, my dear. Perhaps, if I may say so, just a little too thorough. I always think, you know, that one should have a plan. It's like my friend, Mrs. Eldritch; she had such a nice little maid, polished linoleum beautifully, but she was so thorough that she polished the bathroom floors too much, and as Mrs. Eldritch was stepping out of the bath the cork mat slipped from under her and she had a very nasty fall and actually broke her leg! Most awkward, because the bathroom door was locked, of course, and the gardener had to get a ladder and come in through the window—terribly distressing to Mrs. Eldritch, who had always been a very modest woman."

Edward moved restlessly.

Miss Marple said quickly, "Please forgive me. So apt, I know, to fly off at a tangent. But one thing does remind one of another. And sometimes that is helpful. All I was trying to say was that perhaps if we tried to sharpen our wits and think of a likely place—"

Edward said crossly, "You think of one, Miss Marple. Charmian's brains and mine are now only beautiful blanks!"

"Dear, dear. Of course—most tiring for you. If you don't mind I'll just look through all this." She indicated the papers on the table. "That is, if there's nothing private —I don't want to appear to pry."

"Oh, that's all right. But I'm afraid you won't find anything."

She sat down by the table and methodically worked through the sheaf of documents. As she replaced each one, she sorted them automatically into tidy little heaps. When she had finished she sat staring in front of her for some minutes.

Edward asked, not without a touch of malice, "Well, Miss Marple?"

She came to herself with a little start. "I beg your pardon. Most helpful."

"You've found something relevant?"

"Oh no, nothing like that, but I do believe I know what sort of man your Uncle Mathew was. Rather like my own Uncle Henry, I think. Fond of rather obvious jokes. A bachelor, evidently—I wonder why—perhaps an early disappointment? Methodical up to a point, but not very fond of being tied up—so few bachelors are!"

Behind Miss Marple's back Charmian made a sign to Edward. It said, "She's ga-ga."

Miss Marple was continuing happily to talk of her deceased Uncle Henry. "Very fond of puns, he was. And to some people puns are most annoying. A mere play upon words may be very irritating. He was a suspicious man too. Always was convinced the servants were robbing him. And sometimes, of course, they were, but not always. It grew upon him, poor man. Toward the end he suspected them of tampering with his food and finally refused to eat anything but boiled eggs! Said nobody could tamper with the inside of a boiled egg. Dear Uncle Henry, he used to be such a merry soul at one time—very fond of his coffee after dinner. He always used to say, 'This coffee is very Moorish,' meaning, you know, that he'd like a little more."

Edward felt that if he heard any more about Uncle Henry he'd go mad.

"Fond of young people, too," went on Miss Marple, "but inclined to tease them a little, if you know what I mean. Used to put bags of sweets where a child just couldn't reach them."

Casting politeness aside, Charmian said, "I think he sounds horrible!"

"Oh no, dear, just an old bachelor, you know, and not used to children. And he wasn't at all stupid, really. He used to keep a good deal of money in the house, and he had a safe put in. Made a great fuss about it—and how very secure it was. As a result of his talking so much, burglars broke in one night and actually cut a hole in the safe with a chemical device."

"Served him right," said Edward.

"Oh, but there was nothing in the safe," said Miss Marple. "You see, he really kept the money somewhere else—behind some volumes of sermons in the library, as a matter of fact. He said people never took a book of that kind out of the shelf!"

Edward interrupted excitedly, "I say, that's an idea. What about the library?"

But Charmian shook a scornful head. "Do you think I hadn't thought of that? I went through all the books Tuesday of last week, when you went off to Portsmouth. Took them all out, shook them. Nothing there."

Edward sighed. Then, rousing himself, he endeavoured to rid himself tactfully of their disappointing guest. "It's been awfully good of you to come down as you have and try to help us. Sorry it's been all a washout. Feel we trespassed a lot on your time. However—I'll get the car out and you'll be able to catch the three-thirty—"

"Oh," said Miss Marple, "but we've got to find the money, haven't we? You mustn't give up, Mr. Rossiter. 'If at first you don't succeed, try, try, try again.'"

"You mean you're going to go—on trying?"

"Strictly speaking," said Miss Marple, "I haven't begun yet. 'First catch your hare,' as Mrs. Beeton says in her cookery book—a wonderful book but terribly expensive; most of the recipes begin, 'Take a quart of cream and a dozen eggs.' Let me see, where was I? Oh yes. Well, we have, so to speak, caught our hare—the hare being, of course, your Uncle Mathew, and we've only got to decide now where he would have hidden the money. It ought to be quite simple."

"Simple?" demanded Charmian.

"Oh yes, dear. I'm sure he would have done the obvious thing. A secret drawer—that's my solution."

Edward said dryly, "You couldn't put bars of gold in a secret drawer."

"No, no, of course not. But there's no reason to believe the money is in gold."

"He always used to say—"

"So did my Uncle Henry about his safe! So I should strongly suspect that that was just a simple blind. Diamonds, now they could be in a secret drawer quite easily."

"But we've looked in all the secret drawers. We had a cabinetmaker over to examine the furniture."

"Did you, dear? That was clever of you. I should suggest your uncle's own desk would be the most likely. Was it the tall escritoire against the wall there?"

"Yes. And I'll show you." Charmian went over to it. She took down the flap. Inside were pigeonholes and little drawers. She opened a small door in the center and touched a spring inside the left-hand drawer. The bottom of the center recess clicked and slid forward. Charmian drew it out, revealing a shallow well beneath. It was empty.

"Now isn't that a coincidence," exclaimed Miss Marple. "Uncle Henry had a desk just like this, only his was burr walnut and this is mahogany."

"At any rate," said Charmian, "there's nothing there, as you can see."

"I expect," said Miss Marple, "your cabinetmaker was a young man. He didn't know everything. People were very artful when they made hiding places in those days. There's such a thing as a secret inside a secret."

She extracted a hairpin from her neat bun of grey hair. Straightening it out, she stuck the point into what appeared to be a tiny wormhole in one side of the secret recess. With a little difficulty she pulled out a small drawer. In it was a bundle of faded letters and a folded paper.

Edward and Charmian pounced on the find together. With trembling fingers Edward unfolded the paper. He dropped it with an exclamation of disgust.

"A cookery recipe. Baked ham!"

Charmian was untying a ribbon that held the letters together. She drew one out and glanced at it. "Love letters!"

Miss Marple reacted with Victorian gusto. "How interesting! Perhaps the reason your uncle never married."

Charmian read aloud:

"My ever dear Mathew, I must confess that the time seems long indeed since I received your last letter. I try to occupy myself with the various tasks allotted to me, and often say to myself that I am indeed fortunate to see so much of the globe, though little did I think when I went to America that I should voyage off to these far islands!"

Charmian broke off. "Where is it from? Oh, Hawaii!" She went on:

"Alas, these natives are still far from seeing the light. They are in an unclothed and savage state and spend most of their time swimming and dancing, adorning themselves with garlands of flowers. Mr. Gray has made some converts but it is up-hill work and he and Mrs. Gray get sadly discouraged. I try to do all I can to cheer and encourage him, but I, too, am often sad for a reason you can guess, dear Mathew. Alas, absence is a severe trial to a loving heart. Your renewed vows and protestations of affection cheered me greatly. Now and always you have my faithful and devoted heart, dear Mathew, and I remain—

Your true love,
Betty Martin

"P.S.—I address my letter under cover to our mutual friend, Matilda Graves, as usual. I hope Heaven will pardon this little subterfuge."

Edward whistled. "A female missionary! So that was Uncle Mathew's romance. I wonder why they never married?"

"She seems to have gone all over the world," said Charmian, looking through the letters. "Mauritius—all sorts of places. Probably died of yellow fever or something."

A gentle chuckle made them start. Miss Marple was apparently much amused. "Well, well," she said. "Fancy that, now!"

She was reading the recipe for baked ham. Seeing their inquiring glances, she read out: " 'Baked Ham with Spinach. Take a nice piece of gammon, stuff with cloves and cover with brown sugar. Bake in a slow oven. Serve with a border of puréed spinach.'

"What do you think of that now?"

"I think it sounds filthy," said Edward.

"No, no, actually it would be very good—but what do you think of the whole thing?"

A sudden ray of light illuminated Edward's face. "Do you think it's a code—cryptogram of some kind?" He seized it.

"Look here, Charmian, it might be, you know! No reason to put a cooking recipe in a secret drawer otherwise."

"Exactly," said Miss Marple. "Very, very significant."

Charmian said, "I know what it might be—invisible ink! Let's heat it. Turn on the electric fire."

Edward did so. But no signs of writing appeared under the treatment.

Miss Marple coughed. "I really think, you know, that you're making it rather too difficult. The recipe is only an indication, so to speak. It is, I think, the letters that are significant."

"The letters?"

"Especially," said Miss Marple, "the signature."

But Edward hardly heard her. He called excitedly, "Charmian! Come here! She's right. See—the envelopes are old right enough, but the letters themselves were written much later."

"Exactly," said Miss Marple.

"They're only fake old. I bet anything old Uncle Mat faked them himself—"

"Precisely," said Miss Marple.

"The whole thing's a sell. There never was a female missionary. It must be a code."

"My dear, dear children—there's really no need to make it all so difficult. Your uncle was really a very simple man. He had to have his little joke, that was all."

For the first time they gave her their full attention. "Just exactly what do you mean, Miss Marple?" asked Charmian.

"I mean, dear, that you're actually holding the money in your hand this minute."

Charmian stared down.

"The signature, dear. That gives the whole thing away. The recipe is just an indication. Shorn of all the cloves and brown sugar and the rest of it, what is it actually? Why, gammon and spinach to be sure! Gammon and spinach! Meaning—nonsense! So it's clear that it's the letters that are important. And then, if you take into consideration what your uncle did just before he died. He tapped his eye, you said. Well, there you are—that gives you the clue, you see."

Charmian said, "Are we mad, or are you?"

"Surely, my dear, you must have heard the expression meaning that something is not a true picture, or has it quite died out nowadays: *'All my eye and Betty Martin.'* "

Edward gasped, his eyes falling to the letter in his hand. "Betty Martin—"

"Of course, Mr. Rossiter. As you have just said, there isn't—there wasn't any such person. The letters were written by your uncle, and I dare say he got a lot of fun out of writing them! As you say, the writing on the envelopes is much older—in fact, the envelopes couldn't belong to the letters anyway, because the postmark of the one you are holding is eighteen fifty-one."

She paused. She made it very emphatic: "Eighteen fifty-one. And that explains everything, doesn't it?"

"Not to me," said Edward.

"Well, of course," said Miss Marple, "I dare say it wouldn't to me if it weren't for my great-nephew Lionel. Such a dear little boy and a passionate stamp collector. Knows all about stamps. It was he who told me about rare and expensive stamps and that a wonderful new find had come up for auction. And I actually remember his mentioning one stamp—an 1851 blue 2 cent. It realized something like $25,000, I believe. Fancy! I should imagine that the other stamps are something also rare and expensive. No doubt your uncle bought through dealers and was careful to 'cover his tracks,' as they say in detective stories."

Edward groaned. He sat down and buried his face in his hands.

"What's the matter?" demanded Charmian.

"Nothing. It's only the awful thought that, but for Miss Marple, we might have burned these letters in a decent, gentlemanly way!"

"Ah," said Miss Marple, "that's just what these old gentlemen who are fond of their joke never realize. My Uncle Henry, I remember, sent a favourite niece a five-pound note for a Christmas present. He put it inside a Christmas card, gummed the card together, and wrote on it: 'Love and best wishes. Afraid this is all I can manage this year.'

"She, poor girl, was annoyed at what she thought was his meanness and threw it all straight into the fire. So then, of course, he had to give her another."

Edward's feelings toward Uncle Henry had suffered an abrupt and complete change.

"Miss Marple," he said, "I'm going to get a bottle of champagne. We'll all drink the health of your Uncle Henry."

SANCTUARY

The Vicar's wife came round the corner of the vicarage with her arms full of chrysanthemums. A good deal of rich garden soil was attached to her strong brogue shoes and a few fragments of earth were adhering to her nose, but of that fact she was perfectly unconscious.

She had a slight struggle in opening the vicarage gate which hung, rustily, half off its hinges. A puff of wind caught at her battered felt hat, causing it to sit even more rakishly than it had done before. "Bother!" said Bunch.

Christened by her optimistic parents Diana, Mrs. Harmon had become Bunch at an early age for somewhat obvious reasons and the name had stuck to her ever since. Clutching the chrysanthemums, she made her way through the gate to the churchyard and so to the church door.

The November air was mild and damp. Clouds scudded across the sky with patches of blue here and there. Inside, the church was dark and cold; it was unheated except at service times.

"Brrrrrh!" said Bunch expressively. "I'd better get on with this quickly. I don't want to die of cold."

With the quickness born of practice she collected the necessary paraphernalia: vases, water, flower holders. "I wish we had lilies," thought Bunch to herself. "I get so tired of these scraggy chrysanthemums." Her nimble fingers arranged the blooms in their holders.

There was nothing particularly original or artistic about the decorations, for Bunch Harmon herself was neither original nor artistic, but it was a homely and pleasant arrangement. Carrying the vases carefully, Bunch stepped up the aisle and made her way toward the altar. As she did so the sun came out.

It shone through the east window of somewhat crude coloured glass, mostly blue and red—the gift of a wealthy Victorian churchgoer. The effect was almost startling in its sudden opulence. "Like jewels," thought Bunch. Suddenly she stopped, staring ahead of her. On the chancel steps was a huddled dark form.

Putting down the flowers carefully, Bunch went up to it and bent over it. It was a man lying there, huddled over on himself. Bunch knelt down by him and slowly, carefully, she turned him over. Her fingers went to his pulse—a pulse so feeble and fluttering that it told its own story, as did the almost greenish pallor of his face. There was no doubt, Bunch thought, that the man was dying.

He was a man of about forty-five, dressed in a dark, shabby suit. She laid down the limp hand she had picked up and looked at his other hand. This seemed clenched like a fist on his breast. Looking more closely, she saw that the fingers were closed over what seemed to be a large wad or handkerchief which he was holding tightly to his chest. All round the clenched hand there were splashes of a dry brown fluid which, Bunch guessed, was dry blood. Bunch sat back on her heels, frowning.

Up till now the man's eyes had been closed, but at this point they suddenly opened and fixed themselves on Bunch's face. They were neither dazed nor wandering. They seemed fully alive and intelligent. His lips moved, and Bunch bent forward to catch the words, or rather the word. It was only one word that he said:

"Sanctuary."

There was, she thought, just a very faint smile as he breathed out this word. There was no mistaking it, for after a moment he said it again, "Sanctuary . . ."

Then, with a faint, long-drawn-out sigh, his eyes closed again. Once more Bunch's fingers went to his pulse. It was still there, but fainter now and more intermittent. She got up with decision.

"Don't move," she said, "or try to move. I'm going for help."

The man's eyes opened again, but he seemed now to be

fixing his attention on the coloured light that came through the east window. He murmured something that Bunch could not quite catch. She thought, startled, that it might have been her husband's name.

"Julian?" she said. "Did you come here to find Julian?" But there was no answer. The man lay with eyes closed, his breathing coming in slow, shallow fashion.

Bunch turned and left the church rapidly. She glanced at her watch and nodded with some satisfaction. Dr. Griffiths would still be in his surgery. It was only a couple of minutes' walk from the church. She went in, without waiting to knock or ring, passing through the waiting room and into the doctor's surgery.

"You must come at once," said Bunch. "There's a man dying in the church."

Some minutes later Dr. Griffiths rose from his knees after a brief examination.

"Can we move him from here into the vicarage? I can attend to him better there—not that it's any use."

"Of course," said Bunch. "I'll go along and get things ready. I'll get Harper and Jones, shall I? To help you carry him."

"Thanks. I can telephone from the vicarage for an ambulance, but I'm afraid—by the time it comes . . ." He left the remark unfinished.

Bunch said, "Internal bleeding?"

Dr. Griffiths nodded. He said, "How on earth did he come here?"

"I think he must have been here all night," said Bunch, considering. "Harper unlocks the church in the morning as he goes to work, but he doesn't usually come in."

It was about five minutes later when Dr. Griffiths put down the telephone receiver and came back into the morning room where the injured man was lying on quickly arranged blankets on the sofa. Bunch was moving a basin of water and clearing up after the doctor's examination.

"Well, that's that," said Griffiths. "I've sent for an ambulance and I've notified the police." He stood, frowning, looking down on the patient who lay with closed eyes. His left hand was plucking in a nervous, spasmodic way at his side.

"He was shot," said Griffiths. "Shot at fairly close quarters. He rolled his handkerchief up into a ball and plugged the wound with it so as to stop the bleeding."

"Could he have gone far after that happened?" Bunch asked.

"Oh yes, it's quite possible. A mortally wounded man has been known to pick himself up and walk along a street as though nothing had happened and then suddenly collapse five or ten minutes later. So he needn't have been shot in the church. Oh no. He may have been shot some distance away. Of course, he may have shot himself and then dropped the revolver and staggered blindly toward the church. I don't quite know why he made for the church and not for the vicarage."

"Oh, I know that," said Bunch. "He said it: 'Sanctuary.' "

The doctor stared at her. "Sanctuary?"

"Here's Julian," said Bunch, turning her head as she heard her husband's steps in the hall. "Julian! Come here."

The Reverend Julian Harmon entered the room. His vague, scholarly manner always made him appear much older than he really was. "Dear me!" said Julian Harmon, staring in a mild, puzzled manner at the surgical appliances and the prone figure on the sofa.

Bunch explained with her usual economy of words. "He was in the church, dying. He'd been shot. Do you know him, Julian? I thought he said your name."

The vicar came up to the sofa and looked down at the dying man. "Poor fellow," he said, and shook his head. "No, I don't know him. I'm almost sure I've never seen him before."

At that moment the dying man's eyes opened once more. They went from the doctor to Julian Harmon and from him to his wife. The eyes stayed there, staring into Bunch's face. Griffiths stepped forward.

"If you could tell us," he said urgently.

But with his eyes fixed on Bunch, the man said in a weak voice, "Please—please—" And then, with a slight tremor, he died. . . .

Sergeant Hayes licked his pencil and turned the page of his notebook.

"So that's all you can tell me, Mrs. Harmon?"

"That's all," said Bunch. "These are the things out of his coat pockets."

On a table at Sergeant Hayes's elbow was a wallet, a rather battered old watch with the initials W.S., and the return half of a ticket to London. Nothing more.

"You've found out who he is?" asked Bunch.

"A Mr. and Mrs. Eccles phoned up the station. He's her brother, it seems. Name of Sandbourne. Been in a low state of health and nerves for some time. He's been getting worse lately. The day before yesterday he walked out and didn't come back. He took a revolver with him."

"And he came out here and shot himself with it?" said Bunch. "Why?"

"Well, you see, he'd been depressed . . ."

Bunch interrupted him. "I don't mean that. I mean, why here?"

Since Sergeant Hayes obviously did not know the answer to that one he replied in an oblique fashion, "Come out here, he did, on the five-ten bus."

"Yes," said Bunch again. "But why?"

"I don't know, Mrs. Harmon," said Sergeant Hayes. "There's no accounting. If the balance of the mind is disturbed—"

Bunch finished for him. "They may do it anywhere. But it still seems to me unnecessary to take a bus out to a small country place like this. He didn't know anyone here, did he?"

"Not so far as can be ascertained," said Sergeant Hayes. He coughed in an apologetic manner and said, as he rose to his feet, "It may be as Mr. and Mrs. Eccles will come out and see you, ma'am—if you don't mind, that is."

"Of course I don't mind," said Bunch. "It's very natural. I only wish I had something to tell them."

"I'll be getting along," said Sergeant Hayes.

"I'm only so thankful," said Bunch, going with him to the front door, "that it wasn't murder."

A car had drawn up at the vicarage gate. Sergeant Hayes, glancing at it, remarked, "Looks as though that's Mr. and Mrs. Eccles come here now, ma'am, to talk with you."

Bunch braced herself to endure what, she felt, might be rather a difficult ordeal. "However," she thought, "I can always call Julian in to help me. A clergyman's a great help when people are bereaved."

Exactly what she had expected Mr. and Mrs. Eccles to be like, Bunch could not have said, but she was conscious, as she greeted them, of a feeling of surprise. Mr. Eccles was a stout and florid man whose natural manner would have been cheerful and facetious. Mrs. Eccles had a vaguely flashy look about her. She had a small, mean, pursed-up mouth. Her voice was thin and reedy.

"It's been a terrible shock, Mrs. Harmon, as you can imagine," she said.

"Oh, I know," said Bunch. "It must have been. Do sit down. Can I offer you—well, perhaps it's a little early for tea—"

Mr. Eccles waved a pudgy hand. "No, no, nothing for us," he said. "It's very kind of you, I'm sure. Just wanted to . . . well . . . what poor William said and all that, you know?"

"He's been abroad a long time," said Mrs. Eccles, "and I think he must have had some very nasty experiences. Very quiet and depressed he's been, ever since he came home. Said the world wasn't fit to live in and there was nothing to look forward to. Poor Bill, he was always moody."

Bunch stared at them both for a moment or two without speaking.

"Pinched my husband's revolver, he did," went on Mrs. Eccles. "Without our knowing. Then it seems he come out here by bus. I suppose that was nice feeling on his part. He wouldn't have liked to do it in our house."

"Poor fellow, poor fellow," said Mr. Eccles, with a sigh. "It doesn't do to judge."

There was another short pause, and Mr. Eccles said, "Did he leave a message? Any last words, nothing like that?"

His bright, rather piglike eyes watched Bunch closely. Mrs. Eccles, too, leaned forward as though anxious for the reply.

"No," said Bunch quietly. "He came into the church when he was dying, for sanctuary."

Mrs. Eccles said in a puzzled voice, "Sanctuary? I don't think I quite . . ."

Mr. Eccles interrupted. "Holy place, my dear," he said

impatiently. "That's what the vicar's wife means. It's a sin—suicide, you know. I expect he wanted to make amends."

"He tried to say something just before he died," said Bunch. "He began, 'Please,' but that's as far as he got."

Mrs. Eccles put her handkerchief to her eyes and sniffed.

"Oh, dear," she said. "It's terribly upsetting, isn't it?"

"There, there, Pam," said her husband. "Don't take on. These things can't be helped. Poor Willie. Still, he's at peace now. Well, thank you very much, Mrs. Harmon. I hope we haven't interrupted you. A vicar's wife is a busy lady, we know that."

They shook hands with her. Then Eccles turned back suddenly to say, "Oh yes, there's just one other thing. I think you've got his coat here, haven't you?"

"His coat?" Bunch frowned.

Mrs. Eccles said, "We'd like all his things, you know. Sentimental like."

"He had a watch and a wallet and a railway ticket in the pockets," said Bunch. "I gave them to Sergeant Hayes."

"That's all right, then," said Mr. Eccles. "He'll hand them over to us, I expect. His private papers would be in the wallet."

"There was a pound note in the wallet," said Bunch. "Nothing else."

"No letters? Nothing like that?"

Bunch shook her head.

"Well, thank you again, Mrs. Harmon. The coat he was wearing—perhaps the sergeant's got that, too, has he?"

Bunch frowned in an effort of remembrance.

"No," she said. "I don't think . . . let me see. The doctor and I took his coat off to examine his wound." She looked round the room vaguely. "I must have taken it upstairs with the towels and basin."

"I wonder now, Mrs. Harmon, if you don't mind . . . We'd like his coat, you know, the last thing he wore. Well, the wife feels rather sentimental about it."

"Of course," said Bunch. "Would you like me to have it cleaned first? I'm afraid it's rather—well—stained."

"Oh no, no, no, that doesn't matter."

Bunch frowned. "Now I wonder where . . . Excuse me a moment." She went upstairs and it was some few minutes before she returned.

"I'm so sorry," she said breathlessly. "My daily woman must have put it aside with other clothes that were going to the cleaners. It's taken me quite a long time to find it. Here it is. I'll do it up for you in brown paper."

Disclaiming their protests, she did so; then once more effusively bidding her farewell, the Eccles departed.

Bunch went slowly back across the hall and entered the study. The Reverend Julian Harmon looked up and his brow cleared. He was composing a sermon and was fearing that he'd been led astray by the interest of the political relations between Judaea and Persia, in the reign of Cyrus.

"Yes, dear?" he said hopefully.

"Julian," said Bunch, "what's *sanctuary* exactly?"

Julian Harmon gratefully put aside his sermon paper.

"Well," he said, "sanctuary in Roman and Greek temples applied to the *cella* in which stood the statue of a god. The Latin word for altar, *ara,* also means protection." He continued learnedly: "In A.D. 399 the right of sanctuary in Christian churches was finally and definitely recognized. The earliest mention of the right of sanctuary in England is in the Code of Laws issued by Ethelbert in A.D. 600 . . ."

He continued for some time with his exposition but was, as often, disconcerted by his wife's reception of his erudite pronouncement.

"Darling," she said, "you are sweet."

Bending over, she kissed him on the tip of his nose. Julian felt rather like a dog who has been congratulated on performing a clever trick.

"The Eccles have been here," said Bunch.

The vicar frowned. "The Eccles? I don't seem to remember . . ."

"You don't know them. They're the sister and her husband of the man in the church."

"My dear, you ought to have called me."

"There wasn't any need," said Bunch. "They were not in need of consolation. I wonder now." She frowned. "If I put a casserole in the oven tomorrow, can you manage, Julian? I think I shall have to go up to London for the sales."

"The sails?" Her husband looked at her blankly. "Do you mean a yacht or a boat or something?"

Bunch laughed.

"No, darling. There's a special white sale at Burrows and

Portman's. You know, sheets, tablecloths and towels and
glass cloths. I don't know what we do with our glass cloths,
the way they wear through. Besides," she added thoughtfully, "I think I ought to go and see Aunt Jane."

That sweet old lady, Miss Jane Marple, was enjoying the
delights of the metropolis for a fortnight, comfortably installed in her nephew's studio flat.

"So kind of dear Raymond," she murmured. "He and
Joan have gone to America for a fortnight and they insisted
I should come up here and enjoy myself. And now, dear
Bunch, do tell me what it is that's worrying you."

Bunch was Miss Marple's favourite godchild, and the
old lady looked at her with great affection as Bunch,
thrusting her best felt hat further on the back of her head,
started on her story.

Bunch's recital was concise and clear. Miss Marple
nodded her head as Bunch finished. "I see," she said. "Yes,
I see."

"That's why I felt I had to see you," said Bunch. "You
see, not being clever——"

"But you are clever, my dear."

"No, I'm not. Not clever like Julian."

"Julian, of course, has a very solid intellect," said Miss
Marple.

"That's it," said Bunch. "Julian's got the intellect, but on
the other hand, I've got the sense."

"You have a lot of common sense, Bunch, and you're
very intelligent."

"You see, I don't really know what I ought to do. I can't
ask Julian because—well, I mean, Julian's so full of rec-
titude . . ."

This statement appeared to be perfectly understood by
Miss Marple, who said, "I know what you mean, dear. We
women—well, it's different." She went on, "You told me
what happened, Bunch, but I'd like to know first exactly
what you think."

"It's all wrong," said Bunch. "The man who was there in
the church, dying, knew all about sanctuary. He said it just
the way Julian would have said it. I mean he was a well-
read, educated man. And if he'd shot himself, he wouldn't

drag himself into a church afterward and say 'sanctuary.' Sanctuary means that you're pursued, and when you get into a church you're safe. Your pursuers can't touch you. At one time even the law couldn't get at you."

She looked questioningly at Miss Marple. The latter nodded. Bunch went on, "Those people, the Eccles, were quite different. Ignorant and coarse. And there's another thing. That watch—the dead man's watch. It had the initials W.S. on the back of it. But inside—I opened it—in very small lettering there was 'To Walter from his father' and a date. *Walter.* But the Eccles kept talking of him as William or Bill."

Miss Marple seemed about to speak, but Bunch rushed on, "Oh, I know you're not always called the name you're baptized by. I mean, I can understand that you might be christened William and called 'Porky' or 'Carrots' or something. But your sister wouldn't call you William or Bill if your name was Walter."

"You mean that she wasn't his sister?"

"I'm quite sure she wasn't his sister. They were horrid—both of them. They came to the vicarage to get his things and to find out if he'd said anything before he died. When I said he hadn't I saw it in their faces—relief. I think, myself," finished Bunch, "it was Eccles who shot him."

"Murder?" said Miss Marple.

"Yes," said Bunch, "murder. That's why I came to you, darling."

Bunch's remark might have seemed incongruous to an ignorant listener, but in certain spheres Miss Marple had a reputation for dealing with murder.

"He said 'please' to me before he died," said Bunch. "He wanted me to do something for him. The awful thing is I've no idea what."

Miss Marple considered for a moment or two and then pounced on the point that had already occurred to Bunch. "But why was he there at all?" she asked.

"You mean," said Bunch, "if you wanted sanctuary, you might pop into a church anywhere. There's no need to take a bus that only goes four times a day and come out to a lonely spot like ours for it."

"He must have come there for a purpose," Miss Marple

thought. "He must have come to see someone. Chipping Cleghorn's not a big place, Bunch. Surely you must have some idea of who it was he came to see?"

Bunch reviewed the inhabitants of her village in her mind before rather doubtfully shaking her head. "In a way," she said, "it could be anybody."

"He never mentioned a name?"

"He said Julian, or I thought he said Julian. It might have been Julia, I suppose. As far as I know, there isn't any Julia living in Chipping Cleghorn."

She screwed up her eyes as she thought back to the scene. The man lying there on the chancel steps, the light coming through the window with its jewels of red and blue light.

"Jewels," said Bunch suddenly. "Perhaps that's what he said. The light coming through the east window looked like jewels."

"Jewels," said Miss Marple thoughtfully.

"I'm coming now," said Bunch, "to the most important thing of all. The reason why I've really come here today. You see, the Eccles made a great fuss about having his coat. We took it off when the doctor was seeing to him. It was an old, shabby sort of coat—there was no reason they should have wanted it. They pretended it was sentimental, but that was nonsense.

"Anyway, I went up to find it, and as I was going up the stairs I remembered how he'd made a kind of picking gesture with his hand, as though he was fumbling with the coat. So when I got hold of the coat I looked at it very carefully and I saw that in one place the lining had been sewn up again with a different thread. So I unpicked it and I found a little piece of paper inside. I took it out and I sewed it up again properly with thread that matched. I was careful and I don't really think that the Eccles would know I've done it. I don't think so, but I can't be sure. And I took the coat down to them and made some excuse for the delay."

"The piece of paper?" asked Miss Marple.

Bunch opened her handbag. "I didn't show it to Julian," she said, "because he would have said that I ought to have given it to the Eccles. But I thought I'd rather bring it to you instead."

"A cloakroom ticket," said Miss Marple, looking at it. "Paddington Station."

"He had a return ticket to Paddington in his pocket," said Bunch.

The eyes of the two women met.

"This calls for action," said Miss Marple briskly. "But it would be advisable, I think, to be careful. Would you have noticed at all, Bunch dear, whether you were followed when you came to London today?"

"Followed!" exclaimed Bunch. "You don't think—"

"Well, I think it's possible," said Miss Marple. "When anything is possible, I think we ought to take precautions." She rose with a brisk movement. "You came up here ostensibly, my dear, to go to the sales. I think the right thing to do, therefore, would be for us to go to the sales. But before we set out, we might put one or two little arrangements in hand. I don't suppose," Miss Marple added obscurely, "that I shall need the old speckled tweed with the beaver collar just at present. . . ."

It was about an hour and a half later that the two ladies, rather the worse for wear and battered in appearance, and both clasping parcels of hard-won household linen, sat down at a small and sequestered hostelry called the Apple Bough to restore their forces with steak-and-kidney pudding followed by apple tart and custard.

"Really a prewar-quality face towel," gasped Miss Marple, slightly out of breath. "With a J on it too. So fortunate that Raymond's wife's name is Joan. I shall put them aside until I really need them and then they will do for her if I pass on sooner than I expect."

"I really did need the glass cloths," said Bunch. "And they were very cheap, though not as cheap as the ones that woman with the ginger hair managed to snatch from me."

A smart young woman with a lavish application of rouge and lipstick entered the Apple Bough at that moment. After looking round vaguely for a moment or two, she hurried to their table. She laid down an envelope by Miss Marple's elbow.

"There you are, miss," she said briskly.

"Oh, thank you, Gladys," said Miss Marple. "Thank you very much. So kind of you."

"Always pleased to oblige, I'm sure," said Gladys. "Ernie always says to me, 'Everything what's good you learned from that Miss Marple of yours that you were in service with,' and I'm sure I'm always glad to oblige you, miss."

"Such a dear girl," said Miss Marple as Gladys departed again. "Always so willing and so kind."

She looked inside the envelope and then passed it on to Bunch. "Now be very careful, dear," she said. "By the way, is there still that nice young inspector at Melchester that I remember?"

"I don't know," said Bunch. "I expect so."

"Well, if not," said Miss Marple thoughtfully, "I can always ring up the chief constable. I think he would remember me."

"Of course he'd remember you," said Bunch. "Everybody would remember you. You're quite unique." She rose.

Arrived at Paddington, Bunch went to the Parcels Office and produced the cloakroom ticket. A moment or two later a rather shabby old suitcase was passed across to her, and carrying this, she made her way to the platform.

The journey home was uneventful. Bunch rose as the train approached Chipping Cleghorn and picked up the old suitcase. She had just left her carriage when a man, sprinting along the platform, suddenly seized the suitcase from her hand and rushed off with it.

"Stop!" Bunch yelled. "Stop him, stop him. He's taken my suitcase."

The ticket collector who, at this rural station, was a man of somewhat slow processes had just begun to say, "Now, look here, you can't do that—" when a smart blow in the chest pushed him aside, and the man with the suitcase rushed out from the station. He made his way toward a waiting car. Tossing the suitcase in, he was about to climb after it, but before he could move a hand fell on his shoulder, and the voice of Police Constable Abel said, "Now then, what's all this?"

Bunch arrived, panting, from the station. "He snatched my suitcase," she said.

"Nonsense," said the man. "I don't know what this lady means. It's my suitcase. I just got out of the train with it."

"Now, let's get this clear," said Police Constable Abel.

He looked at Bunch with a bovine and impartial stare. Nobody would have guessed that Police Constable Abel and Mrs. Harmon spent long half hours in Police Constable Abel's off time discussing the respective merits of manure and bone meal for rose bushes.

"You say, madam, that this is your suitcase?" said Police Constable Abel.

"Yes," said Bunch. "Definitely."

"And you, sir?"

"I say this suitcase is mine."

The man was tall, dark, and well dressed, with a drawling voice and a superior manner. A feminine voice from inside the car said, "Of course it's your suitcase, Edwin. I don't know what this woman means."

"We'll have to get this clear," said Police Constable Abel. "If it's your suitcase, madam, what do you say is inside it?"

"Clothes," said Bunch. "A long speckled coat with a beaver collar, two wool jumpers, and a pair of shoes."

"Well, that's clear enough," said Police Constable Abel. He turned to the other.

"I am a theatrical costumer," said the dark man importantly. "This suitcase contains theatrical properties which I brought down here for an amateur performance."

"Right, sir," said Police Constable Abel. "Well, we'll just look inside, shall we, and see? We can go along to the police station, or if you're in a hurry, we'll take the suitcase back to the station and open it there."

"It'll suit me," said the dark man. "My name is Moss, by the way. Edwin Moss."

The police constable, holding the suitcase, went back into the station. "Just taking this into the Parcels Office, George," he said to the ticket collector.

Police Constable Abel laid the suitcase on the counter of the Parcels Office and pushed back the clasp. The case was not locked. Bunch and Mr. Edwin Moss stood on either side of him, their eyes regarding each other vengefully.

"Ah!" said Police Constable Abel, as he pushed up the lid.

Inside, neatly folded, was a long, rather shabby tweed coat with a beaver fur collar. There were also two wool jumpers and a pair of country shoes.

"Exactly as you say, madam," said Police Constable Abel, turning to Bunch.

Nobody could have said that Mr. Edwin Moss underdid things. His dismay and compunction were magnificent.

"I do apologize," he said. "I really do apologize. Please believe me, dear lady, when I tell you how very, very sorry I am. Unpardonable—quite unpardonable—my behaviour has been." He looked at his watch. "I must rush now. Probably my suitcase has gone on the train." Raising his hat once more, he said meltingly to Bunch, "Do, do forgive me," and rushed hurriedly out of the Parcels Office.

"Are you going to let him get away?" asked Bunch in a conspiratorial whisper of Police Constable Abel.

The latter slowly closed a bovine eye in a wink.

"He won't get too far, ma'am," he said. "That's to say, he won't get far unobserved, if you take my meaning."

"Oh," said Bunch, relieved.

"That old lady's been on the phone," said Police Constable Abel, "the one as was down here a few years ago. Bright she is, isn't she? But there's been a lot cooking up all today. Shouldn't wonder if the inspector or sergeant was out to see you about it tomorrow morning."

It was the inspector who came, the Inspector Craddock whom Miss Marple remembered. He greeted Bunch with a smile as an old friend.

"Crime in Chipping Cleghorn again," he said cheerfully. "You don't lack for sensation here, do you, Mrs. Harmon?"

"I could do with rather less," said Bunch. "Have you come to ask me questions or are you going to tell me things for a change?"

"I'll tell you some things first," said the inspector. "To begin with, Mr. and Mrs. Eccles have been having an eye kept on them for some time. There's reason to believe they've been connected with several robberies in this part of the world. For another thing, although Mrs. Eccles has a brother called Sandbourne who has recently come back from abroad, the man you found dying in the church yesterday was definitely not Sandbourne."

"I knew that he wasn't," said Bunch. "His name was Walter, to begin with, not William."

The inspector nodded. "His name was Walter St. John,

and he escaped forty-eight hours ago from Charrington Prison."

"Of course," said Bunch softly to herself, "he was being hunted down by the law, and he took sanctuary." Then she asked, "What had he done?"

"I'll have to go back rather a long way. It's a complicated story. Several years ago there was a certain dancer doing turns at the music halls. I don't expect you'll have ever heard of her, but she specialized in an Arabian Night's turn. 'Aladdin in the Cave of Jewels,' it was called.

"She wasn't much of a dancer, I believe, but she was—well—attractive. Anyway, a certain Asiatic royalty fell for her in a big way. Among other things he gave her a very magnificent emerald necklace."

"The historic jewels of a rajah?" murmured Bunch ecstatically.

Inspector Craddock coughed. "Well, a rather more modern version, Mrs. Harmon. The affair didn't last very long, broke up when our potentate's attention was captured by a certain film star whose demands were not quite so modest.

"Zobeida, to give the dancer her stage name, hung on to the necklace, and in due course it was stolen. It disappeared from her dressing room at the theater, and there was a lingering suspicion in the minds of the authorities that she herself might have engineered its disappearance. Such things have been known as a publicity stunt, or indeed from more dishonest motives.

"The necklace was never recovered, but during the course of the investigation the attention of the police was drawn to this man, Walter St. John. He was a man of education and breeding who had come down in the world and who was employed as a working jeweler with a rather obscure firm which was suspected as acting as a fence for jewel robberies.

"There was evidence that this necklace had passed through his hands. It was, however, in connection with the theft of some other jewelry that he was finally brought to trial and convicted and sent to prison. He had not very much longer to serve, so his escape was rather a surprise."

"But why did he come here?" asked Bunch.

"We'd like to know that very much, Mrs. Harmon. Following up his trail, it seems that he went first to London. He didn't visit any of his old associates, but he visited an elderly woman, a Mrs. Jacobs who had formerly been a theatrical dresser. She won't say a word of what he came for, but according to other lodgers in the house, he left carrying a suitcase."

"I see," said Bunch. "He left it in the cloakroom at Paddington and then he came down here."

"By that time," said Inspector Craddock, "Eccles and the man who calls himself Edwin Moss were on his trail. They wanted that suitcase. They saw him get on the bus. They must have driven out in a car ahead of him and been waiting for him when he left the bus."

"And he was murdered?" said Bunch.

"Yes," said Craddock. "He was shot. It was Eccles' revolver, but I rather fancy it was Moss who did the shooting. Now, Mrs. Harmon, what we want to know is, where is the suitcase that Walter St. John actually deposited at Paddington Station?"

Bunch grinned. "I expect Aunt Jane's got it by now," she said. "Miss Marple, I mean. That was her plan. She sent a former maid of hers with a suitcase packed with her things to the cloakroom at Paddington and we exchanged tickets. I collected her suitcase and brought it down by train. She seemed to expect that an attempt would be made to get it from me."

It was Inspector Craddock's turn to grin. "So she said when she rang up. I'm driving up to London to see her. Do you want to come, too, Mrs. Harmon?"

"Wel-l," said Bunch, considering. "Wel-l, as a matter of fact, it's very fortunate. I had a toothache last night so I really ought to go to London to see the dentist, oughtn't I?"

"Definitely," said Inspector Craddock.

Miss Marple looked from Inspector Craddock's face to the eager face of Bunch Harmon. The suitcase lay on the table. "Of course, I haven't opened it," the old lady said. "I wouldn't dream of doing such a thing till somebody official arrived. Besides," she added, with a demurely mischievous Victorian smile, "it's locked."

"Like to make a guess at what's inside, Miss Marple?" asked the inspector.

"I should imagine, you know," said Miss Marple, "that it would be Zobeida's theatrical costumes. Would you like a chisel, Inspector?"

The chisel soon did its work. Both women gave a slight gasp as the lid flew up. The sunlight coming through the window lit up what seemed like an inexhaustible treasure of sparkling jewels, red, blue, green, orange.

"Aladdin's Cave," said Miss Marple. "The flashing jewels the girl wore to dance."

"Ah," said Inspector Craddock. "Now, what's so precious about it, do you think, that a man was murdered to get hold of it?"

"She was a shrewd girl, I expect," said Miss Marple thoughtfully. "She's dead, isn't she, Inspector?"

"Yes, died three years ago."

"She had this valuable emerald necklace," said Miss Marple musingly. "Had the stones taken out of their setting and fastened here and there on her theatrical costume, where everyone would take them for merely coloured rhinestones. Then she had a replica made of the real necklace, and that, of course, was what was stolen. No wonder it never came on the market. The thief soon discovered the stones were false."

"Here is an envelope," said Bunch, pulling aside some of the glittering stones.

Inspector Craddock took it from her and extracted two official-looking papers from it. He read aloud, " 'Marriage certificate between Walter Edmund St. John and Mary Moss.' That was Zobeida's real name."

"So they were married," said Miss Marple. "I see."

"What's the other?" asked Bunch.

"A birth certificate of a daughter, Jewel."

"Jewel?" cried Bunch. "Why, of course. Jewel! Jill! That's it. I see now why he came to Chipping Cleghorn. That's what he was trying to say to me. Jewel. The Mundys, you know. Laburnam Cottage. They look after a little girl for someone. They're devoted to her. She's been like their own granddaughter. Yes, I remember now, her name was Jewel, only, of course, they call her Jill.

"Mrs. Mundy had a stroke about a week ago, and the old man's been very ill with pneumonia. They were both going to go to the infirmary. I've been trying hard to find a good home for Jill somewhere. I didn't want her taken away to an institution.

"I suppose her father heard about it in prison and he managed to break away and get hold of this suitcase from the old dresser he or his wife left it with. I suppose if the jewels really belonged to her mother, they can be used for the child now."

"I should imagine so, Mrs. Harmon. If they're here."

"Oh, they'll be here all right," said Miss Marple cheerfully. . . .

"Thank goodness you're back, dear," said the Reverend Julian Harmon, greeting his wife with affection and a sigh of content. "Mrs. Burt always tries to do her best when you're away, but she really gave me some very peculiar fish cakes for lunch. I didn't want to hurt her feelings so I gave them to Tiglash Pileser, but even he wouldn't eat them, so I had to throw them out of the window."

"Tiglash Pileser," said Bunch, stroking the vicarage cat, who was purring against her knee, "is very particular about what fish he eats. I often tell him he's got a proud stomach!"

"And your tooth, dear? Did you have it seen to?"

"Yes," said Bunch. "It didn't hurt much, and I went to see Aunt Jane again, too . . ."

"Dear old thing," said Julian. "I hope she's not failing at all."

"Not in the least," said Bunch, with a grin.

The following morning Bunch took a fresh supply of chrysanthemums to the church. The sun was once more pouring through the east window, and Bunch stood in the jeweled light on the chancel steps. She said very softly under her breath, "Your little girl will be all right. I'll see that she is. I promise."

Then she tidied up the church, slipped into a pew, and knelt for a few moments to say her prayers before returning to the vicarage to attack the piled-up chores of two neglected days.

GREENSHAW'S FOLLY

The two men rounded the corner of the shrubbery.

"Well, there you are," said Raymond West. "That's It."

Horace Bindler took a deep, appreciative breath.

"How wonderful," he cried. His voice rose in a high screech of esthetic delight, then deepened in reverent awe. "It's unbelievable. Out of this world! A period piece of the best."

"I thought you'd like it," said Raymond West complacently.

"Like it?" Words failed Horace. He unbuckled the strap of his camera and got busy. "This will be one of the gems of my collection," he said happily. "I do think, don't you, that it's rather amusing to have a collection of monstrosities? The idea came to me one night seven years ago in my bath. My last real gem was in the Campo Santo at Genoa, but I really think this beats it. What's it called?"

"I haven't the least idea," said Raymond.

"I suppose it's got a name?"

"It must have. But the fact is that it's never referred to round here as anything but Greenshaw's Folly."

"Greenshaw being the man who built it?"

"Yes. In eighteen sixty or seventy or thereabouts. The local success story of the time. Barefoot boy who had risen to immense prosperity. Local opinion is divided as to why he built this house, whether it was sheer exuberance of wealth or whether it was done to impress his creditors. If the latter, it didn't impress them. He either went bankrupt or the next thing to it. Hence the name, Greenshaw's Folly."

Horace's camera clicked. "There," he said in a satisfied

voice. "Remind me to show you Number Three-ten in my collection. A really incredible marble mantelpiece in the Italian manner." He added, looking at the house, "I can't conceive of how Mr. Greenshaw thought of it all."

"Rather obvious in some ways," said Raymond. "He had visited the châteaux of the Loire, don't you think? Those turrets. And then, rather unfortunately, he seems to have travelled in the Orient. The influence of the Taj Mahal is unmistakable. I rather like the Moorish wing," he added, "and the traces of a Venetian palace."

"One wonders how he ever got hold of an architect to carry out these ideas."

Raymond shrugged his shoulders.

"No difficulty about that, I expect," he said. "Probably the architect retired with a good income for life while poor old Greenshaw went bankrupt."

"Could we look at it from the other side?" asked Horace, "or are we trespassing?"

"We're trespassing all right," said Raymond, "but I don't think it will matter."

He turned toward the corner of the house and Horace skipped after him.

"But who lives here? Orphans or holiday visitors? It can't be a school. No playing fields or brisk efficiency."

"Oh, a Greenshaw lives here still," said Raymond over his shoulder. "The house itself didn't go in the crash. Old Greenshaw's son inherited it. He was a bit of a miser and lived here in a corner of it. Never spent a penny. Probably never had a penny to spend. His daughter lives here now. Old lady—very eccentric."

As he spoke Raymond was congratulating himself on having thought of Greenshaw's Folly as a means of entertaining his guest. These literary critics always professed themselves as longing for a weekend in the country and were wont to find the country extremely boring when they got there. Tomorrow there would be the Sunday papers, and for today Raymond West congratulated himself on suggesting a visit to Greenshaw's Folly to enrich Horace Bindler's well-known collection of monstrosities.

They turned the corner of the house and came out on a neglected lawn. In one corner of it was a large artificial rockery, and bending over it was a figure at the sight of which Horace clutched Raymond delightedly by the arm.

"Do you see what she's got on?" he exclaimed. "A sprigged print dress. Just like a housemaid—when there were housemaids. One of my most cherished memories is staying at a house in the country when I was quite a boy where a real housemaid called you in the morning, all crackling in a print dress and a cap. Yes, my boy, really—a cap. Muslin with streamers. No, perhaps it was the parlourmaid who had the streamers. But anyway, she was a real housemaid and she brought in an enormous brass can of hot water. What an exciting day we're having."

The figure in the print dress had straightened up and turned toward them, trowel in hand. She was a sufficiently startling figure. Unkempt locks of iron-grey fell wispily on her shoulders, and a straw hat, rather like the hats that horses wear in Italy, was crammed down on her head. The coloured print dress she wore fell nearly to her ankles. Out of a weather-beaten, not too clean face, shrewd eyes surveyed them appraisingly.

"I must apologize for trespassing, Miss Greenshaw," said Raymond West, as he advanced toward her, "but Mr. Horace Bindler who is staying with me—"

Horace bowed and removed his hat.

"—is most interested in—er—ancient history and—er—fine buildings."

Raymond West spoke with the ease of a famous author who knows that he is a celebrity, that he can venture where other people may not.

Miss Greenshaw looked up at the sprawling exuberance behind her.

"It *is* a fine house," she said appreciatively. "My grandfather built it—before my time, of course. He is reported as having said that he wished to astonish the natives."

"I'll say he did that, ma'am," said Horace Bindler.

"Mr. Bindler is the well-known literary critic," said Raymond West.

Miss Greenshaw had clearly no reverence for literary critics. She remained unimpressed.

"I consider it," said Miss Greenshaw, referring to the house, "as a monument to my grandfather's genius. Silly fools come here and ask me why I don't sell it and go and live in a flat. What would I do in a flat? It's my home and I

live in it," said Miss Greenshaw. "Always have lived here."
She considered, brooding over the past. "There were three
of us. Laura married the curate. Papa wouldn't give her
any money, said clergymen ought to be unworldly. She
died, having a baby. Baby died too. Nettie ran away with
the riding master. Papa cut her out of his will, of course.
Handsome fellow, Harry Fletcher, but no good. Don't
think Nettie was happy with him. Anyway, she didn't live
long. They had a son. He writes to me sometimes, but of
course he isn't a Greenshaw. I'm the last of the Green-
shaws." She drew up her bent shoulders with a certain pride
and readjusted the rakish angle of the straw hat. Then,
turning, she said sharply:

"Yes, Mrs. Cresswell, what is it?"

Approaching them from the house was a figure that,
seen side by side with Miss Greenshaw, seemed ludicrously
dissimilar. Mrs. Cresswell had a marvellously dressed head
of well-blued hair towering upward in meticulously arranged curls and rolls. It was as though she had dressed
her head to go as a French marquise to a fancy dress party.
The rest of her middle-aged person was dressed in what
ought to have been rustling black silk but was actually one
of the shinier varieties of black rayon. Although she was
not a large woman, she had a well-developed and
sumptuous bosom. Her voice was unexpectedly deep. She
spoke with exquisite diction—only a slight hesitation over
words beginning with *h,* and the final pronunciation of
them with an exaggerated aspirate gave rise to a suspicion
that at some remote period in her youth she might have
had trouble over dropping her *h*'s.

"The fish, madam," said Mrs. Cresswell, "the slice of
cod. It has not arrived. I have asked Alfred to go down for
it and he refuses."

Rather unexpectedly, Miss Greenshaw gave a cackle of
laughter.

"Refuses, does he?"

"Alfred, madam, has been most disobliging."

Miss Greenshaw raised two earth-stained fingers to her
lips, suddenly produced an earsplitting whistle, and at the
same time yelled, "Alfred. Alfred, come here."

Round the corner of the house a young man appeared in
answer to the summons, carrying a spade in his hand. He

had a bold, handsome face, and as he drew near he cast an unmistakably malevolent glance toward Mrs. Cresswell.

"You wanted me, miss?" he said.

"Yes, Alfred. I hear you've refused to go down for the fish. What about it, eh?"

Alfred spoke in a surly voice.

"I'll go down for it if you wants it, miss. You've only got to say."

"I do want it. I want it for my supper."

"Right you are, miss. I'll go right away."

He threw an insolent glance at Mrs. Cresswell, who flushed and murmured below her breath.

"Now that I think of it," said Miss Greenshaw, "a couple of strange visitors are just what we need, aren't they, Mrs. Cresswell?"

Mrs. Cresswell looked puzzled.

"I'm sorry, madam—"

"For you-know-what," said Miss Greenshaw, nodding her head. "Beneficiary to a will mustn't witness it. That's right, isn't it?" She appealed to Raymond West.

"Quite correct," said Raymond.

"I know enough law to know that," said Miss Greenshaw, "and you two are men of standing."

She flung down the trowel on her weeding basket.

"Would you mind coming up to the library with me?"

"Delighted," said Horace eagerly.

She led the way through French windows and through a vast yellow-and-gold drawing room with faded brocade on the walls and dust covers arranged over the furniture, then through a large dim hall, up a staircase, and into a room on the second floor.

"My grandfather's library," she announced.

Horace looked round with acute pleasure. It was a room from his point of view quite full of monstrosities. The heads of sphinxes appeared on the most unlikely pieces of furniture; there was a colossal bronze representing, he thought, Paul and Virginia, and a vast bronze clock with classical motifs of which he longed to take a photograph.

"A fine lot of books," said Miss Greenshaw.

Raymond was already looking at the books. From what he could see from a cursory glance there was no book here of any real interest or, indeed, any book which appeared to have been read. They were all superbly bound sets of the classics as supplied ninety years ago for furnishing a gentleman's library. Some novels of a bygone period were included. But they too showed little signs of having been read.

Miss Greenshaw was fumbling in the drawers of a vast desk. Finally she pulled out a parchment document.

"My will," she explained. "Got to leave your money to someone—or so they say. If I died without a will, I suppose that son of a horse trader would get it. Handsome fellow, Harry Fletcher, but a rogue if ever there was one. Don't see why his son should inherit this place. No," she went on, as though answering some unspoken objection, "I've made up my mind. I'm leaving it to Cresswell."

"Your housekeeper?"

"Yes. I've explained it to her. I make a will leaving her all I've got and then I don't need to pay her any wages. Saves me a lot in current expenses, and it keeps her up to the mark. No giving me notice and walking off at any minute. Very la-di-dah and all that, isn't she? But her father was a working plumber in a very small way. She's nothing to give herself airs about."

By now Miss Greenshaw had unfolded the parchment. Picking up a pen, she dipped it in the inkstand and wrote her signature, *Katherine Dorothy Greenshaw*.

"That's right," she said. "You've seen me sign it, and then you two sign it, and that makes it legal."

She handed the pen to Raymond West. He hesitated a moment, feeling an unexpected repulsion to what he was asked to do. Then he quickly scrawled his well-known autograph, for which his morning's mail usually brought at least six requests.

Horace took the pen from him and added his own minute signature.

"That's done," said Miss Greenshaw.

She moved across to the bookcases and stood looking at them uncertainly, then she opened a glass door, took out a book, and slipped the folded parchment inside.

"I've my own places for keeping things," she said.

"*Lady Audley's Secret,*" Raymond West remarked, catching sight of the title as she replaced the book.

Miss Greenshaw gave another cackle of laughter.

"Best-seller in its day," she remarked. "But not like your books, eh?"

She gave Raymond a sudden friendly nudge in the ribs. Raymond was rather surprised that she even knew he wrote books. Although Raymond West was a "big name" in literature, he could hardly be described as a best-seller. Though softening a little with the advent of middle age, his books dealt bleakly with the sordid side of life.

"I wonder," Horace demanded breathlessly, "if I might just take a photograph of the clock."

"By all means," said Miss Greenshaw. "It came, I believe, from the Paris Exhibition."

"Very probably," said Horace. He took his picture.

"This room's not been used much since my grandfather's time," said Miss Greenshaw. "This desk's full of old diaries of his. Interesting, I should think. I haven't the eyesight to read them myself. I'd like to get them published, but I suppose one would have to work on them a good deal."

"You could engage someone to do that," said Raymond West.

"Could I really? It's an idea, you know. I'll think about it."

Raymond West glanced at his watch.

"We mustn't trespass on your kindness any longer," he said.

"Pleased to have seen you," said Miss Greenshaw graciously. "Thought you were the policeman when I heard you coming round the corner of the house."

"Why a policeman?" demanded Horace, who never minded asking questions.

Miss Greenshaw responded unexpectedly.

"If you want to know the time, ask a policeman," she carolled, and with this example of Victorian wit she nudged Horace in the ribs and roared with laughter.

"It's been a wonderful afternoon." Horace sighed as he and Raymond walked home. "Really, that place has everything. The only thing the library needs is a body. Those old-fashioned detective stories about murder in the library —that's just the kind of library I'm sure the authors had in mind."

"If you want to discuss murder," said Raymond, "you must talk to my Aunt Jane."

"Your Aunt Jane? Do you mean Miss Marple?" Horace felt a little at a loss.

The charming old-world lady to whom he had been introduced the night before seemed the last person to be mentioned in connection with murder.

"Oh yes," said Raymond. "Murder is a specialty of hers."

"How intriguing! What do you really mean?"

"I mean just that," said Raymond. He paraphrased: "Some commit murder, some get mixed up in murder, others have murder thrust upon them. My Aunt Jane comes into the third category."

"You are joking."

"Not in the least. I can refer you to the former Commissioner of Scotland Yard, several chief constables, and one or two hard-working inspectors of the C.I.D."

Horace said happily that wonders would never cease. Over the tea table they gave Joan West, Raymond's wife, Louise Oxley, her niece, and old Miss Marple a résumé of the afternoon's happenings, recounting in detail everything that Miss Greenshaw had said to them.

"But I do think," said Horace, "that there is something a little sinister about the whole setup. That duchess-like creature, the housekeeper—arsenic, perhaps, in the teapot, now that she knows her mistress has made the will in her favour?"

"Tell us, Aunt Jane," said Raymond, "will there be murder or won't there? What do you think?"

"I think," said Miss Marple, winding up her wool with a rather severe air, "that you shouldn't joke about these things as much as you do, Raymond. Arsenic is, of course, quite a possibility. So easy to obtain. Probably present in the tool shed already in the form of weed killer."

"Oh, really, darling," said Joan West affectionately. "Wouldn't that be rather too obvious?"

"It's all very well to make a will," said Raymond. "I don't suppose the poor old thing has anything to leave except that awful white elephant of a house, and who would want that?"

"A film company possibly," said Horace, "or a hotel or an institution?"

"They'd expect to buy it for a song," said Raymond, but Miss Marple was shaking her head.

"You know, dear Raymond, I cannot agree with you there. About the money, I mean. The grandfather was evidently one of those lavish spenders who make money easily but can't keep it. He may have gone broke, as you say, but hardly bankrupt, or else his son would not have had the house. Now the son, as is so often the case, was of an entirely different character from his father. A miser. A man who saved every penny. I should say that in the course of his lifetime he probably put by a very good sum. This Miss Greenshaw appears to have taken after him—to dislike spending money, that is. Yes, I should think it quite likely that she has quite a substantial sum tucked away."

"In that case," said Joan West, "I wonder now—what about Louise?"

They looked at Louise as she sat, silent, by the fire.

Louise was Joan West's niece. Her marriage had recently, as she herself put it, come unstuck, leaving her with two young children and a bare sufficiency of money to keep them on.

"I mean," said Joan, "if this Miss Greenshaw really wants someone to go through diaries and get a book ready for publication . . ."

"It's an idea," said Raymond.

Louise said in a low voice, "It's work I could do—and I think I'd enjoy it."

"I'll write to her," said Raymond.

"I wonder," said Miss Marple thoughtfully, "what the old lady meant by that remark about a policeman?"

"Oh, it was just a joke."

"It reminded me," said Miss Marple, nodding her head vigorously, "yes, it reminded me very much of Mr. Naysmith."

"Who was Mr. Naysmith?" asked Raymond curiously.

"He kept bees," said Miss Marple, "and was very good at doing the acrostics in the Sunday papers. And he liked giving people false impressions just for fun. But sometimes it led to trouble."

Everybody was silent for a moment, considering Mr. Naysmith, but as there did not seem to be any points of resemblance between him and Miss Greenshaw, they decided that dear Aunt Jane was perhaps getting a little bit disconnected in her old age.

Horace Bindler went back to London without having collected any more monstrosities, and Raymond West wrote a letter to Miss Greenshaw telling her that he knew of a Mrs. Louise Oxley who would be competent to undertake work on the diaries. After a lapse of some days a letter arrived, written in spidery old-fashioned handwriting, in which Miss Greenshaw declared herself anxious to avail herself of the services of Mrs. Oxley, and making an appointment for Mrs. Oxley to come and see her.

Louise duly kept the appointment, generous terms were arranged, and she started work the following day.

"I'm awfully grateful to you," she said to Raymond. "It will fit in beautifully. I can take the children to school, go on to Greenshaw's Folly, and pick them up on my way back. How fantastic the whole setup is! That old woman has to be seen to be believed."

On the evening of her first day at work she returned and described her day.

"I've hardly seen the housekeeper," she said. "She came in with coffee and biscuits at half-past eleven, with her mouth pursed up very prunes and prisms, and would hardly speak to me. I think she disapproves deeply of my having been engaged." She went on, "It seems there's quite a feud between her and the gardener, Alfred. He's a local boy and fairly lazy, I should imagine, and he and the housekeeper won't speak to each other. Miss Greenshaw said in her rather grand way, 'There have always been feuds as far as I can remember between the garden and the house staff. It was so in my grandfather's time. There were three men and a boy in the garden then, and eight maids in the house, but there was always friction.' "

On the next day Louise returned with another piece of news.

"Just fancy," she said, "I was asked to ring up the nephew today."

"Miss Greenshaw's nephew?"

"Yes. It seems he's an actor playing in the stock company that's doing a summer season at Boreham-on-Sea. I rang up the theater and left a message asking him to lunch tomorrow. Rather fun, really. The old girl didn't want the housekeeper to know. I think Mrs. Cresswell has done something that's annoyed her."

"Tomorrow another installment of this thrilling serial," murmured Raymond.

"It's exactly like a serial isn't it? Reconciliation with the nephew, blood is thicker than water—another will to be made and the old will destroyed."

"Aunt Jane, you're looking very serious."

"Was I, my dear? Have you heard any more about the policeman?"

Louise looked bewildered. "I don't know anything about a policeman."

"That remark of hers, my dear," said Miss Marple, "must have meant something."

Louise arrived at her work the following day in a cheerful mood. She passed through the open front door—the doors and windows of the house were always open. Miss Greenshaw appeared to have no fear of burglars, and was probably justified, as most things in the house weighed several tons and were of no marketable value.

Louise had passed Alfred in the drive. When she first noticed him he had been leaning against a tree smoking a cigarette, but as soon as he had caught sight of her he had seized a broom and begun diligently to sweep leaves. An idle young man, she thought, but good-looking. His features reminded her of someone. As she passed through the hall on her way upstairs to the library, she glanced at the large picture of Nathaniel Greenshaw which presided over the mantelpiece, showing him in the acme of Victorian prosperity, leaning back in a large armchair, his hands resting on the gold Albert chain across his capacious stomach. As her glance swept up from the stomach to the face with its heavy jowls, its bushy eyebrows and its flourishing black moustache, the thought occurred to her that Nathaniel Greenshaw must have been handsome as a young man. He had looked, perhaps, a little like Alfred. . . .

She went into the library on the second floor, shut the door behind her, opened her typewriter, and got out the diaries from the drawer at the side of her desk. Through the open window she caught a glimpse of Miss Greenshaw below, in a puce-coloured sprigged print, bending over the rockery, weeding assiduously. They had had two wet days, of which the weeds had taken full advantage.

Louise, a town-bred girl, decided that if she ever had a garden, it would never contain a rockery which needed weeding by hand. Then she settled down to her work.

When Mrs. Cresswell entered the library with the coffee tray at half-past eleven, she was clearly in a very bad temper. She banged the tray down on the table and observed to the universe:

"Company for lunch—and nothing in the house! What am I supposed to do, I should like to know? And no sign of Alfred."

"He was sweeping in the drive when I got here," Louise offered.

"I daresay. A nice soft job."

Mrs. Cresswell swept out of the room, slamming the door behind her. Louise grinned to herself. She wondered what "the nephew" would be like.

She finished her coffee and settled down to her work again. It was so absorbing that time passed quickly. Nathaniel Greenshaw, when he started to keep a diary, had succumbed to the pleasures of frankness. Typing out a passage relating to the personal charms of a barmaid in the neighbouring town, Louise reflected that a good deal of editing would be necessary.

As she was thinking this, she was startled by a scream from the garden. Jumping up, she ran to the open window. Below her Miss Greenshaw was staggering away from the rockery toward the house. Her hands were clasped to her breast, and between her hands there protruded a feathered shaft that Louise recognized with stupefaction to be the shaft of an arrow.

Miss Greenshaw's head, in its battered straw hat, fell forward on her breast. She called up to Louise in a failing voice: " . . . shot . . . he shot me . . . with an arrow . . . get help . . ."

Louise rushed to the door. She turned the handle, but the door would not open. It took her a moment or two of futile endeavour to realize that she was locked in. She ran back to the window and called down.

"I'm locked in!"

Miss Greenshaw, her back toward Louise and swaying a little on her feet, was calling up to the housekeeper at a window farther along.

"Ring police . . . telephone . . ."

Then, lurching from side to side like a drunkard, Miss Greenshaw disappeared from Louise's view through the window and staggered into the drawing room on the ground floor. A moment later Louise heard a crash of broken china, a heavy fall, and then silence. Her imagination reconstructed the scene. Miss Greenshaw must have stumbled blindly into a small table with a Sèvres tea set on it.

Desperately Louise pounded on the library door, calling and shouting. There was no creeper or drainpipe outside the window that could help her to get out that way.

Tired at last of beating on the door, Louise returned to the window. From the window of her sitting room farther along the housekeeper's head appeared.

"Come and let me out, Mrs. Oxley. I'm locked in."

"So am I," said Louise.

"Oh, dear, isn't it awful? I've telephoned the police. There's an extension in this room, but what I can't understand, Mrs. Oxley, is our being locked in. I never heard a key turn, did you?"

"No, I didn't hear anything at all. Oh, dear, what shall we do? Perhaps Alfred might hear us." Louise shouted at the top of her voice, "Alfred, Alfred."

"Gone to his dinner as likely as not. What time is it?"

Louise glanced at her watch.

"Twenty-five past twelve."

"He's not supposed to go until half-past, but he sneaks off earlier whenever he can."

"Do you think—do you think—"

Louise meant to ask, "Do you think she's dead?"—but the words stuck in her throat.

There was nothing to do but wait. She sat down on the window sill. It seemed an eternity before the stolid helmeted figure of a police constable came round the corner of the house. She leaned out of the window and he looked up at her, shading his eyes with his hand.

"What's going on here?" he demanded.

From their respective windows Louise and Mrs. Cresswell poured a flood of excited information down on him.

The constable produced a notebook and a pencil. "You ladies ran upstairs and locked yourselves in? Can I have your names, please?"

"Somebody locked us in. Come and let us out."

The constable said reprovingly, "All in good time," and disappeared through the French window below.

Once again time seemed infinite. Louise heard the sound of a car arriving, and after what seemed an hour, but was actually only three minutes, first Mrs. Cresswell and then Louise were released by a police sergeant more alert than the original constable.

"Miss Greenshaw?" Louise's voice faltered. "What—what's happened?"

The sergeant cleared his throat.

"I'm sorry to have to tell you, madam," he said, "what I've already told Mrs. Cresswell here. Miss Greenshaw is dead."

"Murdered," said Mrs. Cresswell. "That's what is it—murder."

The sergeant said dubiously, "Could have been an accident—some country lads shooting arrows."

Again there was the sound of a car arriving.

The sergeant said, "That'll be the M.O.," and he started downstairs.

But it was not the M.O. As Louise and Mrs. Cresswell came down the stairs, a young man stepped hesitatingly through the front door and paused, looking round him with a somewhat bewildered air.

Then, speaking in a pleasant voice that in some way seemed familiar to Louise—perhaps it reminded her of Miss Greenshaw's—he asked, "Excuse me, does—er—does Miss Greenshaw live here?"

"May I have your name if you please?" said the sergeant, advancing upon him.

"Fletcher," said the young man. "Nat Fletcher. I'm Miss Greenshaw's nephew, as a matter of fact."

"Indeed, sir, well—I'm sorry—"

"Has anything happened?" asked Nat Fletcher.

"There's been an—accident. Your aunt was shot with an arrow—penetrated the jugular vein—"

Mrs. Cresswell spoke hysterically and without her usual refinement: "Your h'aunt's been murdered, that's what's 'appened. Your h'aunt's been murdered."

Inspector Welch drew his chair a little nearer to the table and let his gaze wander from one to the other of the four people in the room. It was evening of the same day. He had called at the Wests' house to take Louise Oxley once more over her statement.

"You are sure of the exact words? *Shot—he shot me—with an arrow—get help?*"

Louise nodded.

"And the time?"

"I looked at my watch a minute or two later—it was then twelve twenty-five—"

"Your watch keeps good time?"

"I looked at the clock as well." Louise left no doubt of her accuracy.

The inspector turned to Raymond West.

"It appears, sir, that about a week ago you and a Mr. Horace Bindler were witnesses to Miss Greenshaw's will?"

Briefly Raymond recounted the events of the afternoon visit he and Horace Bindler had paid to Greenshaw's Folly.

"This testimony of yours may be important," said Welch. "Miss Greenshaw distinctly told you, did she, that her will was being made in favour of Mrs. Cresswell, the housekeeper, and that she was not paying Mrs. Cresswell any wages in view of the expectations Mrs. Cresswell had of profiting by her death?"

"That is what she told me—yes."

"Would you say that Mrs. Cresswell was definitely aware of these facts?"

"I should say undoubtedly. Miss Greenshaw made a reference in my presence to beneficiaries not being able to witness a will, and Mrs. Cresswell clearly understood what she meant by it. Moreover, Miss Greenshaw herself told me that she had come to this arrangement with Mrs. Cresswell."

"So Mrs. Cresswell had reason to believe she was an interested party. Motive clear enough in her case, and I dare-

say she'd be our chief suspect now if it wasn't for the fact
that she was securely locked in her room like Mrs. Oxley
here, and also that Miss Greenshaw definitely said a man
shot her—"

"She definitely was locked in her room?"

"Oh yes. Sergeant Cayley let her out. It's a big old-fashioned lock with a big old-fashioned key. The key was in
the lock and there's not a chance that it could have been
turned from inside or any hanky-panky of that kind. No,
you can take it definitely that Mrs. Cresswell was locked
inside that room and couldn't get out. And there were no
bows and arrows in the room and Miss Greenshaw
couldn't in any case have been shot from her window—the
angle forbids it. No, Mrs. Cresswell's out."

He paused, then went on: "Would you say that Miss
Greenshaw, in your opinion, was a practical joker?"

Miss Marple looked up sharply from her corner.

"So the will wasn't in Mrs. Cresswell's favor after all?"
she said.

Inspector Welch looked over at her in a rather surprised
fashion.

"That's a very clever guess of yours, madam," he said.
"No, Mrs. Cresswell isn't named as beneficiary."

"Just like Mr. Naysmith," said Miss Marple, nodding
her head. "Miss Greenshaw told Mrs. Cresswell she was
going to leave her everything and so got out of paying her
wages, and then she left her money to somebody else. No
doubt she was vastly pleased with herself. No wonder she
chortled when she put the will away in *Lady Audley's Secret.*"

"It was lucky Mrs. Oxley was able to tell us about the
will and where it was put," said the inspector. "We might
have had a long hunt for it otherwise."

"A Victorian sense of humour," murmured Raymond
West.

"So she left her money to her nephew after all," said
Louise.

The inspector shook his head.

"No," he said, "she didn't leave it to Nat Fletcher. The
story goes around here—of course, I'm new to the place
and I only get the gossip that's secondhand—but it seems
that in the old days both Miss Greenshaw and her sister

were set on the handsome young riding master, and the sister got him. No, she didn't leave the money to her nephew —" Inspector Welch paused, rubbing his chin. "She left it to Alfred," he said.

"Alfred—the gardener?" Joan spoke in a surprised voice.

"Yes, Mrs. West. Alfred Pollock."

"But why?" cried Louise.

"I daresay," said Miss Marple, "that she thought Alfred Pollock might have a pride in the house, might even want to live in it, whereas her nephew would almost certainly have no use for it whatever and would sell it as soon as he could possibly do so. He's an actor, isn't he? What play exactly is he acting in at present?"

Trust an old lady to wander from the point, thought Inspector Welch; but he replied civilly, "I believe, madam, they are doing a season of Sir James M. Barrie's plays."

"Barrie," said Miss Marple thoughtfully.

"*What Every Woman Knows*," said Inspector Welch, and then blushed. "Name of a play," he said quickly. "I'm not much of a theater-goer myself," he added, "but the wife went along and saw it last week. Quite well done, she said it was."

"Barrie wrote some very charming plays," said Miss Marple, "though I must say that when I went with an old friend of mine, General Easterly, to see Barrie's *Little Mary*"—she shook her head sadly—"neither of us knew where to look."

The inspector, unacquainted with the play *Little Mary*, seemed completely fogged.

Miss Marple explained: "When I was a girl, Inspector, nobody ever mentioned the word stomach."

The inspector looked even more at sea. Miss Marple was murmuring titles under her breath.

"*The Admirable Crichton*. Very clever. *Mary Rose*—a charming play. I cried, I remember. *Quality Street* I didn't care for so much. Then there was *A Kiss for Cinderella*. Oh, of course!"

Inspector Welch had no time to waste on theatrical discussion. He returned to the matter at hand.

"The question is," he said, "did Alfred Pollock know the old lady had made a will in his favour? Did she tell him?"

He added, "You see—there's an archery club over at Boreham—and Alfred Pollock's a member. He's a very good shot indeed with a bow and arrow."

"Then isn't your case quite clear?" asked Raymond West. "It would fit in with the doors being locked on the two women—he'd know just where they were in the house."

The inspector looked at him. He spoke with deep melancholy.

"He's got an alibi," said the inspector.

"I always think alibis are definitely suspicious," Raymond remarked.

"Maybe, sir," said Inspector Welch. "You're talking as a writer."

"I don't write detective stories," said Raymond West, horrified at the mere idea.

"Easy enough to say that alibis are suspicious," went on Inspector Welch, "but unfortunately we've got to deal with facts." He sighed. "We've got three good suspects," he went on. "Three people who, as it happened, were very close upon the scene at the time. Yet the odd thing is that it looks as though none of the three could have done it. The housekeeper I've already dealt with; the nephew, Nat Fletcher, at the moment Miss Greenshaw was shot, was a couple of miles away, filling up his car at a garage and asking his way; as for Alfred Pollock, six people will swear that he entered the Dog and Duck at twenty past twelve and was there for an hour, having his usual bread and cheese and beer."

"Deliberately establishing an alibi," said Raymond West hopefully.

"Maybe," said Inspector Welch, "but if so, he did establish it."

There was a long silence. Then Raymond turned his head to where Miss Marple sat upright and thoughtful.

"It's up to you, Aunt Jane," he said. "The inspector's baffled, the sergeant's baffled, I'm baffled, Joan's baffled, Louise is baffled. But to you, Aunt Jane, it is crystal clear. Am I right?"

"I wouldn't say that," said Miss Marple, "not crystal clear. And murder, dear Raymond, isn't a game. I don't suppose poor Miss Greenshaw wanted to die, and it was a particularly brutal murder. Very well-planned and quite cold-blooded. It's not a thing to make jokes about."

"I'm sorry," said Raymond. "I'm not really as callous as I sound. One treats a thing lightly to take away from the— well, the horror of it."

"That is, I believe, the modern tendency," said Miss Marple. "All these wars, and having to joke about funerals. Yes, perhaps I was thoughtless when I implied that you were callous."

"It isn't," said Joan, "as though we'd known her at all well."

"That is very true," said Miss Marple. "You, dear Joan, did not know her at all. I did not know her at all. Raymond gathered an impression of her from one afternoon's conversation. Louise knew her for only two days."

"Come now, Aunt Jane," said Raymond, "tell us your views. You don't mind, Inspector?"

"Not at all," said the inspector politely.

"Well, my dear, it would seem that we have three people who had—or might have thought they had—a motive to kill the old lady. And three quite simple reasons why none of the three could have done so. The housekeeper could not have killed Miss Greenshaw because she was locked in her room and because her mistress definitely stated that a man shot her. The gardener was inside the Dog and Duck at the time, the nephew at the garage."

"Very clearly put, madam," said the inspector.

"And since it seems most unlikely that any outsider should have done it, where, then, are we?"

"That's what the inspector wants to know," said Raymond West.

"One so often looks at a thing the wrong way round," said Miss Marple apologetically. "If we can't alter the movements or the positions of those three people, then couldn't we perhaps alter the time of the murder?"

"You mean that both my watch and the clock were wrong?" asked Louise.

"No, dear," said Miss Marple, "I didn't mean that at all. I mean that the murder didn't occur when you thought it occurred."

"But I saw it," cried Louise.

"Well, what I have been wondering, my dear, was

whether you weren't meant to see it. I've been asking my-self, you know, whether that wasn't the real reason why you were engaged for this job."

"What do you mean, Aunt Jane?"

"Well, dear, it seems odd. Miss Greenshaw did not like spending money—yet she engaged you and agreed quite willingly to the terms you asked. It seems to me that per-haps you were meant to be there in that library on the sec-ond floor, looking out of the window so that you could be the key witness—someone from outside of irreproachably good character—to fix a definite time and place for the murder."

"But you can't mean," said Louise incredulously, "that Miss Greenshaw intended to be murdered."

"What I mean, dear," said Miss Marple, "is that you didn't really know Miss Greenshaw. There's no real reason, is there, why the Miss Greenshaw you saw when you went up to the ¡.ouse should be the same Miss Greenshaw that Raymond saw a few days earlier? Oh yes, I know," she went on, to prevent Louise's reply, "she was wearing the peculiar old-fashioned print dress and the strange straw hat and had unkempt hair. She corresponded exactly to the de-scription Raymond gave us last weekend. But those two women, you know, were much the same age, height, and size. The housekeeper, I mean, and Miss Greenshaw."

"But the housekeeper is fat!" Louise exclaimed. "She's got an enormous bosom."

Miss Marple coughed.

"But, my dear, surely, nowadays I have seen—er—them myself in shops most indelicately displayed. It is very easy for anyone to have a—a bosom—of any size and dimen-sion."

"What are you trying to say?" demanded Raymond.

"I was just thinking that during the two days Louise was working there, one woman could have played both parts. You said yourself, Louise, that you hardly saw the house-keeper, except for the one minute in the morning when she brought you the tray with coffee. One sees those clever artists on the stage coming in as different characters with only a moment or two to spare, and I am sure the change could have been effected quite easily. That marquise head-dress could be just a wig slipped on and off."

"Aunt Jane! Do you mean that Miss Greenshaw was dead before I started work there?"

"Not dead. Kept under drugs, I should say. A very easy job for an unscrupulous woman like the housekeeper to do. Then she made the arrangements with you and got you to telephone to the nephew to ask him to lunch at a definite time. The only person who would have known that this Miss Greenshaw was not Miss Greenshaw would have been Alfred. And if you remember, the first two days you were working there it was wet, and Miss Greenshaw stayed in the house. Alfred never came into the house because of his feud with the housekeeper. And on the last morning Alfred was in the drive, while Miss Greenshaw was working on the rockery—I'd like to have a look at that rockery."

"Do you mean it was Mrs. Cresswell who killed Miss Greenshaw?"

"I think that after bringing you your coffee, the housekeeper locked the door on you as she went out, then carried the unconscious Miss Greenshaw down to the drawing room, then assumed her 'Miss Greenshaw' disguise and went out to work on the rockery where you could see her from the upstairs window. In due course she screamed and came staggering to the house clutching an arrow as though it had penetrated her throat. She called for help and was careful to say 'he shot me' so as to remove suspicion from the housekeeper—from herself. She also called up to the housekeeper's window as though she saw her there. Then, once inside the drawing room, she threw over a table with porcelain on it, ran quickly upstairs, put on her marquise wig, and was able a few moments later to lean her head out of the window and tell you that she, too, was locked in."

"But she was locked in," said Louise.

"I know. That is where the policeman comes in."

"What policeman?"

"Exactly—what policeman? I wonder, Inspector, if you would mind telling me how and when you arrived on the scene?"

The inspector looked a little puzzled.

"At twelve twenty-nine we received a telephone call from Mrs. Cresswell, housekeeper to Miss Greenshaw, stating that her mistress had been shot. Sergeant Cayley and myself went out there at once in a car and arrived at the house at twelve thirty-five. We found Miss Greenshaw dead and the two ladies locked in their rooms."

"So, you see, my dear," said Miss Marple to Louise, "the police constable you saw wasn't a real police constable at all. You never thought of him again—one doesn't—one just accepts one more uniform as part of the law."

"But who—why?"

"As to who—well, if they are playing *A Kiss for Cinderella*, a policeman is the principal character. Nat Fletcher would only have to help himself to the costume he wears on the stage. He'd ask his way at a garage, being careful to call attention to the time—twelve twenty-five; then he would drive on quickly, leave his car round a corner, slip on his police uniform, and do his 'act.' "

"But why—why?"

"Someone had to lock the housekeeper's door on the outside, and someone had to drive the arrow through Mrs. Greenshaw's throat. You can stab anyone with an arrow just as well as by shooting it—but it needs force."

"You mean they were both in it?"

"Oh yes, I think so. Mother and son as likely as not."

"But Miss Greenshaw's sister died long ago."

"Yes, but I've no doubt Mr. Fletcher married again—he sounds like the sort of man who would. I think it possible that the child died, too, and that this so-called nephew was the second wife's child and not really a relation at all. The woman got the post as housekeeper and spied out the land. Then he wrote to Miss Greenshaw as her nephew and proposed to call on her—he may have even made some joking reference to coming in his policeman's uniform—remember, she said she was expecting a policeman. But I think Miss Greenshaw suspected the truth and refused to see him. He would have been her heir if she had died without making a will—but of course once she had made a will in the housekeeper's favour, as they thought, then it was clear sailing."

"But why use an arrow?" objected Joan. "So very far-fetched."

"Not far-fetched at all, dear. Alfred belonged to an archery club—Alfred was meant to take the blame. The fact that he was in the pub as early as twelve-twenty was most unfortunate from their point of view. He always left a little before his proper time and that would have been just right." She shook her head. "It really seems all wrong —morally, I mean, that Alfred's laziness should have saved his life."

The inspector cleared his throat.

"Well, madam, these suggestions of yours are very interesting. I shall, of course, have to investigate—"

Miss Marple and Raymond West stood by the rockery and looked down at a gardening basket full of dying vegetation.

Miss Marple murmured:

"Alyssum, saxifrage, cystis, thimble campanula . . . Yes, that's all the proof I need. Whoever was weeding here yesterday morning was no gardener—she pulled up plants as well as weeds. So now I know I'm right. Thank you, dear Raymond, for bringing me here. I wanted to see the place for myself."

She and Raymond both looked up at the outrageous pile of Greenshaw's Folly.

A cough made them turn. A handsome young man was also looking at the monstrous house.

"Plaguey big place," he said. "Too big for nowadays—or so they say. I dunno about that. If I won a football pool and made a lot of money, that's the kind of house I'd like to build."

He smiled bashfully at them, then rumpled his hair.

"Reckon I can say so now," said Alfred Pollock. "And a fine house it is, for all they call it Greenshaw's Folly!"

THE CASE OF THE PERFECT MAID

"Oh, if you please, madam, could I speak to you a moment?"

It might be thought that this request was in the nature of an absurdity, since Edna, Miss Marple's little maid, was actually speaking to her mistress at the moment.

Recognizing the idiom, however, Miss Marple said promptly, "Certainly, Edna. Come in and shut the door. What is it?"

Obediently shutting the door, Edna advanced into the room, pleated the corner of her apron between her fingers, and swallowed once or twice.

"Yes, Edna?" said Miss Marple encouragingly.

"Oh, please, ma'am, it's my cousin Gladdie. You see, she's lost her place."

"Dear me, I am sorry to hear that. She was at Old Hall, wasn't she, with the Miss—Misses—Skinner?"

"Yes, ma'am, that's right, ma'am. And Gladdie's very upset about it—very upset indeed."

"Gladys has changed places rather often before, though, hasn't she?"

"Oh yes, ma'am. She's always one for a change, Gladdie is. She never seems to get really settled, if you know what I mean. But she's always been the one to give the notice, you see!"

"And this time it's the other way round?" asked Miss Marple dryly.

"Yes, ma'am, and it's upset Gladdie something awful."

Miss Marple looked slightly surprised. Her recollection of Gladys, who had occasionally come to drink tea in the kitchen on her "days out," was a stout, giggling girl of unshakably equable temperament.

Edna went on: "You see, ma'am, it's the way it happened—the way Miss Skinner looked."

"How," inquired Miss Marple patiently, "did Miss Skinner look?"

This time Edna got well away with her news bulletin.

"Oh, ma'am, it was ever such a shock to Gladdie. You see, one of Miss Emily's brooches was missing, and such a hue and cry for it as never was, and of course, nobody likes a thing like that to happen; it's upsetting, ma'am, if you know what I mean. And Gladdie's helped search everywhere, and there was Miss Lavinia saying she was going to the police about it, and then it turned up again, pushed right to the back of a drawer in the dressing table, and very thankful Gladdie was.

"And the very next day as ever was a plate got broken, and Miss Lavinia, she bounced out right away and told Gladdie to take a month's notice. And what Gladdie feels is it couldn't have been the plate and that Miss Lavinia was just making an excuse of that, and that it must be because of the brooch and they think as she took it and put it back when the police was mentioned, and Gladdie wouldn't do such a thing, not never she wouldn't, and what she feels is as it will get round and tell against her, and it's a very serious thing for a girl as you know, ma'am."

Miss Marple nodded. Though having no particular liking for the bouncing, self-opinioned Gladys, she was quite sure of the girl's intrinsic honesty and could well imagine that the affair must have upset her.

Edna said wistfully, "I suppose, ma'am, there isn't anything you could do about it?"

"Tell her not to be silly," said Miss Marple crisply. "If she didn't take the brooch—which I'm sure she didn't—then she has no cause to be upset."

"It'll get about," said Edna dismally.

Miss Marple said, "I—er—am going up that way this afternoon. I'll have word with the Misses Skinner."

"Oh, thank you, madam," said Edna.

Old Hall was a big Victorian house surrounded by woods and park land. Since it had been proved unlettable and unsalable as it was, an enterprising speculator had divided it into four flats with a central hot-water system, and the use of "the grounds" to be held in common by the tenants. The experiment had been satisfactory. A rich and eccentric old lady and her maid occupied one flat. The old lady had a passion for birds and entertained a feathered gathering to meals every day. A retired Indian judge and his wife rented a second. A very young couple, recently married, occupied the third, and the fourth had been taken only two months ago by two maiden ladies of the name of Skinner. The four sets of tenants were only on the most distant terms with each other, since none of them had anything in common. The landlord had been heard to say that this was an excellent thing. What he dreaded were friendships followed by estrangements and subsequent complaints to him.

Miss Marple was acquainted with all the tenants, though she knew none of them well. The elder Miss Skinner, Miss Lavinia, was what might be termed the working member of the firm. Miss Emily, the younger, spent most of her time in bed, suffering from various complaints which, in the opinion of St. Mary Mead, were largely imaginary. Only Miss Lavinia believed devoutly in her sister's martyrdom and patience under affliction and willingly ran errands and trotted up and down to the village for things that "my sister had suddenly fancied."

It was the view of St. Mary Mead that if Miss Emily suffered half as much as she said she did, she would have sent for Dr. Haydock long ago. But Miss Emily, when this was hinted to her, shut her eyes in a superior way and murmured that her case was not a simple one—the best specialists in London had been baffled by it—and that a wonderful new man had put her on a most revolutionary course of treatment and that she really hoped her health would improve under it. No humdrum G.P. could possibly understand her case.

"And it's my opinion," said the outspoken Miss Hartnell, "that she's very wise not to send for him. Dear Dr. Haydock, in that breezy manner of his, would tell her that there was nothing the matter with her and to get up and not make a fuss! Do her a lot of good!"

Failing such arbitrary treatment, however, Miss Emily continued to lie on sofas, to surround herself with strange little pillboxes, and to reject nearly everything that had been cooked for her and ask for something else—usually something difficult and inconvenient to get.

The door was opened to Miss Marple by "Gladdie," looking more depressed than Miss Marple had ever thought possible. In the sitting room (a quarter of the late drawing room, which had been partitioned into a dining room, drawing room, bathroom, and housemaid's cupboard), Miss Lavinia rose to greet Miss Marple.

Lavinia Skinner was a tall, gaunt, bony female of fifty. She had a gruff voice and an abrupt manner.

"Nice to see you," she said. "Emily's lying down—feeling low today, poor dear. Hope she'll see you—it would cheer her up—but there are times when she doesn't feel up to seeing anybody. Poor dear, she's wonderfully patient."

Miss Marple responded politely. Servants were the main topic of conversation in St. Mary Mead, so it was not difficult to lead the conversation in that direction. Miss Marple said she had heard that that nice girl, Gladys Holmes, was leaving.

Miss Lavinia nodded.

"Wednesday week. Broke things, you know. Can't have that."

Miss Marple sighed and said we all had to put up with things nowadays. It was so difficult to get girls to come to the country. Did Miss Skinner really think it was wise to part with Gladys?

"Know it's difficult to get servants," admitted Miss Lavinia. "The Devereuxs haven't got anybody—but then I don't wonder—always quarrelling, jazz on all night—meals any time—that girl knows nothing of housekeeping. I pity her husband! Then the Larkins have just lost their maid. Of course, what with the judge's temper and his wanting Chota Hazri, as he calls it, at six in the morning, and Mrs. Larkin always fussing, I don't wonder at that, either. Mrs. Carmichael's Janet is a fixture, of course—though in my opinion she's the most disagreeable woman and absolutely bullies the old lady."

"Then don't you think you might reconsider your decision about Gladys. She really is a nice girl. I know all her family; very honest and superior."

Miss Lavinia shook her head.

"I've got my reasons," she said importantly.

Miss Marple murmured: "You missed a brooch, I understand—"

"Now who has been talking? I suppose the girl has. Quite frankly, I'm almost certain she took it. And then got frightened and put it back—but of course one can't say anything unless one is sure." She changed the subject. "Do come and see Miss Emily, Miss Marple. I'm sure it would do her good."

Miss Marple followed meekly to where Miss Lavinia knocked on a door, was bidden enter, and ushered her guest into the best room in the flat, most of the light of which was excluded by half-drawn blinds. Miss Emily was lying in bed, apparently enjoying the half gloom and her own indefinite sufferings.

The dim light showed her to be a thin, indecisive looking creature, with a good deal of greyish yellow hair untidily wound around her head and erupting into curls, the whole thing looking like a bird's nest of which no self-respecting bird could be proud. There was a smell in the room of eau de cologne, stale biscuits, and camphor.

With half-closed eyes and in a thin, weak voice, Emily Skinner explained that this was "one of her bad days."

"The worst of ill-health is," said Miss Emily in a melancholy tone, "that one knows what a burden one is to everyone around one.

"Lavinia is very good to me. Lavvie dear, I do so hate giving trouble, but if my hot-water bottle could only be filled in the way I like it—too full it weighs on me so; on the other hand, if it is not sufficiently filled, it gets cold immediately!"

"I'm sorry, dear. Give it to me. I will empty a little out."

"Perhaps, if you're doing that, it might be refilled. There are no rusks in the house, I suppose—no, no, it doesn't matter. I can do without. Some weak tea and a slice of lemon—no lemons? No, really, I couldn't drink tea without lemon. I think the milk was slightly turned this morning. It has put me right against milk in my tea. It doesn't matter. I can do without my tea. Only I do feel so weak. Oysters, they say, are nourishing. I wonder if I could fancy a few. No, no, too much bother to get hold of them so late in the day. I can fast until tomorrow."

Lavinia left the room murmuring something incoherent about bicycling down to the village.

Miss Emily smiled feebly at her guest and remarked that she did hate giving anyone any trouble.

Miss Marple told Edna that evening that she was afraid her mission had met with no success.

She was rather troubled to find that rumours as to Gladys' dishonesty were already going around the village.

In the post office Miss Wetherby tackled her: "My dear Jane, they gave her a written reference saying she was willing and sober and respectable, but saying nothing about honesty. That seems to me most significant! I hear there was some trouble about a brooch. I think there must be something in it, you know, because one doesn't let a servant go nowadays unless it's something rather grave. They'll find it most difficult to get anyone else. Girls simply will not go to Old Hall. They're nervous coming home on their days out. You'll see, the Skinners won't find anyone else, and then perhaps that dreadful hypochondriac sister will have to get up and do something!"

Great was the chagrin of the village when it was made known that the Misses Skinner had engaged, from an agency, a new maid who, by all accounts, was a perfect paragon.

"A three years' reference recommending her most warmly, she prefers the country and actually asks less wages than Gladys. I really feel we have been most fortunate."

"Well, really," said Miss Marple, to whom these details were imparted by Miss Lavinia in the fishmonger's shop. "It does seem too good to be true."

It then became the opinion of St. Mary Mead that the paragon would cry off at the last minute and fail to arrive.

None of these prognostications came true, however, and the village was able to observe the domestic treasure, by name, Mary Higgins, driving through the village in Reed's taxi to Old Hall. It had to be admitted that her appearance was good. A most respectable-looking woman, very neatly dressed.

When Miss Marple next visited Old Hall, on the occasion of recruiting stall holders for the Vicarage Fete, Mary Higgins opened the door. She was certainly a most superior-looking maid, at a guess forty years of age, with neat black hair, rosy cheeks, a plump figure discreetly arrayed in black with a white apron and cap—"quite the good, old-fashioned type of servant," as Miss Marple explained afterward, and with the proper, inaudible, respectful voice, so different from the loud but adenoidal accents of Gladys.

Miss Lavinia was looking far less harassed than usual and, although she regretted that she could not take a stall, owing to her preoccupation with her sister, she nevertheless tendered a handsome monetary contribution and promised to produce a consignment of penwipers and babies' socks.

Miss Marple commented on her air of well-being.

"I really feel I owe a great deal to Mary. I am so thankful I had the resolution to get rid of that other girl. Mary is really invaluable. Cooks nicely and waits beautifully and keeps our little flat scrupulously clean—mattresses turned over every day. And she is really wonderful with Emily!"

Miss Marple hastily inquired after Emily.

"Oh, poor dear, she has been very much under the weather lately. She can't help it, of course, but it really makes things a little difficult sometimes. Wanting certain things cooked and then, when they come, saying she can't eat now—and then wanting them again half an hour later and everything spoiled and having to be done again. It makes, of course, a lot of work—but fortunately Mary does not seem to mind at all. She's used to waiting on invalids, she says, and understands them. It is such a comfort."

"Dear me," said Miss Marple. "You are fortunate."

"Yes, indeed. I really feel Mary has been sent to us as an answer to prayer."

"She sounds to me," said Miss Marple, "almost too good to be true. I should—well, I should be a little careful if I were you."

Lavinia Skinner failed to perceive the point of this remark. She said, "Oh, I assure you I do all I can to make her comfortable. I don't know what I should do if she left."

"I don't expect she'll leave until she's ready to leave," said Miss Marple and stared very hard at her hostess.

Miss Lavinia said, "If one has no domestic worries, it takes such a load off one's mind, doesn't it? How is your little Edna shaping?"

"She's doing quite nicely. Not like your Mary. Still I do know all about Edna, because she's a village girl."

As she went out into the hall she heard the invalid's voice fretfully raised: "This compress has been allowed to get quite dry—Dr. Allerton particularly said moisture continually renewed. There, there, leave it. I want a cup of tea and a boiled egg—boiled only three minutes and a half, remember, and send Miss Lavinia to me."

The efficient Mary emerged from the bedroom and, saying to Lavinia, "Miss Emily is asking for you, madam," proceeded to open the door for Miss Marple, helping her into her coat and handing her her umbrella in the most irreproachable fashion.

Miss Marple took the umbrella, dropped it, tried to pick it up, and dropped her bag which flew open. Mary politely retrieved various odds and ends—a handkerchief, an engagement book, an old-fashioned leather purse, two shillings, three pennies, and a striped piece of peppermint rock.

Miss Marple received the last with some signs of confusion.

"Oh dear, that must have been Mrs. Clement's little boy. He was sucking it, I remember, and he took my bag to play with. He must have put it inside. It's terribly sticky, isn't it?"

"Shall I take it, madam?"

"Oh, would you? Thank you so much."

Mary stooped to retrieve the last item, a small mirror, upon recovering which Miss Marple exclaimed fervently, "How lucky now that that isn't broken."

She thereupon departed, Mary standing politely by the door holding a piece of striped rock with a completely expressionless face.

For ten days longer St. Mary Mead had to endure

hearing of the excellencies of Miss Lavinia's and Miss Emily's treasure.

On the eleventh day the village awoke to its big thrill.

Mary, the paragon, was missing! Her bed had not been slept in and the front door was found ajar. She had slipped out quietly during the night.

And not Mary alone was missing! Two brooches and five rings of Miss Lavinia's, three rings, a pendant, a bracelet, and four brooches of Miss Emily's were missing also!

It was the beginning of a chapter of catastrophe.

Young Mrs. Devereux had lost her diamonds which she kept in an unlocked drawer and also some valuable furs given to her as a wedding present. The judge and his wife also had had jewelry taken and a certain amount of money. Mrs. Carmichael was the greatest sufferer. Not only had she some very valuable jewels, but she also kept a large sum of money in the flat which had gone. It had been Janet's evening out and her mistress was in the habit of walking round the gardens at dusk, calling to the birds and scattering crumbs. It seemed clear that Mary, the perfect maid, had had keys to fit all the flats!

There was, it must be confessed, a certain amount of ill-natured pleasure in St. Mary Mead. Miss Lavinia had boasted so much of her marvellous Mary.

"And all the time, my dear, just a common thief!"

Interesting revelation followed. Not only had Mary disappeared into the blue, but the agency which had provided her and vouched for her credentials was alarmed to find that the Mary Higgins who had applied to them and whose references they had taken up had, to all intents and purposes, never existed. It was the name of a bona fide servant who had lived with the bona fide sister of a dean, but the real Mary Higgins was existing peacefully in a place in Cornwall.

"Clever, the whole thing," Inspector Slack was forced to admit. "And, if you ask me, that woman works in with a gang. There was a case of much the same kind in Northumberland a year ago. Stuff was never traced and they never caught her. However, we'll do better than that in Much Benham!"

Inspector Slack was always a confident man.

Nevertheless, weeks passed and Mary Higgins remained

triumphantly at large. In vain Inspector Slack redoubled that energy that so belied his name.

Miss Lavinia remained tearful. Miss Emily was so upset and felt so alarmed by her condition that she actually sent for Dr. Haydock.

The whole of the village was terribly anxious to know what he thought of Miss Emily's claims to ill-health but naturally could not ask him. Satisfactory data came to hand on the subject, however, through Mr. Meek, the chemist's assistant, who was walking out with Clara, Mrs. Price-Ridley's maid. It was then known that Dr. Haydock had prescribed a mixture of asafoetida and valerian which, according to Mr. Meek, was the stock remedy for malingerers in the army!

Soon afterward it was learned that Miss Emily, not relishing the medical attention she had had, was declaring that in the state of her health she felt it her duty to be near the specialist in London who understood her case. It was, she said, only fair to Lavinia.

The flat was put up for subletting.

It was a few days after that that Miss Marple, rather pink and flustered, called at the police station in Much Benham and asked for Inspector Slack.

Inspector Slack did not like Miss Marple. But he was aware that the chief constable, Colonel Melchett, did not share that opinion. Rather grudgingly, therefore, he received her.

"Good afternoon, Miss Marple. What can I do for you?"

"Oh, dear," said Miss Marple, "I'm afraid you're in a hurry."

"Lot of work on," said Inspector Slack, "but I can spare a few moments."

"Oh, dear," said Miss Marple. "I hope I shall be able to put what I say properly. So difficult, you know, to explain oneself, don't you think? No, perhaps you don't. But you see, not having been educated in the modern style—just a governess, you know, who taught one the dates of the Kings of England and General Knowledge—and how needles are made and all that. Discursive, you know, but not teaching one to keep to the point. Which is what I want to do. It's about Miss Skinner's maid, Gladys, you know."

"Mary Higgins," said Inspector Slack.

"Oh yes, the second maid. But it's Gladys Holmes I mean —rather an impertinent girl and far too pleased with herself, but really strictly honest, and it's so important that that should be recognized."

"No charge against her so far as I know," said the inspector.

"No, I know there isn't a charge—but that makes it worse. Because, you see, people go on thinking things. Oh, dear—I knew I should explain badly. What I really mean is that the important thing is to find Mary Higgins."

"Certainly," said Inspector Slack. "Have you any ideas on the subject?"

"Well, as a matter of fact, I have," said Miss Marple. "May I ask you a question? Are fingerprints of no use to you?"

"Ah," said Inspector Slack, "that's where she was a bit too artful for us. Did most of her work in rubber gloves or housemaid's gloves, it seems. And she'd been careful— wiped off everything in her bedroom and on the sink. Couldn't find a single fingerprint in the place!"

"If you did have her fingerprints, would it help?"

"It might, madam. They may be known at the Yard. This isn't her first job, I'd say!"

Miss Marple nodded brightly. She opened her bag and extracted a small cardboard box. Inside it, wedged in cotton wool, was a small mirror.

"From my handbag," said Miss Marple. "The maid's prints are on it. I think they should be satisfactory—she touched an extremely sticky substance a moment previously."

Inspector Slack stared.

"Did you get her fingerprints on purpose?"

"Of course."

"You suspected her then?"

"Well, you know it did strike me that she was a little too good to be true. I practically told Miss Lavinia so. But she simply wouldn't take the hint! I'm afraid, you know, Inspector, that I don't believe in paragons. Most of us have our faults—and domestic service shows them up very quickly!"

"Well," said Inspector Slack, recovering his balance,

"I'm obliged to you, I'm sure. We'll send these up to the Yard and see what they have to say."

He stopped. Miss Marple had put her head a little on one side and was regarding him with a good deal of meaning.

"You wouldn't consider, I suppose, Inspector, looking a little nearer home?"

"What do you mean, Miss Marple?"

"It's very difficult to explain, but when you come across a peculiar thing you notice it. Although, often, peculiar things may be the merest trifles. I've felt that all along, you know; I mean about Gladys and the brooch. She's an honest girl; she didn't take that brooch. Then why did Miss Skinner think she did? Miss Skinner's not a fool, far from it! Why was she so anxious to let a girl go who was a good servant when servants are hard to get? It was peculiar, you know. So I wondered. I wondered a good deal. And I noticed another peculiar thing! Miss Emily's a hypochondriac, but she's the first hypochondriac who hasn't sent for some doctor or other at once. Hypochondriacs love doctors. Miss Emily didn't!"

"What are you suggesting, Miss Marple?"

"Well, I'm suggesting, you know, that Miss Lavinia and Miss Emily are peculiar people. Miss Emily spends nearly all her time in a dark room. And if that hair of hers isn't a wig, I—I'll eat my own back switch! And what I say is this—it's perfectly possible for a thin, pale, grey-haired, whining woman to be the same as a black-haired, rosy-cheeked, plump woman. And nobody that I can find ever saw Miss Emily and Mary Higgins at one and the same time.

"Plenty of time to get impressions of all the keys, plenty of time to find out all about the other tenants, and then—get rid of the local girl. Miss Emily takes a brisk walk across country one night and arrives at the station as Mary Higgins next day. And then, at the right moment, Mary Higgins disappears, and off goes the hue and cry after her. I'll tell you where you'll find her, Inspector. On Miss Emily Skinner's sofa! Get her fingerprints if you don't believe me, but you'll find I'm right! A couple of clever thieves, that's what the Skinners are—and no doubt in league with a clever post and rails or fence or whatever you call it. But they won't get away with it this time! I'm not going to have one of our village girl's character for honesty taken away like that! Gladys Holmes is as honest as the day and everybody's going to know it! Good afternoon!"

Miss Marple had stalked out before Inspector Slack had recovered.

"Whew!" he muttered. "I wonder if she's right."

He soon found out that Miss Marple was right again.

Colonel Melchett congratulated Slack on his efficiency, and Miss Marple had Gladys come to tea with Edna and spoke to her seriously on settling down in a good situation when she got one.

THE CASE OF THE CARETAKER

"Well," demanded Dr. Haydock of his patient, "and how goes it today?"

Miss Marple smiled at him wanly from pillows.

"I suppose, really, that I'm better," she admitted, "but I feel so terribly depressed. I can't help feeling how much better it would have been if I had died. After all, I'm an old woman. Nobody wants me or cares about me."

Dr. Haydock interrupted with his usual brusqueness: "Yes, yes, typical after-reaction to this type of 'flu.' What you need is something to take you out of yourself. A mental tonic."

Miss Marple sighed and shook her head.

"And what's more," continued Dr. Haydock, "I've brought my medicine with me!"

He tossed a long envelope onto the bed.

"Just the thing for you. The kind of puzzle that is right up your street."

"A puzzle?" Miss Marple looked interested.

"Literary effort of mine," said the doctor, blushing a little. "Tried to make a regular story of it. 'He said, she said, the girl thought, et cetera.' Facts of the story are true."

"But why a puzzle?" asked Miss Marple.

Dr. Haydock grinned. "Because the interpretation is up to you. I want to see if you're as clever as you always make out."

With that Parthian shot he departed.

Miss Marple picked up the manuscript and began to read.

"And where is the bride?" asked Miss Harmon genially. The village was all agog to see the rich and beautiful young wife that Harry Laxton had brought back from abroad. There was a general indulgent feeling that Harry—wicked young scapegrace—had had all the luck. Everyone had always felt indulgent toward Harry. Even the owners of windows that had suffered from his indiscriminate use of a catapult had found their indignation dissipated by young Harry's abject expression of regret. He had broken windows, robbed orchards, poached rabbits, and later had run into debt—been disentangled and sent off to Africa—and the village, as represented by various aging spinsters, had murmured indulgently, "Ah, well! Wild oats! He'll settle down!"

And now, sure enough, the prodigal had returned—not in affliction, but in triumph. Harry Laxton had "made good," as the saying goes. He had pulled himself together, worked hard, and had finally met and successfully wooed a young Anglo-French girl who was the possessor of a considerable fortune.

Harry might have lived in London, or purchased an estate in some fashionable hunting county, but he preferred to come back to the part of the world that was home to him. And there, in the most romantic way, he purchased the derelict estate in the Dower House of which he had passed his childhood.

Kingsdean House had been unoccupied for nearly seventy years. It had gradually fallen into decay and abandon. An elderly caretaker and his wife lived in the one habitable corner of it. It was a vast, unprepossessing, grandiose mansion, the gardens overgrown with rank vegetation and the trees hemming it in like some gloomy enchanter's den.

The Dower House was a pleasant, unpretentious house and had been let for a long term of years to Major Laxton, Harry's father. As a boy, Harry had roamed over the Kingsdean estate and knew every inch of the tangled woods, and the old house itself had always fascinated him.

Major Laxton had died some years ago, so it might have been thought that Harry would have had no ties to bring him back; nevertheless, it was to the home of his boyhood that Harry brought his bride. The ruined old Kingsdean House was pulled down. An army of builders and contractors swooped down upon the place and in almost a miraculously short space of time—so marvellously does wealth tell

—the new house rose, white and gleaming among the trees.

Next came a posse of gardeners and after them a procession of furniture vans.

The house was ready. Servants arrived. Lastly a costly limousine deposited Harry and Mrs. Harry at the front door.

The village rushed to call, and Mrs. Price, who owned the largest house, and who considered herself to lead society in the place, sent out cards of invitation for a party "to meet the bride."

It was a great event. Several ladies had new frocks for the occasion. Everyone was excited, curious, anxious to see this fabulous creature. They said it was all so like a fairy story!

Miss Harmon, weather-beaten, hearty spinster, threw out her question as she squeezed her way through the crowded drawing-room door. Little Miss Brent, a thin, acidulated spinster, fluttered out information.

"Oh, my dear, quite charming. Such pretty manners. And quite young. Really, you know, it makes one feel quite envious to see someone who has everything like that. Good looks and money and breeding—most distinguished, nothing in the least common about her—and dear Harry so devoted!"

"Ah," said Miss Harmon, "it's early days yet!"

Miss Brent's thin nose quivered appreciatively.

"Oh, my dear, do you really think—"

"We all know what Harry is," said Miss Harmon.

"We know what he was! But I expect now—"

"Ah," said Miss Harmon, "men are always the same. I know them."

"Dear, dear. Poor young thing." Miss Brent looked much happier. "Yes, I expect she'll have trouble with him. Someone ought really to warn her."

"Beasts!" said Clarice Vane indignantly to her uncle, Dr. Haydock. "Absolute beasts some people are."

He looked at her curiously.

She was a tall, dark girl, handsome, warmhearted and impulsive. Her big brown eyes were alight now with indignation as she said, "All these cats—saying things—hinting things."

"About Harry Laxton?"

"Yes. It's like ghouls feasting on dead bodies."

"I daresay, my dear, it does seem like that to you. But you see, they have very little to talk about down here, and so I'm afraid they do tend to dwell upon past scandals. But I'm curious to know why it upsets you so much."

Clarice Vane bit her lip and flushed. She said, in a curiously muffled voice, "They—they look so happy. The Laxtons, I mean. They're young and in love and it's all so lovely for them. I hate to think of it being spoiled by whispers and hints and innuendoes and general beastliness."

"H'm. I see."

Clarice went on: "He was talking to me just now. He's so happy and eager and excited and—yes, thrilled—at having got his heart's desire and rebuilt Kingsdean. He's like a child about it all. And she—well, I don't suppose anything has ever gone wrong in her whole life. She's always had everything. You've seen her. What did you think of her?"

The doctor did not answer at once. For other people, Louise Laxton might be an object of envy. A spoiled darling of fortune. To him she had brought only the refrain of a popular song heard many years ago: "Poor Little Rich Girl . . ."

A small, delicate figure, with flaxen hair curled rather stiffly round her face and big, wistful blue eyes.

Louise was drooping a little. The long stream of congratulations had tired her. She was hoping it might soon be time to go. Perhaps, even now, Harry might say so. She looked at him sideways. So tall and broad-shouldered with his eager pleasure in this horrible dull party.

"Poor little rich girl . . ."

"Ooph!" It was a sigh of relief.

Harry turned to look at his wife amusedly. They were driving away from the party. She said, "Darling, what a frightful party!"

Harry laughed.

"Yes, pretty terrible. Never mind, my sweet. It had to be done, you know. All these old pussies knew me when I lived here as a boy. They'd have been terribly disappointed not to have got a good look at you close up."

Louise made a grimace. She said, "Shall we have to see a lot of them?"

"What? Oh no. They'll come and make ceremonious calls with card cases, and you'll return the calls and then you needn't bother any more. You can have your own friends down or whatever you like."

Louise said, after a minute or two, "Isn't there anyone amusing living down here?"

"Oh yes. There's the County, you know. Though you may find them a bit dull too. Mostly interested in bulbs and dogs and horses. You'll ride, of course. You'll enjoy that. There's a horse over at Eglinton I'd like you to see. A beautiful animal, perfectly trained, no vice in him, but plenty of spirit."

The car slowed down to take the turn into the gates of Kingsdean. Harry wrenched the wheel and swore as a grotesque figure sprang up in the middle of the road and he only just managed to avoid it. It stood there, shaking a fist and shouting after them.

Louise clutched his arm. "Who's that—that horrible old woman?"

Harry's brow was black.

"That's old Murgatroyd. She and her husband were caretakers in the old house. They were there for nearly thirty years."

"Why does she shake her fist at you?"

Harry's face got red.

"She—well, she resented the house being pulled down. And she got the sack, of course. Her husband's been dead two years. They say she got a bit queer after he died."

"Is she—she isn't—starving?"

Louise's ideas were vague and somewhat melodramatic. Riches prevented you from coming into contact with reality.

Harry was outraged.

"Good Lord, Louise, what an idea! I pensioned her off, of course—and handsomely too! Found her a new cottage and everything."

Louise asked, bewildered, "Then why does she mind?"

Harry was frowning, his brows drawn together. "Oh, how should I know? Craziness! She loved the house."

"But it was a ruin, wasn't it?"

"Of course it was—crumbling to pieces—roof leaking—more or less unsafe. All the same, I suppose it meant something to her. She'd been there a long time. Oh, I don't know! The old devil's cracked, I think."

Louise said uneasily, "She—I think she cursed us. Oh, Harry, I wish she hadn't."

It seemed to Louise that her new home was tainted and poisoned by the malevolent figure of one crazy old woman. When she went out in the car, when she rode, when she walked out with the dogs, there was always the same figure waiting. Crouched down on herself, a battered hat over wisps of iron-grey hair, and the slow muttering of imprecations.

Louise came to believe that Harry was right—the old woman was mad. Nevertheless, that did not make things easier. Mrs. Murgatroyd never actually came to the house, nor did she use definite threats, nor offer violence. Her squatting figure remained always just outside the gates. To appeal to the police would have been useless and, in any case, Harry Laxton was averse to that course of action. It would, he said, arouse local sympathy for the old brute. He took the matter more easily than Louise did.

"Don't worry about it, darling. She'll get tired of this silly cursing business. Probably she's only trying it on."

"She isn't, Harry. She—she hates us! I can feel it. She—she's ill-wishing us."

"She's not a witch, darling, although she may look like one! Don't be morbid about it all."

Louise was silent. Now that the first excitement of settling in was over, she felt curiously lonely and at a loose end. She had been used to life in London and the Riviera. She had no knowledge of or taste for English country life. She was ignorant of gardening, except for the final act of "doing the flowers." She did not really care for dogs. She was bored by such neighbours as she met. She enjoyed riding best, sometimes with Harry, sometimes, when he was busy about the estate, by herself. She hacked through the woods and lanes, enjoying the easy paces of the beautiful horse that Harry had bought for her. Yet even Prince Hal, most sensitive of chestnut steeds, was wont to shy and snort as he carried his mistress past that huddled figure of a malevolent old woman.

One day Louise took her courage in both hands. She was out walking. She had passed Mrs. Murgatroyd, pretending not to notice her, but suddenly she swerved back and went right up to her. She said, a little breathlessly, "What is it? What's the matter? What do you want?"

The old woman blinked at her. She had a cunning, dark gypsy face, with wisps of iron-grey hair, and bleared, suspicious eyes. Louise wondered if she drank.

She spoke in a whining and yet threatening voice: "What do I want, you ask? What, indeed! That which has been took away from me. Who turned me out of Kingsdean House? I'd lived there, girl and woman, for near on forty years. It was a black deed to turn me out, and it's black bad luck it'll bring to you and him!"

Louise said, "You've got a very nice cottage and—"

She broke off. The old woman's arms flew up. She screamed, "What's the good of that to me? It's my own place I want and my own fire as I sat beside all them years. And as for you and him, I'm telling you there will be no happiness for you in your new fine house. It's the black sorrow will be upon you! Sorrow and death and my curse. May your fair face rot."

Louise turned away and broke into a little stumbling run. She thought, "I must get away from here! We must sell the house! We must go away."

At the moment such a solution seemed easy to her. But Harry's utter incomprehension took her aback. He exclaimed, "Leave here? Sell the house? Because of a crazy old woman's threats? You must be mad."

"No, I'm not. But she—she frightens me. I know something will happen."

Harry Laxton said grimly, "Leave Mrs. Murgatroyd to me. I'll settle her!"

A friendship had sprung up between Clarice Vane and young Mrs. Laxton. The two girls were much of an age, though dissimilar both in character and in tastes. In Clarice's company Louise found reassurance. Clarice was so

self-reliant, so sure of herself. Louise mentioned the matter
of Mrs. Murgatroyd and her threats, but Clarice seemed to
regard the matter as more annoying than frightening.

"It's so stupid, that sort of thing," she said. "And really
very annoying for you."

"You know, Clarice, I—I feel quite frightened sometimes. My heart gives the most awful jumps."

"Nonsense, you mustn't let a silly thing like that get you
down. She'll soon tire of it."

Louise was silent for a minute or two. Clarice said,
"What's the matter?"

Louise paused for a minute, then her answer came with
a rush: "I hate this place! I hate being here. The woods
and this house, and the awful silence at night, and the
queer noise owls make. Oh, and the people and everything."

"The people. What people?"

"The people in the village. Those prying, gossiping old
maids."

Clarice said sharply, "What have they been saying?"

"I don't know. Nothing particular. But they've got nasty
minds. When you've talked to them you feel you wouldn't
trust anybody—not anybody at all."

Clarice said harshly, "Forget them. They've nothing to
do but gossip. And most of the muck they talk they just in-
vent."

Louise said, "I wish we'd never come here. But Harry
adores it so." Her voice softened. Clarice thought, "How
she adores him."

She said abruptly, "I must go now."

"I'll send you back in the car. Come again soon."

Clarice nodded. Louise felt comforted by her new
friend's visit. Harry was pleased to find her more cheerful
and from then on urged her to have Clarice often to the
house.

Then one day he said, "Good news for you, darling."

"Oh, what?"

"I've fixed the Murgatroyd. She's got a son in America,
you know. Well, I've arranged for her to go out and join
him. I'll pay her passage."

"Oh, Harry, how wonderful. I believe I might get to like
Kingsdean after all."

"Get to like it? Why, it's the most wonderful place in the world!"

Louise gave a little shiver. She could not rid herself of her superstitious fear so easily.

If the ladies of St. Mary Mead had hoped for the pleasure of imparting information about her husband's past to the bride, this pleasure was denied them by Harry Laxton's own prompt action.

Miss Harmon and Clarice Vane were both in Mr. Edge's shop, the one buying moth balls and the other a packet of boracic, when Harry Laxton and his wife came in.

After greeting the two ladies, Harry turned to the counter and was just demanding a toothbrush when he stopped in mid-speech and exclaimed heartily, "Well, well, just see who's here! Bella, I do declare."

Mrs. Edge, who had hurried out from the back parlour to attend the congestion of business, beamed back cheerfully at him, showing her big white teeth. She had been a dark, handsome girl and was still a reasonably handsome woman, though she had put on weight and the lines of her face had coarsened, but her large brown eyes were full of warmth as she answered, "Bella it is, Mr. Harry, and pleased to see you after all these years."

Harry turned to his wife.

"Bella's an old flame of mine, Louise," he said. "Head-over-ears in love with her, wasn't I, Bella?"

"That's what you say," said Mrs. Edge.

Louise laughed. She said, "My husband's very happy seeing all his old friends again."

"Ah," said Mrs. Edge, "we haven't forgotten you, Mr. Harry. Seems like a fairy tale to think of you married and building up a new house instead of that ruined old Kingsdean House."

"You look very well and blooming," said Harry, and Mrs. Edge laughed and said there was nothing wrong with her and what about that toothbrush?

Clarice watching the baffled look on Miss Harmon's face, said to herself exultantly, "Oh, well done, Harry. You've spiked their guns."

Dr. Haydock said abruptly to his niece Clarice, "What's

all this nonsense about old Mrs. Murgatroyd hanging about Kingsdean and shaking her fist and cursing the new regime?"

"It isn't nonsense. It's quite true. It's upset Louise a good deal."

"Tell her she needn't worry—when the Murgatroyds were caretakers they never stopped grumbling about the place—they only stayed because Murgatroyd drank and couldn't get another job."

"I'll tell her," said Clarice doubtfully, "but I don't think she'll believe you. The old woman fairly screams with rage."

"Always used to be fond of Harry as a boy. I can't understand it."

Clarice said, "Oh well—they'll be rid of her soon. Harry's paying her passage to America."

Three days later Louise was thrown from her horse and killed.

Two men in a baker's van were witnesses of the accident. They saw Louise ride out of the gates, saw the old woman spring up and stand in the road, waving her arms and shouting, saw the horse start, swerve, and then bolt madly down the road, flinging Louise Laxton over his head.

One of them stood over the unconscious figure, not knowing what to do, while the other rushed to the house to get help.

Harry Laxton came running out, his face ghastly. They took off a door of the van and carried her on it to the house. She died without regaining consciousness and before the doctor arrived.

(End of Dr. Haydock's manuscript.)

When Dr. Haydock arrived the following day, he was pleased to note that there was a pink flush in Miss Marple's cheek and decidedly more animation in her manner.

"Well," he said, "what's the verdict?"

"What's the problem?" countered Miss Marple.

"Oh, my dear lady, do I have to tell you that?"

"I suppose," said Miss Marple, "that it's the curious conduct of the caretaker. Why did she behave in that very odd way? People do mind being turned out of their old homes.

But it wasn't her home. In fact, she used to complain and grumble while she was there. Yes, it certainly looks very fishy. What became of her, by the way?"

"Took flight to Liverpool. The accident scared her. Thought she'd wait there for her boat."

"All very convenient for somebody," said Miss Marple.

"Yes, I think the 'Problem of the Caretaker's Conduct' can be solved easily enough. Bribery, was it not?"

"That's your solution?"

"Well, if it wasn't natural for her to behave in that way, she must have been 'putting on an act,' as people say, and that means that somebody paid her to do what she did."

"And you know who that somebody was?"

"Oh, I think so. Money again, I'm afraid. And I've always noticed that gentlemen always tend to admire the same type."

"Now I'm out of my depth."

"No, no, it all hangs together. Harry Laxton admired Bella Edge, a dark, vivacious type. Your niece Clarice was the same. But the poor little wife was quite a different type —fair-haired and clinging—not his type at all. So he must have married her for her money. And murdered her for her money too!"

"You use the word murder?"

"Well, he sounds the right type. Attractive to women and quite unscrupulous. I suppose he wanted to keep his wife's money and marry your niece. He may have been seen talking to Mrs. Edge. But I don't fancy he was attached to her any more. Though I daresay he made the poor woman think he was, for ends of his own. He soon had her well under his thumb, I fancy."

"How exactly did he murder her, do you think?"

Miss Marple stared ahead of her for some minutes with dreamy blue eyes.

"It was very well timed—with the baker's van as witness. They could see the old woman and, of course, they'd put down the horse's fright to that. But I should imagine, myself, that an air gun, or perhaps a catapult—he used to be good with a catapult. Yes, just as the horse came through the gate. The horse bolted, of course, and Mrs. Laxton was thrown."

She paused, frowning.

"The fall might have killed her. But he couldn't be sure of that. And he seems the sort of man who would lay his plans carefully and leave nothing to chance. After all, Mrs. Edge could get him something suitable without her husband knowing. Otherwise why would Harry bother with her? Yes, I think he had some powerful drug handy, that could be administered before you arrived. After all, if a woman is thrown from her horse and has serious injuries and dies without recovering consciousness, well—a doctor wouldn't normally be suspicious, would he? He'd put it down to shock or something."

Dr. Haydock nodded.

"Why did you suspect?" asked Miss Marple.

"It wasn't any particular cleverness on my part," said Dr. Haydock. "It was just the trite, well-known fact that a murderer is so pleased with his cleverness that he doesn't take proper precautions. I was just saying a few consolatory words to the bereaved husband—and feeling sorry for the fellow, too—when he flung himself down on the settee to do a bit of play-acting and a hypodermic syringe fell out of his pocket.

"He snatched it up and looked so scared that I began to think. Harry Laxton didn't drug; he was in perfect health. What was he doing with a hypodermic syringe? I did the autopsy with a view to certain possibilities. I found strophanthin. The rest was easy. There was strophanthin in Laxton's possession, and Bella Edge, questioned by the police, broke down and admitted to having got it for him. And finally old Mrs. Murgatroyd confessed that it was Harry Laxton who had put her up to the cursing stunt."

"And your niece got over it?"

"Yes, she was attracted by the fellow, but it hadn't gone far."

The doctor picked up his manuscript.

"Full marks to you, Miss Marple—and full marks to me for my prescription. You're looking almost yourself again."

THE BLUE GERANIUM

"When I was down here last year—" said Sir Henry Clithering, and stopped.

His hostess, Mrs. Bantry, looked at him curiously.

The ex-Commissioner of Scotland Yard was staying with old friends of his, Colonel and Mrs. Bantry, who lived near St. Mary Mead.

Mrs. Bantry, pen in hand, had just asked his advice as to who should be invited to make a sixth guest at dinner that evening.

"Yes?" said Mrs. Bantry encouragingly. "When you were here last year?"

"Tell me," said Sir Henry, "do you know a Miss Marple?"

Mrs. Bantry was surprised. It was the last thing she had expected.

"Know Miss Marple? Who doesn't! The typical old maid of fiction. Quite a dear, but hopelessly behind the times. Do you mean you would like me to ask her to dinner?"

"You are surprised?"

"A little, I must confess. I should hardly have thought you—but perhaps there's an explanation?"

"The explanation is simple enough. When I was down here last year we got into the habit of discussing unsolved mysteries—there were five or six of us. We each supplied a story to which we knew the answer, but nobody else did. It was supposed to be an exercise in the deductive faculties—to see who could get nearest the truth."

"Well?"

"Like in the old story—we hardly realized that Miss Marple was playing; but we were very polite about it—

didn't want to hurt the old dear's feelings. And now comes the cream of the jest. The old lady outdid us every time!"

"But how extraordinary! Why, dear old Miss Marple has hardly ever been out of St. Mary Mead."

"Ah! But according to her, that has given her unlimited opportunities of observing human nature—under the microscope, as it were."

"I suppose there's something in that," conceded Mrs. Bantry. "One would at least know the petty side of people. But I don't think we have any really exciting criminals in our midst. I think we must try her with Arthur's ghost story after dinner. I'd be thankful if she'd find a solution to that."

"I didn't know that Arthur believed in ghosts?"

"Oh, he doesn't. That's what worries him so. And it happened to a friend of his, George Pritchard—a most prosaic person. It's really rather tragic for poor George. Either this extraordinary story is true—or else—"

"Or else what?"

Mrs. Bantry did not answer. After a minute or two she said irrelevantly:

"You know, I like George—everyone does. One can't believe that he—but people do do such extraordinary things."

Sir Henry nodded. He knew, better than Mrs. Bantry, the extraordinary things that people did.

So it came about that that evening Mrs. Bantry looked around her dinner table (shivering a little as she did so, because the dining room, like most English dining rooms, was extremely cold) and fixed her gaze on the very upright old lady sitting on her husband's right. Miss Marple wore black lace mittens; an old lace fichu was draped round her shoulders and another piece of lace surmounted her white hair. She was talking animatedly to the elderly doctor, Dr. Lloyd, about the workhouse and the suspected shortcomings of the district nurse.

Mrs. Bantry marvelled anew. She even wondered whether Sir Henry had been making an elaborate joke—but there seemed no point in that. Incredible that what he had said could be really true.

Her glance went on and rested affectionately on her red-faced broad-shouldered husband as he sat talking horses to

Jane Helier, the beautiful and popular actress. Jane, more beautiful (if that were possible) off the stage than on, opened enormous blue eyes and murmured at discreet intervals, "Really?" "Oh, fancy!" "How extraordinary!" She knew nothing whatever about horses and cared less.

"Arthur," said Mrs. Bantry, "you're boring poor Jane to distraction. Leave your horses alone and tell her your ghost story instead. You know . . . George Pritchard."

"Eh, Dolly? Oh, but I don't know—"

"Sir Henry wants to hear it too. I was telling him something about it this morning. It would be interesting to hear what everyone has to say about it."

"Oh, do!" said Jane. "I love ghost stories."

"Well—" Colonel Bantry hesitated. "I've never believed much in the supernatural. But this . . .

"I don't think any of you know George Pritchard. He's one of the best. His wife—well, she's dead now, poor woman. I'll just say this much: she didn't give George any too easy a time when she was alive. She was one of those semi-invalids—I believe she really had something wrong with her, but whatever it was, she played it for all it was worth. She was capricious, exacting, unreasonable. She complained from morning to night. George was expected to wait on her hand and foot, and everything he did was always wrong."

"She was a dreadful woman," said Mrs. Bantry with conviction.

"I don't quite know how this business started. George was rather vague about it. I gather Mrs. Pritchard had always had a weakness for fortunetellers, palmists, clairvoyants—anything of that sort. George didn't mind. If she found amusement in it, well and good. But he refused to go into rhapsodies himself, and that was another grievance.

"A succession of hospital nurses was always passing through the house, Mrs. Pritchard usually becoming dissatisfied with them after a few weeks. One young nurse had been very keen on this fortunetelling stunt, and for a time Mrs. Pritchard had been very fond of her. Then she suddenly fell out with her and insisted on her going. She had back another nurse who had been with her previously—an older woman, experienced and tactful in dealing with a neurotic patient. Nurse Copling, according to George, was

a very good sort—a sensible woman to talk to. She put up
with Mrs. Pritchard's tantrums and nerve storms with complete indifference.

"Mrs. Pritchard always lunched upstairs, and it was usual at lunch time for George and the nurse to come to some
arrangement for the afternoon. Strictly speaking, the nurse
went off from two to four, but 'to oblige,' as the phrase
goes, she would sometimes take her time off after tea if
George wanted to be free for the afternoon. On this occasion she mentioned that she was going to see a sister at
Golders Green and might be a little late returning.
George's face fell, for he had arranged to play a round of
golf. Nurse Copling, however, reassured him.

" 'We'll neither of us be missed, Mr. Pritchard.' A twinkle came into her eye. 'Mrs. Pritchard's going to have more
exciting company than ours.'

" 'Who's that?'

" 'Wait a minute.' Nurse Copling's eyes twinkled more
than ever. 'Let me get it right. *Zarida, Psychic Reader of
the Future.*'

" 'That's a new one, isn't it?' groaned George.

" 'Quite new. I believe my predecessor, Nurse Carstairs,
sent her along. Mrs. Pritchard hasn't seen her yet. She
made me write, fixing an appointment for this afternoon.'

" 'Well, at any rate, I shall get my golf,' said George,
and he went off with the kindliest feelings toward Zarida,
the reader of the future.

"On his return to the house, he found Mrs. Pritchard in
a state of great agitation. She was, as usual, lying on her invalid couch, and she had a bottle of smelling salts in her
hand which she sniffed at frequent intervals.

" 'George,' she exclaimed, 'what did I tell you about this
house? The moment I came into it, I felt there was something wrong! Didn't I tell you so at the time?'

"Repressing his desire to reply, 'You always do,' George
said, 'No, can't say I remember it.'

" 'You never do remember anything that has to do with
me. Men are all extraordinarily callous—but I really believe that you are even more insensitive than most.'

"Oh, come now, Mary dear, that's not fair."

" 'Well, as I was telling you, this woman knew at once!

She—she actually blenched—if you know what I mean—as she came in at that door, and she said, "There is evil here —evil and danger. I feel it." '

"Very unwisely George laughed.

" 'Well, you have had your money's worth this afternoon.'

"His wife closed her eyes and took a long sniff from her smelling bottle.

" 'How you hate me! You would jeer and laugh if I were dying.'

"George protested, and after a minute or two she went on.

" 'You may laugh, but I shall tell you the whole thing. This house is definitely dangerous to me—the woman said so.'

"George's formerly kind feeling toward Zarida underwent a change. He knew his wife was perfectly capable of insisting on moving to a new house if the caprice got hold of her.

" 'What else did she say?' he asked.

" 'She couldn't tell me very much. She was so upset. One thing she did say. I had some violets in a glass. She pointed at them and cried out:

" 'Take those away. No blue flowers—never have blue flowers. Blue flowers are fatal to you—remember that."

" 'And you know,' added Mrs. Pritchard, 'I always have told you that blue as a colour is repellent to me. I feel a natural instinctive sort of warning against it.'

"George was much too wise to remark that he had never heard her say so before. Instead he asked what the mysterious Zarida was like. Mrs. Pritchard entered with gusto upon a description.

" 'Black hair in coiled knobs over her ears—her eyes were half closed—great black rims round them—she had a black veil over her mouth and chin—she spoke in a kind of singing voice with a marked foreign accent—Spanish, I think—'

" 'In fact, all the usual stock in trade,' said George cheerfully.

"His wife immediately closed her eyes.

" 'I feel extremely ill,' she said. 'Ring for Nurse. Unkindness upsets me, as you know only too well.'

"It was two days later that Nurse Copling came to George with a grave face.

" 'Will you come to Mrs. Pritchard, please. She has had a letter which upsets her greatly.'

"He found his wife with the letter in her hand. She held it out to him.

" 'Read it,' she said.

"George read it. It was on heavily scented paper, and the writing was big and black.

I have seen the Future. Be warned before it is too late. Beware of the full moon. The Blue Primrose means Warning; the Blue Hollyhock means Danger; the Blue Geranium means Death. . . .

"Just about to burst out laughing, George caught Nurse Copling's eye. She made a quick warning gesture. He said rather awkwardly, 'The woman's probably trying to frighten you, Mary. Anyway, there aren't such things as blue primroses and blue geraniums.'

"But Mrs. Pritchard began to cry and say her days were numbered. Nurse Copling came out with George upon the landing.

" 'Of all the silly tomfoolery,' he burst out.

" 'I suppose it is.'

"Something in the nurse's tone struck him, and he stared at her in amazement.

" 'Surely, Nurse, you don't believe—'

" 'No, no, Mr. Pritchard. I don't believe in reading the future—that's nonsense. What puzzles me is the meaning of this. Fortunetellers are usually out for what they can get. But this woman seems to be frightening Mrs. Pritchard with no advantage to herself. I can't see the point. There's another thing—'

" 'Yes?'

" 'Mrs. Pritchard says that something about Zarida was faintly familiar to her.'

" 'Well?'

" 'Well, I don't like it, Mr. Pritchard, that's all.'

" 'I didn't know you were so superstitious, Nurse.'

" 'I'm not superstitious, but I know when a thing is fishy.'

"It was about four days after this that the first incident happened. To explain it to you, I shall have to describe Mrs. Pritchard's room—"

"You'd better let me do that," interrupted Mrs. Bantry. "It was papered with one of these new wallpapers where you apply clumps of flowers to make a kind of herbaceous border. The effect is almost like being in a garden— though, of course, the flowers are all wrong. I mean they simply couldn't be in bloom all at the same time—"

"Don't let a passion for horticultural accuracy run away with you, Dolly," said her husband. "We all know you're an enthusiastic gardener."

"Well, it is absurd," protested Mrs. Bantry. "To have bluebells and daffodils and lupins and hollyhocks and Michaelmas daisies all grouped together."

"Most unscientific," said Sir Henry. "But to proceed with the story . . ."

"Well, among these massed flowers were primroses, clumps of yellow and pink primroses, and—oh, go on, Arthur, this is your story."

Colonel Bantry took up the tale.

"Mrs. Pritchard rang her bell violently one morning. The household came running—thought she was in extremis; not at all. She was violently excited and pointing at the wallpaper, and there, sure enough, was one blue primrose in the midst of the others . . ."

"Oh!" said Miss Helier, "how creepy!"

"The question was: Hadn't the blue primrose always been there? That was George's suggestion and the nurse's. But Mrs. Pritchard wouldn't have it at any price. She had never noticed it till that very morning, and the night before had been full moon. She was very upset about it."

"I met George Pritchard that same day and he told me about it," said Mrs. Bantry. "I went to see Mrs. Pritchard and did my best to ridicule the whole thing, but without success. I came away really concerned, and I remember I met Jean Instow and told her about it. Jean is a queer girl. She said, 'So she's really upset about it?' I told her that I thought the woman was perfectly capable of dying of fright—she was really abnormally superstitious.

"I remember Jean rather startled me with what she said next. She said, 'Well, that might be all for the best,

mightn't it?' And she said it so coolly, in so matter-of-fact
a tone, that I was really—well, shocked. Of course I know
it's done nowadays—to be brutal and outspoken, but I
never get used to it. Jean smiled at me rather oddly and
said, 'You don't like my saying that—but it's true. What
use is Mrs. Pritchard's life to her? None at all, and it's hell
for George Pritchard. To have his wife frightened out of
existence would be the best thing that could happen to
him.' I said, 'George is most awfully good to her always.'
And she said, 'Yes, he deserves a reward, poor dear. He's a
very attractive person, George Pritchard. The last nurse
thought so—the pretty one—what was her name? Carstairs. That was the cause of the row between her and Mrs.
P.'

"Now I didn't like hearing Jean say that. Of course, one
had wondered—"

Mrs. Bantry paused significantly.

"Yes, dear," said Miss Marple placidly. "One always
does. Is Miss Instow a pretty girl? I suppose she plays
golf?"

"Yes. She's good at all games. And she's nice-looking,
attractive-looking, very fair with a healthy skin and nice
steady blue eyes. Of course, we always have felt that she
and George Pritchard—I mean, if things had been different
—they are so well suited to one another."

"And they were friends?" asked Miss Marple.

"Oh yes. Great friends."

"Do you think, Dolly," said Colonel Bantry plaintively,
"that I might be allowed to go on with my story?"

"Arthur," said Mrs. Bantry resignedly, "wants to get
back to his ghosts."

"I had the rest of the story from George himself," went
on the colonel. "There's no doubt that Mrs. Pritchard got
the wind up badly toward the end of the next month. She
marked off on a calendar the day when the moon would be
full, and on that night she had both the nurse and then
George into her room and made them study the wallpaper
carefully. There were pink hollyhocks and red ones, but
there were no blue among them. Then when George left
the room she locked the door—"

"And in the morning there was a large blue hollyhock,"
said Miss Helier joyfully.

"Quite right," said Colonel Bantry. "Or at any rate, nearly right. One flower of a hollyhock just above her head had turned blue. It staggered George, and of course, the more it staggered him the more he refused to take the thing seriously. He insisted that the whole thing was some kind of a practical joke. He ignored the evidence of the locked door and the fact that Mrs. Pritchard discovered the change before anyone—even Nurse Copling—was admitted.

"It staggered George, and it made him unreasonable. His wife wanted to leave the house, and he wouldn't let her. He was inclined to believe in the supernatural for the first time, but he wasn't going to admit it. He usually gave in to his wife, but this time he wouldn't. Mary was not to make a fool of herself, he said. The whole thing was the most infernal nonsense.

"And so the next month sped away. Mrs. Pritchard made less protest than one would have imagined. I think she was superstitious enough to believe that she couldn't escape her fate. She repeated again and again: 'The blue primrose—warning. The blue hollyhock—danger. The blue geranium—death.' And she would lie looking at the clump of pinky-red geraniums nearest her bed.

"The whole business was pretty nervy. Even the nurse caught the infection. She came to George two days before full moon and begged him to take Mrs. Pritchard away. George was angry.

" 'If all the flowers on that wall turned into blue devils, it couldn't kill anyone!' he shouted.

" 'It might. Shock has killed people before now.'

" 'Nonsense,' said George.

"George has always been a shade pigheaded. You can't drive him. I believe he had a secret idea that his wife worked the changes herself and that it was all some morbid, hysterical plan of hers.

"Well, the fatal night came. Mrs. Pritchard locked her door as usual. She was very calm—in almost an exalted state of mind. The nurse was worried by her state—and wanted to give her a stimulant, an injection of strychnine, but Mrs. Pritchard refused. In a way, I believe, she was enjoying herself. George said she was."

"I think that's quite possible," said Mrs. Bantry. "There

must have been a strange sort of glamour about the whole thing."

"There was no violent ringing of a bell the next morning. Mrs. Pritchard usually woke about eight. When, at eight-thirty, there was no sign from her, Nurse rapped loudly on the door. Getting no reply, she fetched George and insisted on the door being broken open. They did so with the help of a chisel.

"One look at the still figure on the bed was enough for Nurse Copling. She sent George to telephone for the doctor, but it was too late. Mrs. Pritchard, he said, must have been dead at least eight hours. Her smelling salts lay by her hand on the bed, and on the wall beside her one of the pinky-red geraniums was a bright deep blue."

"Horrible," said Miss Helier with a shiver.

Sir Henry was frowning.

"No additional details?"

Colonel Bantry shook his head, but Mrs. Bantry spoke quickly.

"The gas."

"What about the gas?" asked Sir Henry.

"When the doctor arrived there was a slight smell of gas, and sure enough, he found the gas ring in the fireplace very slightly turned on, but so little that it couldn't have mattered."

"Did Mr. Pritchard and the nurse not notice it when they first went in?"

"The nurse said she did notice a slight smell. George said he didn't notice gas, but something made him feel very queer and overcome; but he put that down to shock—and probably it was. At any rate, there was no question of gas poisoning. The smell was scarcely noticeable."

"And that's the end of the story?"

"No, it isn't. One way and another, there was a lot of talk. The servants, you see, had overheard things—had heard, for instance, Mrs. Pritchard telling her husband that he hated her and would jeer if she were dying. And also more recent remarks. She said one day, apropos of his refusing to leave the house, 'Very well. When I am dead, I hope everyone will realize that you have killed me.' And as ill luck would have it, he had been mixing some weed killer for the garden paths the very day before. One of the younger servants had seen him and had afterward seen him taking up a glass of hot milk to his wife.

"The talk spread and grew. The doctor had given a certificate—I don't know exactly in what terms—shock, syncope, heart failure, probably some medical term meaning nothing much. However, the poor lady had not been a month in her grave before an exhumation order was applied for and granted."

"And the result of the autopsy was nil, I remember," said Sir Henry gravely. "A case, for once, of smoke without fire."

"The whole thing is really very curious," said Mrs. Bantry. "That fortuneteller, for instance—Zarida. At the address where she was supposed to be, no one had ever heard of any such person!"

"She appeared once—out of the blue," said her husband, "and then utterly vanished. Out of the blue—that's rather good!"

"And what is more," continued Mrs. Bantry, "little Nurse Carstairs, who was supposed to have recommended her, had never even heard of her."

They looked at each other.

"It's a mysterious story," said Dr. Lloyd. "One can make guesses, but to guess—"

He shook his head.

"Has Mr. Pritchard married Miss Instow?" asked Miss Marple in her gentle voice.

"Now why do you ask that?" inquired Sir Henry.

Miss Marple opened gentle blue eyes.

"It seems to me so important," she said. "Have they married?"

Colonel Bantry shook his head.

"We—well, we expected something of the kind—but it's eighteen months now. I don't believe they even see much of each other."

"That is important," said Miss Marple. "Very important."

"Then you think the same as I do," said Mrs. Bantry. "You think—"

"Now, Dolly," said her husband. "It's unjustifiable—what you're going to say. You can't go about accusing people without a shadow of proof."

"Don't be so—so manly, Arthur. Men are always afraid to say anything. Anyway, this is all between ourselves. It's just a wild, fantastic idea of mine that possibly—only possibly—Jean Instow disguised herself as a fortuneteller. Mind you, she may have done it for a joke. I don't for a minute think that she meant any harm; but if she did do it, and if Mrs. Pritchard was foolish enough to die of fright—well, that's what Miss Marple meant, wasn't it?"

"No, dear, not quite," said Miss Marple. "You see, if I were going to kill anyone—which, of course, I wouldn't dream of doing for a minute, because it would be very wicked, and besides, I don't like killing—not even wasps, though I know it has to be, and I'm sure the gardener does it as humanely as possible. Let me see, what was I saying?"

"If you wished to kill anyone," prompted Sir Henry.

"Oh yes. Well, if I did, I shouldn't be at all satisfied to trust to fright. I know one reads of people dying of it, but it seems a very uncertain sort of thing, and the most nervous people are far more brave than one really thinks they are. I should like something definite and certain and make a thoroughly good plan about it."

"Miss Marple," said Sir Henry, "you frighten me. I hope you will never wish to remove me. Your plans would be too good."

Miss Marple looked at him reproachfully.

"I thought I had made it clear that I would never contemplate such wickedness," she said. "No, I was trying to put myself in the place of—er—a certain person."

"Do you mean George Pritchard?" asked Colonel Bantry. "I'll never believe it of George—though, mind you, even the nurse believes it. I went and saw her about a month afterward, at the time of the exhumation. She didn't know how it was done—in fact, she wouldn't say anything at all—but it was clear enough that she believed George to be in some way responsible for his wife's death. She was convinced of it."

"Well," said Dr. Lloyd, "perhaps she wasn't so far wrong. And mind you, a nurse often knows. She can't say—she's got no proof—but she knows."

Sir Henry leaned forward.

"Come now, Miss Marple," he said persuasively. "You're lost in a daydream. Won't you tell us all about it?"

Miss Marple started and turned pink.

"I beg your pardon," she said. "I was just thinking about our district nurse. A most difficult problem."

"More difficult than the problem of a blue geranium?"

"It really depends on the primroses," said Miss Marple. "I mean, Mrs. Bantry said they were yellow and pink. If it was a pink primrose that turned blue, of course, that fits in perfectly. But if it happened to be a yellow one—"

"It was a pink one," said Mrs. Bantry.

She stared. They all stared at Miss Marple.

"Then that seems to settle it," said Miss Marple. She shook her head regretfully. "And the wasp season and everything. And of course the gas."

"It reminds you, I suppose, of countless village tragedies?" said Sir Henry.

"Not tragedies," said Miss Marple. "And certainly nothing criminal. But it does remind me a little of the trouble we are having with the district nurse. After all, nurses are human beings, and what with having to be so correct in their behaviour and wearing those uncomfortable collars and being so thrown with the family—well, can you wonder that things sometimes happen?"

A glimmer of light broke upon Sir Henry.

"You mean Nurse Carstairs?"

"Oh no. Not Nurse Carstairs. Nurse Copling. You see, she had been there before and very much thrown with Mr. Pritchard, who you say is an attractive man. I daresay she thought, poor thing—well, we needn't go into that. I don't suppose she knew about Miss Instow, and of course afterward, when she found out, it turned her against him and she tried to do all the harm she could. Of course, the letter really gave her away, didn't it?"

"What letter?"

"Well, she wrote to the fortuneteller at Mrs. Pritchard's request, and the fortuneteller came, apparently in answer to the letter. But later it was discovered that there never had been such a person at that address. So that shows that Nurse Copling was in it. She only pretended to write—so what could be more likely than that she was the fortuneteller herself?"

"I never saw the point about the letter," said Sir Henry. "That's a most important point, of course."

"Rather a bold step to take," said Miss Marple, "because Mrs. Pritchard might have recognized her in spite of the disguise—though of course if she had, the nurse could have pretended it was a joke."

"What did you mean," said Sir Henry, "when you said that if you were a certain person, you would not have trusted to fright?"

"One couldn't be sure that way," said Miss Marple. "No, I think that the warnings and the blue flowers were, if I may use a military term"—she laughed self-consciously—"just camouflage."

"And the real thing?"

"I know," said Miss Marple apologetically, "that I've got wasps on the brain. Poor things, destroyed in their thousands—and usually on such a beautiful summer's day. But I remember thinking, when I saw the gardener shaking up the cyanide of potassium in a bottle with water, how like smelling salts it looked. And if it were ·put in a smelling-salt bottle and substituted for the real one—well, the poor lady was in the habit of using her smelling salts. Indeed, you said they were found by her hand. Then, of course, while Mr. Pritchard went to telephone to the doctor, the nurse would change it for the real bottle, and she'd just turn on the gas a little bit to mask any smell of almonds and in case anyone felt queer, and I always have heard that cyanide leaves no trace if you wait long enough. But, of course, I may be wrong, and it may have been something entirely different in the bottle, but that doesn't really matter, does it?"

Miss Marple paused, a little out of breath.

Jane Helier leaned forward and said, "But the blue geranium and the other flowers?"

"Nurses always have litmus paper, don't they?" said Miss Marple, "for—well, for testing. Not a very pleasant subject. We won't dwell on it. I have done a little nursing myself." She grew delicately pink. "Blue turns red with acids, and red turns blue with alkalies. So easy to paste some red litmus over a red flower—near the bed, of course. And then, when the poor lady used her smelling salts, the strong ammonia fumes would turn it blue. Really most ingenious. Of course, the geranium wasn't blue when they first broke into the room—nobody noticed it till afterward. When nurse changed the bottles, she held the sal ammoniac against the wallpaper for a minute, I expect."

"You might have been there, Miss Marple," said Sir Henry.

"What worries me," said Miss Marple, "is poor Mr. Pritchard and that nice girl, Miss Instow. Probably both suspecting each other and keeping apart—and life so very short."

She shook her head.

"You needn't worry," said Sir Henry. "As a matter of fact, I have something up my sleeve. A nurse has been arrested on a charge of murdering an elderly patient who had left her a legacy. It was done with cyanide of potassium substituted for smelling salts. Nurse Copling trying the same trick again. Miss Instow and Mr. Pritchard need have no doubts as to the truth."

"Now isn't that nice?" cried Miss Marple. "I don't mean about the new murder, of course. That's very sad and shows how much wickedness there is in the world and that if once you give away—which reminds me, I must finish my little conversation with Dr. Lloyd about the village nurse."

THE COMPANION

"Now, Dr. Lloyd," said Miss Helier, "don't you know any creepy stories?"

She smiled at him—the smile that nightly bewitched the theater-going public. Jane Helier was sometimes called the most beautiful woman in England, and jealous members of her own profession were in the habit of saying to each other: "Of course Jane's not an artist. She can't act—if you know what I mean. It's those eyes!"

And those "eyes" were at this minute fixed appealingly on the grizzled elderly bachelor doctor who, for the last five years, had ministered to the ailments of the village of St. Mary Mead.

With an unconscious gesture, the doctor pulled down his waistcoat (inclined of late to be uncomfortably tight) and racked his brains hastily, so as not to disappoint the lovely creature who addressed him so confidently.

"I feel," said Jane dreamily, "that I would like to wallow in crime this evening."

"Splendid," said Colonel Bantry, her host. "Splendid, splendid." And he laughed a loud, hearty military laugh. "Eh, Dolly?"

His wife, hastily recalled to the exigencies of social life (she had been planning her spring border), agreed enthusiastically.

"Of course it's splendid," she said heartily but vaguely. "I always thought so."

"Did you, my dear?" said old Miss Marple, and her eyes twinkled a little.

"We don't get much in the creepy line—and still less in

the criminal line—in St. Mary Mead, you know, Miss Helier," said Dr. Lloyd.

"You surprise me," said Sir Henry Clithering. The ex-Commissioner of Scotland Yard turned to Miss Marple. "I always understood from our friend here that St. Mary Mead is a positive hotbed of crime and vice."

"Oh, Sir Henry!" protested Miss Marple, a spot of colour coming into her cheeks. "I'm sure I never said anything of the kind. The only thing I ever said was that human nature is much the same in a village as anywhere else, only one has opportunities and leisure for seeing it at closer quarters."

"But you haven't always lived here," said Jane Helier, still addressing the doctor. "You've been in all sorts of queer places all over the world—places where things happen!"

"That is so, of course," said Dr. Lloyd, still thinking desperately. "Yes, of course . . . Yes . . . Ah! I have it!"

He sank back with a sigh of relief.

"It is some years ago now—I had almost forgotten. But the facts were really very strange—very strange indeed. And the final coincidence which put the clue into my hand was strange also."

Miss Helier drew her chair a little nearer to him, applied some lipstick, and waited expectantly. The others also turned interested faces toward him.

"I don't know whether any of you know the Canary Islands," began the doctor.

"They must be wonderful," said Jane Helier. "They're in the South Seas, aren't they? Or is it the Mediterranean?"

"I've called in there on my way to South Africa," said the colonel. "The Peak of Teneriffe is a fine sight with the setting sun on it."

"The incident I am describing happened in the island of Grand Canary, not Teneriffe. It is a good many years ago now. I had had a breakdown in health and was forced to give up my practice in England to go abroad. I practised in Las Palmas, which is the principal town of Grand Canary. In many ways I enjoyed the life out there very much. The climate was mild and sunny, there was excellent surf bathing (and I am an enthusiastic bather), and the sea life of the port attracted me. Ships from all over the world put in at Las Palmas. I used to walk along the mole every morning, far more interested than any member of the fair sex could be in a street of hat shops.

"As I say, ships from all over the world put in at Las Palmas. Sometimes they stay a few hours, sometimes a day or two. In the principal hotel there, the Metropole, you will see people of all races and nationalities—birds of passage. Even the people going to Teneriffe usually come here and stay a few days before crossing to the other island.

"My story begins there, in the Metropole Hotel, one Thursday evening in January. There was a dance going on and I and a friend had been sitting at a small table watching the scene. There was a fair sprinkling of English and other nationalities, but the majority of the dancers were Spanish; and when the orchestra struck up a tango, only half a dozen couples of the latter nationality took the floor. They all danced well and we looked on and admired. One woman in particular excited our lively admiration. Tall, beautiful, and sinuous, she moved with the grace of a half-tamed leopardess. There was something dangerous about her. I said as much to my friend and he agreed.

"'Women like that,' he said, 'are bound to have a history. Life will not pass them by.'

"'Beauty is perhaps a dangerous possession,' I said.

"'It's not only beauty,' he insisted. 'There is something else. Look at her again. Things are bound to happen to that woman, or because of her. As I said, life will not pass her by. Strange and exciting events will surround her. You've only got to look at her to know it.'

"He paused and then added with a smile:

"'Just as you've only got to look at those two women over there and know that nothing out of the way could ever happen to either of them! They are made for a safe and uneventful existence.'

"I followed his eyes. The two women he referred to were travellers who had just arrived—a Holland Lloyd boat had put into port that evening, and the passengers were just beginning to arrive.

"As I looked at them I saw at once what my friend meant. They were two English ladies—the thoroughly nice travelling English that you do find abroad. Their ages, I should say, were round about forty. One was fair and a little—just a little—too plump; the other was dark and a little—again just a little—inclined to scragginess. They were what is called well-preserved, quietly and inconspicuously dressed in well-cut tweeds, and innocent of any kind of make-up. They had that air of quiet assurance which is the birthright of well-bred Englishwomen. There was nothing remarkable about either of them. They were like thousands of their sisters. They would doubtless see what they wished to see, assisted by Baedeker, and be blind to everything else. They would use the English library and attend the English church in any place they happened to be, and it was quite likely that one or both of them sketched a little. And as my friend said, nothing exciting or remarkable would ever happen to either of them, though they might quite likely travel half over the world. I looked from them back to our sinuous Spanish woman with her half-closed smouldering eyes and I smiled."

"Poor things," said Jane Helier with a sigh. "But I do think it's so silly of people not to make the most of themselves. That woman in Bond Street—Valentine—is really wonderful. Audrey Denman goes to her; and have you seen her in *The Downward Step*? As the schoolgirl in the first act she's really marvellous. And yet Audrey is fifty if she's a day. As a matter of fact, I happen to know she's really nearer sixty."

"Go on," said Mrs. Bantry to Dr. Lloyd. "I love stories about sinuous Spanish dancers. It makes me forget how old and fat I am."

"I'm sorry," said Dr. Lloyd apologetically. "But you see, as a matter of fact, this story isn't about the Spanish woman."

"It isn't?"

"No. As it happens, my friend and I were wrong. Nothing in the least exciting happened to the Spanish beauty. She married a clerk in a shipping office, and by the time I left the island she had had five children and was getting very fat."

"Just like that girl of Israel Peters," commented Miss Marple. "The one who went on the stage and had such good legs that they made her principal boy in the pantomime. Everyone said she'd come to no good, but she married a commercial traveller and settled down splendidly."

"The village parallel," murmured Sir Henry softly.

"No," went on the doctor, "my story is about the two English ladies."

"Something happened to them?" breathed Miss Helier.

"Something happened to them—and the very next day too."

"Yes?" said Mrs. Bantry encouragingly.

"Just for curiosity, as I went out that evening, I glanced at the hotel register. I found the names easily enough. Miss Mary Barton and Miss Amy Durrant of Little Paddocks, Caughton Weir, Bucks. I little thought then how soon I was to encounter the owners of those names again—and under what tragic circumstances.

"The following day I had arranged to go for a picnic with some friends. We were to motor across the island, taking our lunch, to a place called (as far as I remember—it is so long ago) Las Nieves, a well-sheltered bay where we could bathe if we felt inclined. This programme we duly carried out, except that we were somewhat late in starting, so that we stopped on the way and picnicked, going on to Las Nieves afterward for a swim before tea.

"As we approached the beach, we were at once aware of a tremendous commotion. The whole population of the small village seemed to be gathered on the shore. As soon as they saw us they rushed toward the car and began explaining excitedly. My Spanish not being very good, it took me a few minutes to understand, but at last I got it.

"Two of the mad English ladies had gone in to bathe, and one had swum out too far and got into difficulties. The other had gone after her and had tried to bring her in, but her strength in turn had failed and she, too, would have drowned had not a man rowed out in a boat and brought in rescuer and rescued—the latter beyond help.

"As soon as I got the hang of things I pushed the crowd aside and hurried down the beach. I did not at first recognize the two women. The plump figure in the tight green rubber bathing cap awoke no chord of recognition as she looked up anxiously. She was kneeling beside the body of her friend, making somewhat amateurish attempts at artificial respiration. When I told her that I was a doctor she gave a sigh of relief, and I ordered her off at once to one of the cottages for a rubdown and dry clothing. One of the ladies in my party went with her. I myself worked unavailingly on the body of the drowned woman. Life was only too clearly extinct, and in the end I had reluctantly to give in.

"I rejoined the others in the small fisherman's cottage and there I had to break the sad news. The survivor was attired now in her own clothes, and I immediately recognized her as one of the two arrivals of the night before. She received the sad news fairly calmly, and it was evidently the horror of the whole thing that struck her more than any great personal feeling.

" 'Poor Amy,' she said. 'Poor, poor Amy. She had been looking forward to the bathing here so much. And she was a good swimmer too. I can't understand it. What do you think it can have been, Doctor?'

" 'Possibly cramp. Will you tell me exactly what happened?'

" 'We had both been swimming about for some time—twenty minutes, I should say. Then I thought I would go in, but Amy said she was going to swim out once more. She did so, and suddenly I heard her call and realized she was calling for help. I swam out as fast as I could. She was still afloat when I got to her, but she clutched at me wildly and we both went under. If it hadn't been for that man coming out with his boat, I should have been drowned too.'

" 'That has happened fairly often,' I said. 'To save anyone from drowning is not an easy affair.'

" 'It seems so awful,' continued Miss Barton. 'We only arrived yesterday and were so delighting in the sunshine and our little holiday. And now this—this terrible tragedy occurs.'

"I asked her then for particulars about the dead woman, explaining that I would do everything I could for her, but that the Spanish authorities would require full information. This she gave me readily enough.

"The dead woman, Miss Amy Durrant, was her companion and had come to her about five months previously. They had got on very well together, but Miss Durrant had spoken very little about her people. She had been left an orphan at an early age and had been brought up by an uncle and had earned her own living since she was twenty-one.

"And so that was that," went on the doctor. He paused and said again, but this time with a certain finality in his voice, "And so that was that."

"I don't understand," said Jane Helier. "Is that all? I mean, it's very tragic, I suppose, but isn't—well, it isn't what I call creepy."

"I think there's more to follow," said Sir Henry.

"Yes," said Dr. Lloyd, "there's more to follow. You see, right at the time there was one queer thing. Of course, I asked questions of the fishermen, et cetera, as to what they'd seen. They were eyewitnesses. And one woman had rather a funny story. I didn't pay any attention to it at the time, but it came back to me afterward. She insisted, you see, that Miss Durrant wasn't in difficulties when she called out. The other swam out to her and, according to this woman, deliberately held Miss Durrant's head under water. I didn't, as I say, pay much attention. It was such a fantastic story, and these things look so differently from the shore. Miss Barton might have tried to make her friend lose consciousness, realizing that the latter's panic-stricken clutching would drown them both. You see, according to the Spanish woman's story, it looked as though—well, as though Miss Barton was deliberately trying to drown her companion.

"As I say, I paid very little attention to this story at the time. It came back to me later. Our great difficulty was to find out anything about this woman, Amy Durrant. She didn't seem to have any relations. Miss Barton and I went through her things together. We found one address and wrote there, but it proved to be simply a room she had taken in which to keep some of her things. The landlady knew nothing, had only seen her when she took the room. Miss Durrant had remarked at the time that she always liked to have one place she could call her own to which she could return at any moment. There were one or two nice pieces of old furniture and some bound numbers of Academy pictures, and a trunk full of pieces of material bought at sales, but no personal belongings. She had mentioned to the landlady that her father and mother had died in India when she was a child and that she had been brought up by an uncle who was a clergyman, but she did not say if he was her father's or her mother's brother, so the name was no guide.

"It wasn't exactly mysterious, it was just unsatisfactory. There must be many lonely women, proud and reticent, in just that position. There were a couple of photographs among her belongings in Las Palmas—rather old and faded, and they had been cut to fit the frames they were in, so that there was no photographer's name upon them, and there was an old daguerreotype which might have been her mother or more probably her grandmother.

"Miss Barton had had two references with her. One she had forgotten; the other name she recollected after an effort. It proved to be that of a lady who was now abroad, having gone to Australia. She was written to. Her answer, of course, was a long time in coming, and I may say that when it did arrive there was no particular help to be gained from it. She said Miss Durrant had been with her as companion and had been most efficient and that she was a very charming woman, but that she knew nothing of her private affairs or relations.

"So there it was—as I say, nothing unusual, really. It was just the two things together that aroused my uneasiness. This Amy Durrant of whom no one knew anything, and the Spanish woman's queer story. Yes, and I'll add a third thing: When I was first bending over the body and Miss Barton was walking away toward the huts, she looked back. Looked back with an expression on her face that I can only describe as one of poignant anxiety—a kind of anguished uncertainty that imprinted itself on my brain.

"It didn't strike me as anything unusual at the time. I put it down to her terrible distress over her friend. But, you see, later I realized that they weren't on those terms. There was no devoted attachment between them, no terrible grief. Miss Barton was fond of Amy Durrant and shocked by her death—that was all.

"But, then, why that terrible poignant anxiety? That was the question that kept coming back to me. I had not been mistaken in that look. And almost against my will an answer began to shape itself in my mind. Supposing the Spanish woman's story were true; supposing that Mary Barton wilfully and in cold blood tried to drown Amy Durrant.

She succeeds in holding her under water while pretending to be saving her. She is rescued by a boat. They are on a lonely beach far from anywhere. And then I appear—the last thing she expects. A doctor! And an English doctor! She knows well enough that people who have been under water far longer than Amy Durrant have been revived by artificial respiration. But she has to play her part—to go off, leaving me alone with her victim. And as she turns for one last look, a terrible poignant anxiety shows in her face. Will Amy Durrant come back to life and tell what she knows?"

"Oh!" said Jane Helier. "I'm thrilled now."

"Viewed in that aspect, the whole business seemed more sinister, and the personality of Amy Durrant became more mysterious. Who was Amy Durrant? Why should she, an insignificant paid companion, be murdered by her employer? What story lay behind that fatal bathing expedition? She had entered Mary Barton's employment only a few months before. Mary Barton had brought her abroad, and the very day after they landed the tragedy had occurred. And they were both nice commonplace, refined Englishwomen! The whole thing was fantastic, and I told myself so. I had been letting my imagination run away with me."

"You didn't do anything, then?" asked Miss Helier.

"My dear young lady, what could I do? There was no evidence. The majority of the eyewitnesses told the same story as Miss Barton. I had built up my own suspicions out of a fleeting expression which I might quite possibly have imagined. The only thing I could and did do was to see that the widest inquiries were made for the relations of Amy Durrant. The next time I was in England I even went and saw the landlady of her room, with the results I have told you."

"But you felt there was something wrong," said Miss Marple.

Dr. Lloyd nodded.

"Half the time I was ashamed of myself for thinking so. Who was I to go suspecting this nice, pleasant-mannered English lady of a foul and cold-blooded crime? I did my best to be as cordial as possible to her during the short time she stayed on the island. I helped her with the Spanish authorities. I did everything I could do as an Englishman to help a compatriot in a foreign country, and yet I am convinced that she knew I suspected and disliked her."

"How long did she stay out here?" asked Miss Marple.

"I think it was about a fortnight. Miss Durrant was buried there, and it must have been about ten days later when she took a boat back to England. The shock had upset her so much that she felt she couldn't spend the winter there as she had planned. That's what she said."

"Did it seem to have upset her?" asked Miss Marple.

The doctor hesitated.

"Well, I don't know that it affected her appearance at all," he said cautiously.

"She didn't, for instance, grow fatter?" asked Miss Marple.

"Do you know—it's a curious thing your saying that. Now I come to think back, I believe you're right. She—yes, she did seem, if anything, to be putting on weight."

"How horrible," said Jane Helier with a shudder. "It's like—it's like fattening on your victim's blood."

"And yet, in another way, I may be doing her an injustice," went on Dr. Lloyd. "She certainly said something before she left which pointed in an entirely different direction. There may be, I think there are, consciences which work very slowly—which take some time to awaken to the enormity of the deed committed.

"It was the evening before her departure from the Canaries. She had asked me to go and see her and had thanked me very warmly for all I had done to help her. I, of course, made light of the matter, said I had only done what was natural under the circumstances, and so on. There was a pause after that, and then she suddenly asked me a question.

" 'Do you think,' she asked, 'that one is ever justified in taking the law into one's own hands?'

"I replied that that was rather a difficult question but that, on the whole, I thought not. The law was the law, and we had to abide by it.

" 'Even when it is powerless?'

" 'I don't quite understand.'

" 'It's difficult to explain, but one might do something that is considered definitely wrong—that is considered a crime, even, for a very good and sufficient reason.'

"I replied dryly that possibly several criminals had thought that in their time, and she shrank back.

" 'But that's horrible,' she murmured. 'Horrible.'

"And then with a change of tone she asked me to give her something to make her sleep. She had not been able to sleep properly since—she hesitated—since that terrible shock.

" 'You're sure it is that? There is nothing worrying you? Nothing on your mind?'

" 'On my mind? What should be on my mind?'

"She spoke fiercely and suspiciously.

" 'Worry is a cause of sleeplessness sometimes,' I said lightly.

"She seemed to brood for a moment.

" 'Do you mean worrying over the future, or worrying over the past, which can't be altered?'

" 'Either.'

" 'Only it wouldn't be any good worrying over the past. You couldn't bring back— Oh, what's the use? One mustn't think. One must not think.'

"I prescribed a mild sleeping draught and made my adieu. As I went away I wondered not a little over the words she had spoken. 'You couldn't bring back—' What? Or who?

"I think that last interview prepared me in a way for what was to come. I didn't expect it, of course, but when it happened, I wasn't surprised. Because, you see, Mary Barton struck me all along as a conscientious woman—not a weak sinner, but a woman with convictions, who would act up to them, and who would not relent as long as she still believed in them. I fancied that in that last conversation we had she was beginning to doubt her own convictions. I know her words suggested to me that she was feeling the first faint beginnings of that terrible soul-searcher—remorse.

"The thing happened in Cornwall, in a small watering place, rather deserted at that season of the year. It must have been—let me see—late March. I read about it in the papers. A lady had been staying at a small hotel there—a Miss Barton. She had been very odd and peculiar in her manner. That had been noticed by all. At night she would walk up and down her room, muttering to herself, and not allowing the people on either side of her to sleep. She had called on the vicar one day and had told him that she had a communication of the gravest importance to make to him. She had, she said, committed a crime. Then, instead of proceeding, she had stood up abruptly and said she would call another day. The vicar put her down as being slightly unbalanced and did not take her self-accusation seriously.

"The very next morning she was found to be missing from her room. A note was left addressed to the coroner. It ran as follows:

> I tried to speak to the vicar yesterday, to confess all, but was not allowed. She would not let me. I can make amends only one way—a life for a life; and my life must go the same way as hers did. I, too, must drown in the deep sea. I believed I was justified. I see now that that was not so. If I desire Amy's forgiveness, I must go to her. Let no one be blamed for my death—Mary Barton.

"Her clothes were found lying on the beach in a secluded cove near by, and it seemed clear that she had undressed there and swum resolutely out to sea where the current was known to be dangerous, sweeping one down the coast.

"The body was not discovered, but after a time leave was given to presume death. She was a rich woman, her estate being proved at a hundred thousand pounds. Since she died intestate, it all went to her next of kin—a family of cousins in Australia. The papers made discreet references to the tragedy in the Canary Islands, putting forward the theory that the death of Miss Durrant had unhinged her friend's brain. At the inquest the usual verdict of 'Suicide while temporarily insane' was returned.

"And so the curtain falls on the tragedy of Amy Durrant and Mary Barton."

There was a long pause and then Jane Helier gave a great gasp.

"Oh, but you mustn't stop there—just in the most interesting part. Go on."

"But you see, Miss Helier, this isn't a serial story. This is real life, and real life stops just where it chooses."

"But I don't want it to," said Jane. "I want to know."

"This is where we use our brains, Miss Helier," explained Sir Henry. "Why did Mary Barton kill her companion? That's the problem Dr. Lloyd has set us."

"Oh well," said Miss Helier, "she might have killed her for lots of reasons. I mean—oh, I don't know. She might have got on her nerves, or else she got jealous, although Dr. Lloyd doesn't mention any men, but still on the boat out—well, you know what everyone says about boats and sea voyages."

Miss Helier paused, slightly out of breath, and it was borne in upon her audience that the outside of Jane's charming head was distinctly superior to the inside.

"I would like to have a lot of guesses," said Mrs. Bantry. "But I suppose I must confine myself to one. Well, I think that Miss Barton's father made all his money out of ruining Amy Durrant's father, so Amy determined to have her revenge. Oh no, that's the wrong way around. How tiresome! Why does the rich employer kill the humble companion? I've got it. Miss Barton had a young brother who shot himself for love of Amy Durrant. Miss Barton waits her time. Amy comes down in the world. Miss B. engages her as companion and takes her to the Canaries and accomplishes her revenge. How's that?"

"Excellent," said Sir Henry. "Only we don't know that Miss Barton ever had a young brother."

"We deduce that," said Mrs. Bantry. "Unless she had a young brother there's no motive. So she must have had a young brother. Do you see, Watson?"

"That's all very fine, Dolly," said her husband. "But it's only a guess."

"Of course it is," said Mrs. Bantry. "That's all we can do —guess. We haven't got any clues. Go on, dear, have a guess yourself."

"Upon my word, I don't know what to say. But I think there's something in Miss Helier's suggestion that they fell out about a man. Look here, Dolly, it was probably some high church parson. They both embroidered him a cope or something, and he wore the Durrant woman's first. Depend upon it, it was something like that. Look how she went off to a parson at the end. These women all lose their heads over a good-looking clergyman. You hear of it over and over again."

"I think I must try and make my explanation a little more subtle," said Sir Henry, "though I admit it's only a guess. I suggest that Miss Barton was always mentally unhinged. There are more cases like that than you would imagine. Her mania grew stronger and she began to believe it her duty to rid the world of certain persons—possibly what is termed unfortunate females. Nothing much is known about Miss Durrant's past. So very possibly she *had* a past—an 'unfortunate' one. Miss Barton learns of this and decides on extermination. Later the righteousness of her act begins to trouble her and she is overcome by remorse. Her end shows her to be completely unhinged. Now, do say you agree with me, Miss Marple."

"I'm afraid I don't, Sir Henry," said Miss Marple, smiling apologetically. "I think her end shows her to have been a very clever and resourceful woman."

Jane Helier interrupted with a little scream.

"Oh! I've been so stupid. May I guess again? Of course it must have been that. Blackmail! The companion woman was blackmailing her. Only I don't see why Miss Marple says it was clever of her to kill herself. I can't see that at all."

"Ah!" said Sir Henry. "You see, Miss Marple knew a case just like it in St. Mary Mead."

"You always laugh at me, Sir Henry," said Miss Marple reproachfully. "I must confess it does remind me, just a little, of old Mrs. Trout. She drew the old-age pension, you know, for three old women who were dead, in different parishes."

"It sounds like a most complicated and resourceful crime," said Sir Henry. "But it doesn't seem to me to throw any light upon our present problem."

"Of course not," said Miss Marple. "It wouldn't—to you. But some of the families were very poor, and the old-age pension was a great boon to the children. I know it's difficult for anyone outside to understand. But what I really meant was that the whole thing hinged upon one old woman being so like any other old woman."

"Eh?" said Sir Henry, mystified.

"I always explain things so badly. What I mean is that when Dr. Lloyd described the two ladies first, he didn't know which was which, and I don't suppose anyone else in the hotel did. They would have, of course, after a day or so, but the very next day one of the two was drowned, and if the one who was left said she was Miss Barton, I don't suppose it would ever occur to anyone that she mightn't be."

"You think— Oh! I see," said Sir Henry slowly.

"It's the only natural way of thinking of it. Dear Mrs. Bantry began that way just now. Why should the rich employer kill the humble companion? It's so much more likely to be the other way about. I mean—that's the way things happen."

"Is it?" said Sir Henry. "You shock me."

"But of course," went on Miss Marple, "she would have to wear Miss Barton's clothes, and they would probably be a little tight on her, so that her general appearance would look as though she had got a little fatter. That's why I asked that question. A gentleman would be sure to think it was the lady who had got fatter and not the clothes that had got smaller—though that isn't quite the right way of putting it."

"But if Amy Durrant killed Miss Barton, what did she gain by it?" asked Mrs. Bantry. "She couldn't keep up the deception for ever."

"She only kept it up for another month or so," pointed out Miss Marple. "And during that time I expect she travelled, keeping away from anyone who might know her. That's what I meant by saying that one lady of a certain age looks so like another. I don't suppose the different photograph on her passport was ever noticed—you know what passports are. And then in March she went down to this Cornish place and began to act queerly and draw attention to herself so that when people found her clothes on the beach and read her last letter they shouldn't think of the common-sense conclusion."

"Which was?" asked Sir Henry.

"No body," said Miss Marple firmly. "That's the thing that would stare you in the face, if there weren't such a lot of red herrings to draw you off the trail—including the suggestion of foul play and remorse. No body. That was the real significant fact."

"Do you mean—" said Mrs. Bantry, "do you mean that there wasn't any remorse? That there wasn't—that she didn't drown herself?"

"Not she!" said Miss Marple "It's just Mrs. Trout over again. Mrs. Trout was very good at red herrings, but she met her match in me. And I can see through your remorse-driven Miss Barton. Drown herself? Went off to Australia, if I'm any good at guessing."

"You are, Miss Marple," said Dr. Lloyd. "Undoubtedly you are. Now it again took me quite by surprise. Why, you could have knocked me down with a feather that day in Melbourne."

"Was that what you spoke of as a final coincidence?"

Dr. Lloyd nodded.

"Yes, it was rather rough luck on Miss Barton—or Miss Amy Durrant—whatever you like to call her. I became a ship's doctor for a while, and landing in Melbourne, the first person I saw as I walked down the street was the lady I thought had been drowned in Cornwall. She saw the game was up as far as I was concerned, and she did the bold thing—took me into her confidence. A curious woman, completely lacking, I suppose, in some moral sense. She was the eldest of a family of nine, all wretchedly poor. They had applied once for help to their rich cousin in England and been repulsed, Miss Barton having quarrelled with their father. Money was wanted desperately, for the three youngest children were delicate and wanted expensive medical treatment. Amy Barton then and there seems to have decided on her plan of cold-blooded murder. She set out for England, working her passage over as a children's nurse. She obtained the situation of companion to Miss Barton, calling herself Amy Durrant. She engaged a room and put some furniture into it so as to create more of a personality for herself. The drowning plan was a sudden inspiration. She had been waiting for some opportunity to present itself. Then she staged the final scene of the drama and returned to Australia, and in due time she and her brothers and sisters inherited Miss Barton's money as next of kin."

"A very bold and perfect crime," said Sir Henry. "Almost the perfect crime. If it had been Miss Barton who had died in the Canaries, suspicion might attach to Amy Durrant and her connection with the Barton family might have been discovered; but the change of identity and the double crime, as you may call it, effectually did away with that. Yes, almost the perfect crime."

"What happened to her?" asked Mrs. Bantry. "What did you do in the matter, Dr. Lloyd?"

"I was in a very curious position, Mrs. Bantry. Of evidence, as the law understands it, I still had very little. Also, there were certain signs, plain to me as a medical man, that though strong and vigorous in appearance, the lady was not long for this world. I went home with her and saw the rest of the family—a charming family, devoted to their eldest sister and without an idea in their heads that she might prove to have committed a crime. Why bring sorrow on them when I could prove nothing? The lady's admission to me was unheard by anyone else. I let nature take its course. Miss Amy Barton died six months after my meeting with her. I have often wondered if she was cheerful and unrepentant up to the last."

"Surely not," said Mrs. Bantry.

"I expect so," said Miss Marple. "Mrs. Trout was."

Jane Helier gave herself a little shake.

"Well," she said, "it's very, very thrilling. I don't quite understand now who drowned which. And how does this Mrs. Trout come into it?"

"She doesn't, my dear," said Miss Marple. "She was only a person—not a very nice person—in the village."

"Oh!" said Jane. "In the village. But nothing ever happens in a village, does it?" She sighed. "I'm sure I shouldn't have any brains at all if I lived in a village."

THE FOUR SUSPECTS

The conversation hovered round undiscovered and unpunished crimes. Everyone in turn vouchsafed an opinion: Colonel Bantry, his plump amiable wife, Jane Helier, Dr. Lloyd, and even old Miss Marple. The one person who did not speak was the one best fitted in most people's opinion to do so. Sir Henry Clithering, ex-Commissioner of Scotland Yard, sat silent, twisting his moustache—or rather stroking it—and half smiling, as though at some inward thought that amused him.

"Sir Henry," said Mrs. Bantry at last, "if you don't say something, I shall scream. Are there a lot of crimes that go unpunished, or are there not?"

"You're thinking of newspaper headlines, Mrs. Bantry. SCOTLAND YARD AT FAULT AGAIN. And a list of unsolved mysteries to follow."

"Which really, I suppose, form a very small percentage of the whole?" said Dr. Lloyd.

"Yes, that is so. The hundreds of crimes that are solved and the perpetrators punished are seldom heralded and sung. But that isn't quite the point at issue, is it? When you talk of undiscovered crimes and unsolved crimes, you are talking of two different things. In the first category come all the crimes that Scotland Yard never hears about, the crimes that no one even knows have been committed."

"But I suppose there aren't very many of those?" said Mrs. Bantry.

"Aren't there?"

"Sir Henry! You don't mean there are?"

"I should think," said Miss Marple thoughtfully, "that there must be a very large number."

The charming old lady, with her old-world, unruffled air, made her statement in a tone of the utmost placidity.

"My dear Miss Marple," said Colonel Bantry.

"Of course," said Miss Marple, "a lot of people are stupid. And stupid people get found out, whatever they do. But there are quite a number of people who aren't stupid, and one shudders to think of what they might accomplish unless they had very strongly rooted principles."

"Yes," said Sir Henry, "there are a lot of people who aren't stupid. How often does some crime come to light simply by reason of a bit of unmitigated bungling, and each time one asks oneself the question: If this hadn't been bungled, would anyone ever have known?"

"But that's very serious, Clithering," said Colonel Bantry. "Very serious, indeed."

"Is it?"

"What do you mean, is it? Of course it's serious."

"You say crime goes unpunished, but does it? Unpunished by the law perhaps, but cause and effect works outside the law. To say that every crime brings its own punishment is by way of being a platitude, and yet in my opinion nothing can be truer."

"Perhaps, perhaps," said Colonel Bantry. "But that doesn't alter the seriousness—the—er—seriousness—" He paused, rather at a loss.

Sir Henry Clithering smiled.

"Ninety-nine people out of a hundred are doubtless of your way of thinking," he said. "But you know, it isn't really guilt that is important—it's innocence. That's the thing that nobody will realize."

"I don't understand," said Jane Helier.

"I do," said Miss Marple. "When Mrs. Trent found half a crown missing from her bag, the person it affected most was the daily woman, Mrs. Arthur. Of course the Trents thought it was her, but being kindly people and knowing she had a large family and a husband who drinks, well—they naturally didn't want to go to extremes. But they felt differently toward her, and they didn't leave her in charge of the house when they went away, which made a great difference to her; and other people began to get a feeling about her too. And then it suddenly came out that it was the governess. Mrs. Trent saw her through a door reflected in a mirror. The purest chance—though I prefer to call it Providence. And that, I think, is what Sir Henry means. Most people would be only interested in who took the money, and it turned out to be the most unlikely person— just like in detective stories! But the real person it was life and death to was poor Mrs. Arthur, who had done nothing. That's what you mean, isn't it, Sir Henry?"

"Yes, Miss Marple, you've hit off my meaning exactly. Your charwoman person was lucky in the instance you relate. Her innocence was shown. But some people may go through a lifetime crushed by the weight of a suspicion that is really unjustified."

"Are you thinking of some particular instance, Sir Henry?" asked Mrs. Bantry shrewdly.

"As a matter of fact, Mrs. Bantry, I am. A very curious case. A case where we believe murder to have been committed, but with no possible chance of ever proving it."

"Poison, I suppose," breathed Jane. "Something untraceable."

Dr. Lloyd moved restlessly and Sir Henry shook his head.

"No, dear lady. Not the secret arrow poison of the South American Indians! I wish it were something of that kind. We have to deal with something much more prosaic—so prosaic, in fact, that there is no hope of bringing the deed home to its perpetrator. An old gentleman who fell downstairs and broke his neck; one of those regrettable accidents which happen every day."

"But what happened really?"

"Who can say?" Sir Henry shrugged his shoulders. "A push from behind? A piece of cotton or string tied across the top of the stairs and carefully removed afterward? That we shall never know."

"But you do think that it—well, wasn't an accident? Now why?" asked the doctor.

"That's rather a long story, but—well, yes, we're pretty sure. As I said, there's no chance of being able to bring the deed home to anyone—the evidence would be too flimsy. But there's the other aspect of the case—the one I was speaking about. You see, there were four people who might have done the trick. One's guilty, but the other three are innocent. And unless the truth is found out, those three are going to remain under the terrible shadow of doubt."

"I think," said Mrs. Bantry, "that you'd better tell us your long story."

"I needn't make it so very long after all," said Sir Henry. "I can at any rate condense the beginning. That deals with a German secret society—the *Schwartze Hand*—something after the lines of the Camorra or what is most people's idea of the Camorra. A scheme of blackmail and terrorization. The thing started quite suddenly after the war and spread to an amazing extent. Numberless people were victimized by it. The authorities were not successful in coping with it, for its secrets were jealously guarded, and it was almost impossible to find anyone who could be induced to betray them.

"Nothing much was ever known about it in England, but in Germany it was having a most paralyzing effect. It was finally broken up and dispersed through the efforts of one man, a Dr. Rosen, who had at one time been very prominent in Secret Service work. He became a member, penetrated its inmost circle, and was, as I say, instrumental in bringing about its downfall.

"But he was, in consequence, a marked man, and it was deemed wise that he should leave Germany—at any rate for a time. He came to England, and we had letters about him from the police in Berlin. He came and had a personal interview with me. His point of view was both dispassionate and resigned. He had no doubts of what the future held for him.

" 'They will get me, Sir Henry,' he said. 'Not a doubt of it.' He was a big man with a fine head and a very deep voice, with only a slight guttural intonation to tell of his nationality. 'That is a foregone conclusion. It does not matter, I am prepared. I faced the risk when I undertook this business. I have done what I set out to do. The organization can never be gotten together again. But there are many members of it at liberty, and they will take the only revenge they can—my life. It is simply a question of time, but I am anxious that that time should be as long as possible. You see, I am collecting and editing some very interesting material—the result of my life's work. I should like, if possible, to be able to complete my task.'

"He spoke very simply, with a certain grandeur which I could not but admire. I told him we would take all precautions, but he waved my words aside.

" 'Some day, sooner or later, they will get me,' he repeated. 'When that day comes, do not distress yourself. You will, I have no doubt, have done all that is possible.'

"He then proceeded to outline his plans which were simple enough. He proposed to take a small cottage in the country where he could live quietly and go on with his work. In the end he selected a village in Somerset—King's Gnaton, which was seven miles from a railway station and singularly untouched by civilization. He bought a very charming cottage, had various improvements and alterations made, and settled down there most contentedly. His household consisted of his niece, Greta; a secretary; an old German servant who had served him faithfully for nearly forty years; and an outside handy man and gardener who was a native of King's Gnaton."

"The four suspects," said Dr. Lloyd softly.

"Exactly. The four suspects. There is not much more to tell. Life went on peacefully at King's Gnaton for five months and then the blow fell. Dr. Rosen fell down the stairs one morning and was found dead about half an hour later. At the time the accident must have taken place, Gertrud was in her kitchen with the door closed and heard nothing—so she says. Fräulein Greta was in the garden, planting some bulbs—again, so she says. The gardener, Dobbs, was in the small potting shed having his elevenses —so he says: and the secretary was out for a walk, and once more there is only his own word for it. No one had an alibi—no one can corroborate anyone else's story. But one thing is certain. No one from outside could have done it, for a stranger in the little village of King's Gnaton would be noticed without fail. Both the back and the front doors were locked, each member of the household having his own key. So you see it narrows down to those four. And yet each one seems to be above suspicion. Greta, his own brother's child. Gertrud, with forty years of faithful service. Dobbs, who has never been out of King's Gnaton. And Charles Templeton, the secretary—"

"Yes," said Colonel Bantry, "what about him? He seems the suspicious person to my mind. What do you know about him?"

"It is what I knew about him that put him completely out of court—at any rate, at the time," said Sir Henry gravely. "You see, Charles Templeton was one of my own men."

"Oh!" said Colonel Bantry, considerably taken aback.

"Yes. I wanted to have someone on the spot, and at the same time I didn't want to cause talk in the village. Rosen really needed a secretary. I put Templeton on the job. He's a gentleman, he speaks German fluently, and he's altogether a very able fellow."

"But, then, which do you suspect?" asked Mrs. Bantry in a bewildered tone. "They all seem so—well, impossible."

"Yes, so it appears. But you can look at the thing from another angle. Fräulein Greta was his niece and a very lovely girl, but the war has shown us time and again that brother can turn against sister, or father against son, and so on, and the loveliest and gentlest of young girls did some of the most amazing things. The same thing applies to Gertrud, and who knows what other forces might be at work in her case? A quarrel, perhaps, with her master, a growing resentment all the more lasting because of the long faithful years behind her. Elderly women of that class can be amazingly bitter sometimes. And Dobbs? Was he right outside it because he had no connection with the family? Money will do much. In some way Dobbs might have been approached and bought.

"For one thing seems certain: Some message or some order must have come from outside. Otherwise, why five months' immunity? No, the agents of the society must have been at work. Not yet sure of Rosen's perfidy, they delayed till the betrayal had been traced to him beyond any possible doubt. And then, all doubts set aside, they must have sent their message to the spy within the gates—the message that said, 'Kill.' "

"How nasty!" said Jane Helier, and shuddered.

"But how did the message come? That was the point I tried to elucidate—the one hope of solving my problem. One of those four people must have been approached or communicated with in some way. There would be no delay

—I knew that; as soon as the command came, it would be carried out. That was a peculiarity of the *Schwartze Hand*.

"I went into the question, went into it in a way that will probably strike you as being ridiculously meticulous. Who had come to the cottage that morning? I eliminated nobody. Here is the list."

He took an envelope from his pocket and selected a paper from its contents.

"The butcher, bringing some neck of mutton. Investigated and found correct.

"The grocer's assistant, bringing a packet of corn flour, two pounds of sugar, a pound of butter, and a pound of coffee. Also investigated and found correct.

"The postman, bringing two circulars for Fräulein Rosen, a local letter for Gertrud, three letters for Dr. Rosen, one with a foreign stamp, and two letters for Mr. Templeton, one also with a foreign stamp."

Sir Henry paused and then took a sheaf of documents from the envelope.

"It may interest you to see these for yourself. They were handed me by the various people concerned or collected from the wastepaper basket. I need hardly say they've been tested by experts for invisible ink, et cetera. No excitement of that kind is possible."

Everyone crowded round to look. The catalogues were respectively from a nurseryman and from a prominent London fur establishment. The two bills addressed to Dr. Rosen were a local one for seeds for the garden and one from a London stationery firm. The letter addressed to him ran as follows:

> My Dear Rosen—Just back from Dr. Helmuth Spath's. I saw Edgar Jackson the other day. He and Amos Perry have just come back from Tsingtau. In all Honesty I can't say I envy them the trip. Let me have news of you soon. As I said before: Beware of a certain person. You know who I mean, though you don't agree.—Yours,
>
> Georgina.

"Mr. Templeton's mail consisted of this bill which, as you see, is an account rendered from his tailor, and a letter from a friend in Germany," went on Sir Henry. "The latter, unfortunately, he tore up while out on his walk. Finally we have the letter received by Gertrud."

> Dear Mrs. Swartz,—We're hoping as how you be able to come the social on friday evening. the vicar says has he hopes you will—one and all being welcome. The resipy for the ham was very good, and I thanks you for it. Hoping as this finds you well and that we shall see you friday i remain
>
> > Yours faithfully,
> > Emma Greene.

Dr. Lloyd smiled a little over this and so did Mrs. Bantry.

"I think the last letter can be put out of court," said Dr. Lloyd.

"I thought the same," said Sir Henry, "but I took the precaution of verifying that there was a Mrs. Greene and a church social. One can't be too careful, you know."

"That's what our friend Miss Marple always says," said Dr. Lloyd, smiling. "You're lost in a daydream, Miss Marple. What are you thinking out?"

Miss Marple gave a start.

"So stupid of me," she said. "I was just wondering why the word Honesty in Dr. Rosen's letter was spelled with a capital H."

Mrs. Bantry picked it up.

"So it is," she said. "Oh!"

"Yes, dear," said Miss Marple. "I thought you'd notice!"

"There's a definite warning in that letter," said Colonel Bantry. "That's the first thing caught my attention. I notice more than you'd think. Yes, a definite warning—against whom?"

"There's rather a curious point about that letter," said Sir Henry. "According to Templeton, Dr. Rosen opened the letter at breakfast and tossed it across to him, saying he didn't know who the fellow was from Adam."

"But it wasn't a fellow," said Jane Helier. "It was signed 'Georgina.'"

"It's difficult to say which it is," said Dr. Lloyd. "It

might be Georgey, but it certainly looks more like Georgina. Only it strikes me that the writing is a man's."

"You know, that's interesting," said Colonel Bantry. "His tossing it across the table like that and pretending he knew nothing about it. Wanted to watch somebody's face. Whose face—the girl's? Or the man's?"

"Or even the cook's?" suggested Mrs. Bantry. "She might have been in the room bringing in the breakfast. But what I don't see is . . . it's most peculiar—"

She frowned over the letter. Miss Marple drew closer to her. Miss Marple's finger went out and touched the sheet of paper. They murmured together.

"But why did the secretary tear up the other letter?" asked Jane Helier suddenly. "It seems—oh, I don't know— it seems queer. Why should he have letters from Germany? Although, of course, if he's above suspicion, as you say—"

"But Sir Henry didn't say that," said Miss Marple quickly, looking up from her murmured conference with Mrs. Bantry. "He said four suspects. So that shows that he includes Mr. Templeton. I'm right, am I not, Sir Henry?"

"Yes, Miss Marple. I have learned one thing through bitter experience. Never say to yourself that anyone is above suspicion. I gave you reasons just now why three of these people might after all be guilty, unlikely as it seemed. I did not at that time apply the same process to Charles Templeton. But I came to it at last through pursuing the rule I have just mentioned. And I was forced to recognize this: That every army and every navy and every police force has a certain number of traitors within its ranks, much as we hate to admit the idea. And I examined dispassionately the case against Charles Templeton.

"I asked myself very much the same questions as Miss Helier has just asked. Why should he, alone of all the house, not be able to produce the letter he had received—a letter, moreover, with a German stamp on it. Why should he have letters from Germany?

"The last question was an innocent one, and I actually put it to him. His reply came simply enough. His mother's sister was married to a German. The letter had been from a German girl cousin. So I learned something I did not know before—that Charles Templeton had relations with people in Germany. And that put him definitely on the list of suspects—very much so. He is my own man—a lad I have always liked and trusted; but in common justice and fairness I must admit that he heads that list.

"But there it is—I do not know! I do not know . . . And in all probability I never shall know. It is not a question of punishing a murderer. It is a question that to me seems a hundred times more important. It is the blighting, perhaps, of an honourable man's whole career . . . because of suspicion—a suspicion that I dare not disregard."

Miss Marple coughed and said gently:

"Then, Sir Henry, if I understand you rightly, it is this young Mr. Templeton only who is so much on your mind?"

"Yes, in a sense. It should, in theory, be the same for all four, but that is not actually the case. Dobbs, for instance —suspicion may attach to him in my mind, but it will not actually affect his career. Nobody in the village has ever had any idea that old Dr. Rosen's death was anything but an accident. Gertrud is slightly more affected. It must make, for instance, a difference in Fräulein Rosen's attitude toward her. But that, possibly, is not of great importance to her.

"As for Greta Rosen—well, here we come to the crux of the matter. Greta is a very pretty girl and Charles Templeton is a good-looking young man, and for five months they were thrown together with no outer distractions. The inevitable happened. They fell in love with each other—even if they did not come to the point of admitting the fact in words.

"And then the catastrophe happens. It is three months ago now, and a day or two after I returned, Greta Rosen came to see me. She had sold the cottage and was returning to Germany, having finally settled up her uncle's affairs. She came to me personally, although she knew I had retired, because it was really about a personal matter she wanted to see me. She beat about the bush a little, but at last it all came out. What did I think? That letter with the German stamp—she had worried about it and worried about it—the one Charles had torn up. Was it all right? Surely it must be all right. Of course she believed his story, but—oh, if she only knew! If she knew—for certain.

"You see? The same feeling: the wish to trust—but the horrible lurking suspicion, thrust resolutely to the back of the mind, but persisting nevertheless. I spoke to her with absolute frankness and asked her to do the same. I asked her whether she had been on the point of caring for Charles and he for her.

" 'I think so,' she said. 'Oh yes, I know it was so. We were so happy. Every day passed so contentedly. We knew —we both knew. There was no hurry—there was all the time in the world. Some day he would tell me he loved me, and I should tell him that I, too— Ah! But you can guess! And now it is all changed. A black cloud has come between us—we are constrained, when we meet we do not know what to say. It is, perhaps, the same with him as with me . . . We are each saying to ourselves, "If I were sure!" That is why, Sir Henry, I beg of you to say to me, "You may be sure, whoever killed your uncle, it was not Charles Templeton!" Say it to me! Oh, say it to me! I beg—I beg!'

"I couldn't say it to her. They'll drift farther and farther apart, those two—with suspicion like a ghost between them —a ghost that can't be laid."

He leaned back in his chair; his face looked tired and grey. He shook his head once or twice despondently.

"And there's nothing more can be done, unless—" He sat up straight again and a tiny whimsical smile crossed his face.—"unless Miss Marple can help us. Can't you, Miss Marple? I've a feeling that letter might be in your line, you know. The one about the church social. Doesn't it remind you of something or someone that makes everything perfectly plain? Can't you do something to help two helpless young people who want to be happy?"

Behind the whimsicality there was something earnest in his appeal. He had come to think very highly of the mental powers of this frail, old-fashioned maiden lady. He looked across at her with something very like hope in his eyes.

Miss Marple coughed and smoothed her lace.

"It does remind me a little of Annie Poultny," she admitted. "Of course the letter is perfectly plain—both to Mrs. Bantry and myself. I don't mean the church-social letter, but the other one. You living so much in London and not being a gardener, Sir Henry, would not have been likely to notice."

"Eh?" said Sir Henry. "Notice what?"

Mrs. Bantry reached out a hand and selected a catalogue. She opened it and read aloud with gusto:

" 'Dr. Helmuth Spath. Pure lilac, a wonderfully fine flower, carried on exceptionally long and stiff stem. Splendid for cutting and garden decoration. A novelty of striking beauty.

" 'Edgar Jackson. Beautifully shaped chrysanthemum-like flower of a distinct brick-red colour.

" 'Amos Perry. Brilliant red, highly decorative.

" 'Tsingtau. Brilliant orange-red, showy garden plant and lasting cut flower.

" 'Honesty—' "

"With a capital H, you remember," murmured Miss Marple.

" 'Honesty. Rose and white shades, enormous perfect-shaped flower.' "

Mrs. Bantry flung down the catalogue and said with immense explosive force:

"Dahlias!"

"And their initial letters spell 'Death,' " explained Miss Marple.

"But the letter came to Dr. Rosen himself," objected Sir Henry.

"That was the clever part of it," said Miss Marple. "That and the warning in it. What would he do, getting a letter from someone he didn't know, full of names he didn't know. Why, of course, toss it over to his secretary."

"Then, after all—"

"Oh no!" said Miss Marple. "Not the secretary. Why, that's what makes it so perfectly clear that it wasn't him. He'd never have let that letter be found if so. And equally he'd never have destroyed a letter to himself with a German stamp on it. Really, his innocence is—if you'll allow me to use the word—just shining."

"Then who—"

"Well, it seems almost certain—as certain as anything can be in this world. There was another person at the breakfast table, and she would—quite naturally under the circumstances—put out her hand for the letter and read it. And that would be that. You remember that she got a gardening catalogue by the same post—"

"Greta Rosen," said Sir Henry slowly. "Then her visit to me—"

"Gentlemen never see through these things," said Miss Marple. "And I'm afraid they often think we old women are—well, cats, to see things the way we do. But there it is. One does know a great deal about one's own sex, unfortunately. I've no doubt there was a barrier between them. The young man felt a sudden inexplicable repulsion. He suspected purely through instinct, and couldn't hide the suspicion. And I really think that the girl's visit to you was just pure spite. She was safe enough really, but she just went out of her way to fix your suspicions definitely on poor Mr. Templeton. You weren't nearly so sure about him until after her visit."

"I'm sure it was nothing that she said—" began Sir Henry.

"Gentlemen," said Miss Marple calmly, "never see through these things."

"And that girl—" He stopped. "She commits a cold-blooded murder and gets off scot-free!"

"Oh no, Sir Henry," said Miss Marple. "Not scot-free. Neither you nor I believe that. Remember what you said not long ago. No. Greta Rosen will not escape punishment. To begin with, she must be in with a very queer set of people—blackmailers and terrorists—associates who will do her no good and will probably bring her to a miserable end. As you say, one mustn't waste thoughts on the guilty—it's the innocent who matter. Mr. Templeton, who I daresay will marry that German cousin, his tearing up her letter looks —well, it looks suspicious—using the word in quite a different sense from the one we've been using all the evening. A little as though he were afraid of the other girl noticing or asking to see it? Yes, I think there must have been some little romance there. And then there's Dobbs—though, as you say, I daresay it won't much matter to him. His elevenses are probably all he thinks about. And then there's that poor old Gertrud—the one who reminded me of Annie Poultny. Poor Annie Poultny. Fifty years' faithful service and suspected of making away with Miss Lamb's will, though nothing could be proved. Almost broke the poor creature's faithful heart. And then after she was dead it came to light in the secret drawer of the tea caddy where old Miss Lamb had put it herself for safety. But too late then for poor Annie.

"That's what worries me so about that poor old German woman. When one is old, one becomes embittered very easily. I felt much more sorry for her than for Mr. Templeton, who is young and good-looking and evidently a favourite with the ladies. You will write to her, won't you, Sir Henry, and just tell her that her innocence is established beyond doubt? Her dear old master dead, and she no doubt brooding and feeling herself suspected of . . . Oh! It won't bear thinking about!"

"I will write, Miss Marple," said Sir Henry. He looked at her curiously. "You know, I shall never quite understand you. Your outlook is always a different one from what I expect."

"My outlook, I'm afraid, is a very petty one," said Miss Marple humbly. "I hardly ever go out of St. Mary Mead."

"And yet you have solved what may be called an international mystery," said Sir Henry. "For you have solved it. I am convinced of that."

Miss Marple blushed, then bridled a little.

"I was, I think, well educated for the standard of my day. My sister and I had a German governess—a Fräulein. A very sentimental creature. She taught us the language of flowers—a forgotten study nowadays, but most charming. A yellow tulip, for instance, means 'Hopeless Love,' while a China aster means 'I Die of Jealousy at Your Feet.' That letter was signed Georgina, which I seem to remember as dahlia in German, and that of course made the whole thing perfectly clear. I wish I could remember the meaning of dahlia, but alas, that eludes me. My memory is not what it was."

"At any rate, it didn't mean 'Death.' "

"No, indeed. Horrible, is it not? There are very sad things in the world."

"There are," said Mrs. Bantry with a sigh. "It's lucky one has flowers and one's friends."

"She puts us last, you observe," said Dr. Lloyd.

"A man used to send me purple orchids every night to the theater," said Jane dreamily.

" 'I Await Your Favours'—that's what that means," said Miss Marple brightly.

Sir Henry gave a peculiar sort of cough and turned his head away.

Miss Marple gave a sudden exclamation.

"I've remembered. Dahlias mean 'Treachery and Misrepresentation.' "

"Wonderful," said Sir Henry. "Absolutely wonderful."

And he sighed.

MOTIVE v. OPPORTUNITY

Mr. Petherick, the solicitor, cleared his throat rather more importantly than usual and beamed appreciatively over his eyeglasses.

"The story I am about to tell is a perfectly simple and straightforward one and can be followed by any layman."

"No legal quibbles, now," said Miss Marple, shaking a knitting needle at him.

"Certainly not," said Mr. Petherick.

"Ah well, I am not so sure, but let's hear the story."

"It concerns a former client of mine. I will call him Mr. Clode—Simon Clode. He was a man of considerable wealth and lived in a large house not very far from here. He had had one son killed in the war and this son had left one child, a little girl. Her mother had died at her birth, and on her father's death she had come to live with her grandfather who at once became passionately attached to her. Little Chris could do anything she liked with her grandfather. I have never seen a man more completely wrapped up in a child, and I cannot describe to you his grief and despair when, at the age of eleven, the child contracted pneumonia and died.

"Poor Simon Clode was inconsolable. A brother of his had recently died in poor circumstances and Simon Clode had generously offered a home to his brother's children— two girls, Grace and Mary, and a boy, George. But though kind and generous to his nephew and nieces, the old man never expended on them any of the love and devotion he had accorded to his little grandchild. Employment was found for George Clode in a bank nearby, and Grace married a clever young research chemist of the name of Philip

Garrod. Mary, who was a quiet, self-contained girl, lived at home and looked after her uncle. She was, I think, fond of him in her quiet, undemonstrative way. And to all appearances things went on very peacefully. I may say that after the death of little Christobel, Simon Clode came to me and instructed me to draw up a new will. By this will his fortune, a very considerable one, was divided equally between his nephew and nieces, a third share to each.

"Time went on. Chancing to meet George Clode one day, I inquired for his uncle, whom I had not seen for some time. To my surprise George's face clouded over. 'I wish you could put some sense into Uncle Simon,' he said ruefully. His honest but not very brilliant countenance looked puzzled and worried. 'This spirit business is getting worse and worse.'

" 'What spirit business?' I asked, very much surprised.

"Then George told me the whole story. How Mr. Clode had gradually got interested in the subject and how on the top of this interest he had chanced to meet an American medium, a Mrs. Eurydice Spragg. This woman, whom George did not hesitate to characterize as an out-and-out swindler, had gained an immense ascendency over Simon Clode. She was practically always in the house, and many séances were held in which the spirit of Christobel manifested itself to the doting grandfather.

"I may say here and now that I do not belong to the ranks of those who cover spiritualism with ridicule and scorn. I am a believer in evidence. And I think that when we have an impartial mind and weigh the evidence in favour of spiritualism there remains much that cannot be put down to fraud or lightly set aside. Therefore, as I say, I am neither a believer nor an unbeliever. There is certain testimony with which one cannot afford to disagree.

"On the other hand, spiritualism lends itself very easily to fraud and imposture, and from all young George Clode told me about this Mrs. Eurydice Spragg I felt more and more convinced that Simon Clode was in bad hands and that Mrs. Spragg was probably an impostor of the worst type. The old man, shrewd as he was in practical matters, would be easily imposed on where his love for his dead grandchild was concerned.

"Turning things over in my mind, I felt more and more

uneasy. I was fond of the young Clodes, Mary and George, and I realized that this Mrs. Spragg and her influence over their uncle might lead to trouble in the future.

"At the earliest opportunity I made a pretext for calling on Simon Clode. I found Mrs. Spragg installed as an honoured and friendly guest. As soon as I saw her my worst apprehensions were fulfilled. She was a stout woman of middle age, dressed in a flamboyant style. Very full of cant phrases about 'our dear ones who have passed over,' and other things of the kind.

"Her husband was also staying in the house, Mr. Absalom Spragg, a thin, lank man with a melancholy expression and extremely furtive eyes. As soon as I could, I got Simon Clode to myself and sounded him tactfully on the subject. He was full of enthusiasm. Eurydice Spragg was wonderful! She had been sent to him directly in answer to prayer! She cared nothing for money; the joy of helping a heart in affliction was enough for her. She had quite a mother's feeling for little Chris. He was beginning to regard her almost as a daughter. Then he went on to give me details— how he had heard his Chris's voice speaking—how she was well and happy with her father and mother. He went on to tell other sentiments expressed by the child, which in my remembrance of little Christobel seemed to me highly unlikely. She laid stress on the fact that 'Father and Mother loved dear Mrs. Spragg.'

" 'But, of course,' he broke off, 'you are a scoffer, Petherick.'

" 'No, I am not a scoffer. Very far from it. Some of the men who have written on the subject are men whose testimony I would accept unhesitatingly, and I should accord any medium recommended by them respect and credence. I presume that this Mrs. Spragg is well vouched for?'

"Simon went into ecstasies over Mrs. Spragg. She had been sent to him by Heaven. He had come across her at the watering place where he had spent two months in the summer. A chance meeting, with what a wonderful result!

"I went away very dissatisfied. My worst fears were realized, but I did not see what I could do. After a good deal of thought and deliberation I wrote to Philip Garrod who had, as I mentioned, just married the eldest Clode girl, Grace. I set the case before him—of course, in the most carefully guarded language. I pointed out the danger of such a woman gaining ascendency over the old man's mind. And I suggested that Mr. Clode should be brought into contact if possible with some reputable spiritualistic circles. This, I thought, would not be a difficult matter for Philip Garrod to arrange.

"Garrod was prompt to act. He realized, which I did not, that Simon Clode's health was in a very precarious condition, and as a practical man he had no intention of letting his wife or her sister and brother be despoiled of the inheritance which was so rightly theirs. He came down the following week, bringing with him as a guest no other than the famous Professor Longman. Longman was a scientist of the first order, a man whose association with spiritualism compelled the latter to be treated with respect. Not only a brilliant scientist, he was a man of the utmost uprightness and probity.

"The result of the visit was most unfortunate. Longman, it seemed, had said very little while he was there. Two séances were held—under what conditions I do not know. Longman was noncommittal all the time he was in the house, but after his departure he wrote a letter to Philip Garrod. In it he admitted that he had not been able to detect Mrs. Spragg in fraud; nevertheless, his private opinion was that the phenomena were not genuine. Mr. Garrod, he said, was at liberty to show this letter to his uncle if he thought fit, and he suggested that he himself should put Mr. Clode in touch with a medium of perfect integrity.

"Philip Garrod had taken this letter straight to his uncle, but the result was not what he had anticipated. The old man flew into a towering rage. It was all a plot to discredit Mrs. Spragg who was a maligned and injured saint! She had told him already what bitter jealousy there was of her in this country. He pointed out that Longman was forced to say he had not detected fraud. Eurydice Spragg had come to him in the darkest hour of his life, had given him help and comfort, and he was prepared to espouse her cause even if it meant quarrelling with every member of the family. She was more to him than anyone else in the world.

"Philip Garrod was turned out of the house with scant ceremony, but as a result of his rage Clode's own health took a decided turn for the worst. For the last month he had kept to his bed pretty continuously, and now there seemed every possibility of his being a bedridden invalid until such time as death should release him. Two days after Philip's departure I received an urgent summons and went hurriedly over. Clode was in bed and looked even to my layman's eye very ill indeed. He was gasping for breath.

" 'This is the end of me,' he said. 'I feel it. Don't argue with me, Petherick. But before I die I am going to do my duty by the one human being who has done more for me than anyone else in the world. I want to make a fresh will.'

" 'Certainly,' I said. 'If you will give me your instructions now, I will draft out a will and send it to you.'

" 'That won't do,' he said. 'Why, man, I might not live through the night. I have written out what I want here'— he fumbled under his pillow—'and you can tell me if it is right.'

"He produced a sheet of paper with a few words roughly scribbled on it in pencil. It was quite simple and clear. He left £5000 to each of his nieces and nephew and the residue of his vast property outright to Eurydice Spragg 'in gratitude and admiration.'

"I didn't like it, but there it was. There was no question of unsound mind; the old man was as sane as anybody.

"He rang the bell for two of the servants. They came promptly. The housemaid, Emma Gaunt, was a tall middle-aged woman who had been in service there for many years and who had nursed Clode devotedly. With her came the cook, a fresh buxom young woman of thirty. Simon Clode glared at them both from under his bushy eyebrow

" 'I want you to witness my will. Emma, get me my fountain pen.'

"Emma went over obediently to the desk.

" 'Not that left-hand drawer, girl,' said old Simon irritably. 'Don't you know it is in the right-hand one?'

" 'No, it is here, sir,' said Emma, producing it.

" 'Then you must have put it away wrong last time,' grumbled the old man. 'I can't stand things not being kept in their proper places.'

"Still grumbling, he took the pen from her and copied his own rough draft, amended by me, on to a fresh piece of paper. Then he signed his name. Emma Gaunt and the cook, Lucy David, also signed. I folded the will up and put it into a long blue envelope. It was necessarily, you understand, written on an ordinary piece of paper.

"Just as the servants were turning to leave the room Clode lay back on the pillows with a gasp and a distorted face. I bent over him anxiously, and Emma Gaunt came quickly back. However, the old man recovered and smiled weakly.

" 'It is all right, Petherick, don't be alarmed. At any rate, I shall die easy now, having done what I wanted to.'

"Emma Gaunt looked inquiringly at me as if to know whether she could leave the room. I nodded reassuringly and she went out—first stopping to pick up the blue envelope which I had let slip to the ground in my moment of anxiety. She handed it to me and I slipped it into my coat pocket and then she went out.

" 'You are annoyed, Petherick,' said Simon Clode. 'You are prejudiced, like everybody else.'

" 'It is not a question of prejudice,' I said. 'Mrs. Spragg may be all she claims to be. I should see no objection to you leaving her a small legacy as a memento of gratitude, but I tell you frankly, Clode, that to disinherit your own flesh and blood in favor of a stranger is wrong.'

"With that I turned to depart. I had done what I could and made my protest.

"Mary Clode came out of the drawing room and met me in the hall.

" 'You will have tea before you go, won't you? Come in here.' And she led me into the drawing room.

"A fire was burning on the hearth and the room looked cosy and cheerful. She relieved me of my overcoat just as her brother, George, came into the room. He took it from her and laid it across a chair at the far end of the room, then he came back to the fireside where we drank tea. During the meal a question arose about some point concerning the estate. Simon Clode said he didn't want to be bothered with it and had left it to George to decide. George was rather nervous about trusting to his own judgment. At my suggestion, we adjourned to the study after tea and I looked over the papers in question. Mary Clode accompanied us.

"A quarter of an hour later I prepared to take my departure. Remembering that I had left my overcoat in the drawing room, I went there to fetch it. The only occupant of the room was Mrs. Spragg, who was kneeling by the chair on which the overcoat lay. She seemed to be doing something rather unnecessary to the cretonne cover. She rose with a very red face as we entered.

" 'That cover never did sit right,' she complained. 'My! I could make a better fit myself.'

"I took up my overcoat and put it on. As I did so I noticed that the envelope containing the will had fallen out of the pocket and was lying on the floor. I replaced it in my pocket, said good-bye, and took my departure.

"On arrival at my office, I will describe my next actions carefully. I removed my overcoat and took the will from the pocket. I had it in my hand and was standing by the table when my clerk came in. Somebody wished to speak to me on the telephone, and the extension to my desk was out of order. I accordingly accompanied him to the outer office and remained there for about five minutes engaged in conversation over the telephone.

"When I emerged, I found my clerk waiting for me.

" 'Mr. Spragg has called to see you, sir. I showed him into your office.'

"I went there to find Mr. Spragg sitting by the table. He rose and greeted me in a somewhat unctuous manner, then proceeded to a long discursive speech. In the main it seemed to be an uneasy justification of himself and his wife. He was afraid people were saying, et cetera, et cetera. His wife had been known from her babyhood upward for the pureness of her heart and her motives . . . and so on and so on. I was, I am afraid, rather curt with him. In the end I think he realized that his visit was not being a success and he left somewhat abruptly. I then remembered that I had left the will lying on the table. I took it, sealed the envelope, and wrote on it and put it away in the safe.

"Now I come to the crux of my story. Two months later Mr. Simon Clode died. I will not go into long-winded discussions. I will just state the bare facts. When the sealed envelope containing the will was opened it was found to contain a sheet of blank paper."

He paused, looking around the circle of interested faces. He smiled himself with a certain enjoyment.

"You appreciate the point, of course? For two months the sealed envelope had lain in my safe. It could not have been tampered with then. No, the time limit was a very short one. Between the moment the will was signed and my locking it away in the safe. Now who had had the opportunity, and to whose interests would it be to do so?

"I will recapitulate the vital points in a brief summary: The will was signed by Mr. Clode, placed by me in an envelope—so far so good. It was then put by me in my overcoat pocket. That overcoat was taken from me by Mary and handed by her to George, who was in full sight of me while handling the coat. During the time that I was in the study Mrs. Eurydice Spragg would have had plenty of time to extract the envelope from the coat pocket and read its contents and, as a matter of fact, finding the envelope on the ground and not in the pocket seemed to point to her having done so. But here we come to a curious point: she had the opportunity of substituting the blank paper, but no motive. The will was in her favour, and by substituting a blank piece of paper she despoiled herself of the heritage she had been so anxious to gain. The same applies to Mr. Spragg. He too had the opportunity. He was left alone with the document in question for some two or three minutes in my office. But again, it was not to his advantage to do so. So we are faced with this curious problem: the two people who had the opportunity of substituting a blank piece of paper had no motive for doing so, and the two people who had a motive had no opportunity. By the way, I would not exclude the housemaid, Emma Gaunt, from suspicion. She was devoted to her young master and mistress and detested the Spraggs. She would, I feel sure, have been quite equal to attempting the substitution if she had thought of it. But although she actually handled the envelope when she picked it up from the floor and handed it to me, she certainly had no opportunity of tampering with its contents and she could not have substituted another envelope by some sleight of hand (of which, anyway, she would not be capable) because the envelope in question was brought into the house by me and no one there would be likely to have a duplicate."

He looked round, beaming on the assembly.

"Now, there is my little problem. I have, I hope, stated it clearly, I should be interested to hear your views."

To everyone's astonishment Miss Marple gave vent to a long and prolonged chuckle. Something seemed to be amusing her immensely.

"What is the matter, Aunt Jane? Can't we share the joke?" said Raymond.

"I was thinking of little Tommy Symonds, a naughty little boy, I am afraid, but sometimes very amusing. One of those children with innocent, childlike faces who are always up to some mischief or other. I was thinking how last week in Sunday school he said, 'Teacher, do you say yolk of eggs is white or yolk of eggs are white?' And Miss Durston explained that anyone would say 'yolks of eggs are white, or yolk of egg is white'—and naughty Tommy said: 'Well, I should say yolk of egg is yellow!' Very naughty of him, of course, and as old as the hills. I knew that one as a child."

"Very funny, my dear Aunt Jane," Raymond said gently, "but surely that has nothing to do with the very interesting story that Mr. Petherick has been telling us."

"Oh yes, it has," said Miss Marple. "It is a catch! And so is Mr. Petherick's story a catch. So like a lawyer! Ah, my dear old friend!" She shook a reproving head at him.

"I wonder if you really know," said the lawyer with a twinkle.

Miss Marple wrote a few words on a piece of paper, folded them up, and passed them across to him.

Mr. Petherick unfolded the paper, read what was written on it, and looked across at her appreciatively.

"My dear friend," he said, "is there anything you do not know?"

"I knew that as a child," said Miss Marple. "Played with it too."

"I feel rather out of this," said Sir Henry. "I feel sure that Mr. Petherick has some clever legal legerdemain up his sleeve."

"Not at all," said Mr. Petherick. "Not at all. It is a perfectly fair, straightforward proposition. You must not pay any attention to Miss Marple. She has her own way of looking at things."

"We should be able to arrive at the truth," said Raymond West a trifle vexedly. "The facts certainly seem plain enough. Five persons actually touched that envelope. The Spraggs clearly could have meddled with it, but equally clearly they did not do so. There remains the other three. Now, when one sees the marvellous ways that conjurers have of doing things before one's eyes, it seems to me that that paper could have been extracted and another substituted by George Clode during the time he was carrying the overcoat to the far end of the room."

"Well, I think it was the girl," said Joyce. "I think the housemaid ran down and told her what was happening and she got hold of another blue envelope and just substituted the one for the other."

Sir Henry shook his head. "I disagree with you both," he said slowly. "These sorts of things are done by conjurers, and they are done on the stage and in novels, but I think they would be impossible to do in real life, especially under the shrewd eyes of a man like my friend Mr. Petherick here. But I have an idea—it is only an idea and nothing more. We know that Professor Longman had just been down for a visit and that he said very little. It is only reasonable to suppose that the Spraggs may have been very anxious as to the result of that visit. If Simon Clode did not take them into his confidence, which is quite probable, they may have viewed his sending for Mr. Petherick from quite another angle. They may have believed that Mr. Clode had already made a will which benefited Eurydice Spragg and that this new one might be for the express purpose of cutting her out as a result of Professor Longman's revelations, or alternatively, as you lawyers say, Philip Garrod had impressed on his uncle the claims of his own flesh and blood. In that case, suppose Mrs. Spragg prepared to effect a substitution. This she does, but Mr. Petherick coming in at an unfortunate moment, she has no time to read the real document and hastily destroys it by fire in case the lawyer should discover his loss."

Joyce shook her head very decidedly.

"She would never burn it without reading it."

"The solution is rather a weak one," admitted Sir Henry. "I suppose—er—Mr. Petherick did not assist Providence himself."

The suggestion was only a laughing one, but the little lawyer drew himself up in offended dignity.

"A most improper suggestion," he said with some asperity.

"What does Dr. Pender say?" asked Sir Henry.

"I cannot say I have any very clear ideas. I think the substitution must have been effected by either Mrs. Spragg or her husband, possibly for the motive that Sir Henry suggests. If she did not read the will until after Mr. Petherick had departed, she would then be in somewhat of a dilemma, since she could not own up to her action in the matter. Possibly she would place it among Mr. Clode's papers where she thought it would be found after his death. But why it wasn't found I don't know. It might be a mere speculation this—that Emma Gaunt came across it—and out of misplaced devotion to her employers—deliberately destroyed it."

"I think Dr. Pender's solution is the best of all," said Joyce. "Is it right, Mr. Petherick?"

The lawyer shook his head.

"I will go on where I left off. I was dumbfounded and quite as much at sea as all of you are. I don't think I should ever have guessed the truth—probably not—but I was enlightened. It was cleverly done too.

"I went and dined with Philip Garrod about a month later, and in the course of our after-dinner conversation he mentioned an interesting case that had recently come to his notice.

" 'I should like to tell you about it, Petherick, in confidence, of course.'

" 'Quite so,' I replied.

" 'A friend of mine who had expectations from one of his relatives was greatly distressed to find that that relative had thoughts of benefiting a totally unworthy person. My friend, I am afraid, is a trifle unscrupulous in his methods. There was a maid in the house who was greatly devoted to the interests of what I may call the legitimate party. My friend gave her very simple instructions. He gave her a fountain pen, duly filled. She was to place this in a drawer in the writing table in her master's room, but not the usual drawer where the pen was generally kept. If her master asked her to witness his signature to any document and asked her to bring him his pen, she was to bring him not the right one, but this one which was an exact duplicate of it. That was all she had to do. He gave her no other information. She was a devoted creature and she carried out his instructions faithfully.'

"He broke off and said:

" 'I hope I am not boring you, Petherick.'

" 'Not at all,' I said. 'I am keenly interested.'

"Our eyes met.

" 'My friend is, of course, not known to you,' he said.

" 'Of course not,' I replied.

" 'Then that is all right,' said Philip Garrod.

"He paused, then said smilingly, 'You see the point? The pen was filled with what is commonly known as evanescent ink—a solution of starch in water to which a few drops of iodine has been added. This makes a deep blue-black fluid, but the writing disappears entirely in four or five days.' "

Miss Marple chuckled.

"Disappearing ink," she said. "I knew it. Many is the time I have played with it as a child."

And she beamed round on them all, pausing to shake a finger once more at Mr. Petherick.

"But all the same it's a catch, Mr. Petherick," she said. "Just like a lawyer."

THE THUMBMARK OF ST. PETER

"And now, Aunt Jane, it is up to you," said Raymond West.

"Yes, Aunt Jane, we are expecting something really spicy," chimed in Joyce Lemprière.

"Now, you are laughing at me, my dears," said Miss Marple placidly. "You think that because I have lived in this out-of-the-way spot all my life I am not likely to have had any very interesting experiences."

"God forbid that I should ever regard village life as peaceful and uneventful," said Raymond with fervour. "Not after the revelations we have heard from you! The cosmopolitan world seems a mild and peaceful place compared with St. Mary Mead."

"Well, my dear," said Miss Marple, "human nature is much the same everywhere, and, of course, one has opportunities of observing it at closer quarters in a village."

"You really are unique, Aunt Jane," cried Joyce. "I hope you don't mind me calling you Aunt Jane?" she added. "I don't know why I do it."

"Don't you, my dear?" said Miss Marple.

She looked up for a moment or two with something quizzical in her glance, which made the blood flame to the girl's cheeks. Raymond West fidgeted and cleared his throat in a somewhat embarrassed manner.

Miss Marple looked at them both and smiled again and bent her attention once more to her knitting.

"It is true, of course, that I have lived what is called a very uneventful life, but I have had a lot of experiences in solving different little problems that have arisen. Some of them have been really quite ingenious, but it would be no

good telling them to you, because they are about such un-
important things that you would not be interested—just
things like: Who cut the meshes of Mrs. Jones's string bag?
And why Mrs. Sims only wore her new fur coat once. Very
interesting things, really, to any student of human nature.
No, the only experience that I can remember that would be
of interest to you is the one about my poor niece Mabel's
husband.

"It is about ten or fifteen years ago now, and happily it
is all over and done with, and everyone has forgotten about
it. People's memories are very short—a lucky thing, I always think."

Miss Marple paused and murmured to herself:

"I must just count this row. The decreasing is a little
awkward. One, two, three, four, five, and then three purl;
that is right. Now, what was I saying? Oh yes, about poor
Mabel.

"Mabel was my niece. A nice girl, really a very nice girl,
but just a trifle what one might call silly. Rather fond of
being melodramatic and of saying a great deal more than
she meant whenever she was upset. She married a Mr.
Denman when she was twenty-two, and I am afraid it was
not a very happy marriage. I had hoped very much that the
attachment would not come to anything, for Mr. Denman
was a man of very violent temper—not the kind of man
who would be patient with Mabel's foibles—and I also
learned that there was insanity in his family. However,
girls were just as obstinate then as they are now, and as
they always will be. And Mabel married him.

"I didn't see very much of her after her marriage. She
came to stay with me once or twice, and they asked me
there several times, but, as a matter of fact, I am not very
fond of staying in other people's houses, and I always managed to make some excuse. They had been married ten
years when Mr. Denman died suddenly. There were no
children, and he left all his money to Mabel. I wrote, of
course, and offered to come to Mabel if she wanted me;
but she wrote back a very sensible letter, and I gathered
that she was not altogether overwhelmed by grief. I
thought that was only natural, because I knew they had not
been getting on together for some time. It was not until
about three months afterward that I got a most hysterical

letter from Mabel, begging me to come to her, and saying that things were going from bad to worse and she couldn't stand it much longer.

"So, of course," continued Miss Marple, "I put Clara on board wages and sent the plate and the King Charles tankard to the bank, and I went off at once. I found Mabel in a very nervous state. The house, Myrtle Dene, was a fairly large one, very comfortably furnished. There was a cook and a house-parlourmaid, as well as a nurse-attendant to look after old Mr. Denman, Mabel's husband's father, who was what is called 'not quite right in the head.' Quite peaceful and well-behaved, but distinctly odd at times. As I say, there was insanity in the family.

"I was really shocked to see the change in Mabel. She was a mass of nerves, twitching all over, yet I had the greatest difficulty in making her tell me what the trouble was. I got at it, as one always does get at these things, indirectly. I asked her about some friends of hers she was always mentioning in her letters, the Gallaghers. She said, to my surprise, that she hardly ever saw them nowadays. Other friends whom I mentioned elicited the same remark. I spoke to her then of the folly of shutting herself up and brooding, and especially of the silliness of cutting herself adrift from her friends. Then she came bursting out with the truth.

" 'It is not my doing, it is theirs. There is not a soul in the place who will speak to me now. When I go down the High Street they all get out of the way so that they shan't have to meet me or speak to me. I am like a kind of leper. It is awful, and I can't bear it any longer. I shall have to sell the house and go abroad. Yet why should I be driven away from home like this? I have done nothing.'

"I was more disturbed than I can tell you. I was knitting a comforter for old Mrs. Hay at the time, and in my perturbation I dropped two stitches and never discovered it until long after.

" 'My dear Mabel,' I said, 'you amaze me. But what is the cause of all this?'

"Even as a child Mabel was always difficult. I had the greatest difficulty in getting her to give me a straightforward answer to my question. She would only say vague things about wicked talk and idle people who had nothing better to do than gossip, and people who put ideas into the other people's heads.

" 'That is all quite clear to me,' I said. 'There is evidently some story being circulated about you. But what that story is you must know as well as anyone. And you are going to tell me.'

" 'It is so wicked,' moaned Mabel.

" 'Of course it is wicked,' I said briskly. 'There is nothing that you can tell me about people's minds that would astonish or surprise me. Now, Mabel, will you tell me in plain English what people are saying about you?'

"Then it all came out.

"It seemed that Geoffrey Denman's death, being quite sudden and unexpected, gave rise to various rumours. In fact—and in plain English as I had put it to her—people were saying that she had poisoned her husband.

"Now, as I expect you know, there is nothing more cruel than talk, and there is nothing more difficult to combat. When people say things behind your back there is nothing you can refute or deny, and the rumours go on growing and growing, and no one can stop them. I was quite certain of one thing: Mabel was quite incapable of poisoning anyone. And I didn't see why life should be ruined for her and her home made unbearable just because in all probability she had been doing something silly and foolish.

" 'There is no smoke without fire,' I said. 'Now, Mabel, you have got to tell me what started people off on this tack. There must have been something.'

"Mabel was very incoherent and declared there was nothing—nothing at all, except, of course, that Geoffrey's death had been very sudden. He had seemed quite well at supper that evening and had taken violently ill in the night. The doctor had been sent for, but the poor man had died a few minutes after the doctor's arrival. Death had been thought to be the result of eating poisoned mushrooms.

" 'Well,' I said, 'I suppose a sudden death of that kind might start tongues wagging, but surely not without some additional facts. Did you have a quarrel with Geoffrey or anything of that kind?'

"She admitted that she had had a quarrel with him on the preceding morning at breakfast time.

" 'And the servants heard it, I suppose?' I asked.

" 'They weren't in the room.'

" 'No, my dear,' I said, 'but they probably were fairly near the door outside.'

"I knew the carrying power of Mabel's high-pitched, hysterical voice only too well. Geoffrey Denman, too, was a man given to raising his voice loudly when angry.

" 'What did you quarrel about?' I asked.

" 'Oh, the usual things. It was always the same things over and over again. Some little thing would start us off, and then Geoffrey became impossible and said abominable things, and I told him what I thought of him.'

" 'There had been a lot of quarrelling, then?' I asked.

" 'It wasn't my fault—'

" 'My dear child,' I said, 'it doesn't matter whose fault it was. That is not what we are discussing. In a place like this everybody's private affairs are more or less public property. You and your husband were always quarrelling. You had a particularly bad quarrel one morning, and that night your husband died suddenly and mysteriously. Is that all, or is there anything else?'

" 'I don't know what you mean by anything else,' said Mabel sullenly.

" 'Just what I say, my dear. If you have done anything silly, don't, for heaven's sake, keep it back now. I only want to do what I can to help you.'

" 'Nothing and nobody can help,' said Mabel wildly, 'except death.'

" 'Have a little more faith in Providence, dear,' I said. 'Now then, Mabel, I know perfectly well there is something else that you are keeping back.'

"I always did know, even when she was a child, when she was not telling me the whole truth. It took a long time, but I got it out at last. She had gone down to the chemist's that morning and had bought some arsenic. She had had, of course, to sign the book for it. Naturally the chemist had talked.

" 'Who is your doctor?' I asked.

" 'Dr. Rawlinson.'

"I knew him by sight. Mabel had pointed him out to me the other day. To put it in perfectly plain language, he was what I would describe as an old dodderer. I have had too much experience of life to believe in the infallibility of doctors. Some of them are clever men and some of them are not, and half the time the best of them don't know what is the matter with you. I have no truck with doctors and their medicines myself.

"I thought things over, and then I put my bonnet on and went to call on Dr. Rawlinson. He was just what I had thought him—a nice old man, kindly, vague, and so short-sighted as to be pitiful, slightly deaf, and, withal, touchy and sensitive to the last degree. He was on his high horse at once when I mentioned Geoffrey Denman's death, talked for a long time about various kinds of fungi, edible and otherwise. He had questioned the cook, and she had admitted that one or two of the mushrooms cooked had been 'a little queer,' but as the shop had sent them she thought they must be all right. The more she thought about them since, the more she was convinced that their appearance was unusual.

" 'She would be,' I said. 'They would start by being quite like mushrooms in appearance, and they would end by being orange with purple spots.'

"I gathered that Denman had been past speech when the doctor got to him. He was incapable of swallowing and had died within a few minutes. The doctor seemed perfectly satisfied with the certificate he had given. But how much of that was obstinacy and how much of it was genuine belief I could not be sure.

"I went straight home and asked Mabel quite frankly why she had bought arsenic.

" 'You must have had some idea in your mind,' I pointed out.

"Mabel burst into tears. 'I wanted to make away with myself,' she moaned. 'I was too unhappy. I thought I would end it all.'

" 'Have you the arsenic still?' I asked.

" 'No, I threw it away.'

"I sat there turning things over and over in my mind.

" 'What happened when he was taken ill? Did he call you?'

" 'No.' She shook her head. 'He rang the bell violently. He must have rung several times. At last Dorothy, the house-parlourmaid, heard it, and she waked the cook up, and they came down. When Dorothy saw him she was frightened. He was rambling and delirious. She left the cook with him and came rushing to me. I got up and went to him. Of course, I saw at once he was dreadfully ill. Unfortunately Brewster, who looks after old Mr. Denman, was away for the night, so there was no one who knew what to do. I sent Dorothy off for the doctor, and cook and I stayed with him, but after a few minutes I couldn't bear it any longer; it was too dreadful. I ran away back to my room and locked the door.'

" 'Very selfish and unkind of you,' I said, 'and no doubt that conduct of yours has done nothing to help you since, you may be sure of that. Cook will have repeated it everywhere. Well, well, this is a bad business.'

"Next I spoke to the servants. The cook wanted to tell me about the mushrooms, but I stopped her. I was tired of these mushrooms. Instead, I questioned both of them very closely about their master's condition on that night. They both agreed that he seemed to be in great agony, that he was unable to swallow, and he could only speak in a strangled voice, and when he did speak it was only rambling—nothing sensible.

" 'What did he say when he was rambling?' I asked curiously.

" 'Something about some fish, wasn't it?' She turned to the other.

"Dorothy agreed.

" 'A heap of fish,' she said. 'Some nonsense like that. I could see at once he wasn't in his right mind, poor gentleman.'

"There didn't seem to be any sense to be made out of that. As a last resource I went up to see the nurse-attendant, Brewster, who was a gaunt, middle-aged woman of about fifty.

" 'It is a pity that I wasn't here that night,' she said. 'Nobody seems to have tried to do anything for him until the doctor came.'

" 'I suppose he was delirious,' I said doubtfully, 'but that is not a symptom of ptomaine poisoning, is it?'

" 'It depends,' said Brewster.

"I asked her how her patient was getting on.

"She shook her head.

" 'He is pretty bad,' she said.

" 'Weak?'

" 'Oh no, he is strong enough physically—all but his eyesight. That is failing badly. He may outlive all of us, but his mind is failing very fast now. I had already told both Mr. and Mrs. Denman that he ought to be in an institution, but Mrs. Denman wouldn't hear of it at any price.'

"I will say for Mabel that she always had a kindly heart.

"Well, there the thing was. I thought it over in every aspect, and at last I decided that there was only one thing to be done. In view of rumours that were going about, permission must be applied for to exhume the body, and a proper post-mortem must be made and lying tongues quieted once and for all. Mabel, of course, made a fuss, mostly on sentimental grounds—disturbing the dead man in his peaceful grave, et cetera, et cetera—but I was firm.

"I won't make a long story of this part of it. We got the order and they did the autopsy, or whatever they call it, but the result was not so satisfactory as it might have been. There was no trace of arsenic—that was all to the good— but the actual words of the report were that there was nothing to show by what means deceased had come to his death.

"So, you see, that didn't lead us out of trouble altogether. People went on talking—about rare poisons impossible to detect and rubbish of that sort. I had seen the pathologist who had done the post-mortem, and I had asked him several questions, though he tried his best to get out of answering most of them; but I got out of him that he considered it highly unlikely that the poisoned mushrooms were the cause of death. An idea was simmering in my mind, and I asked him what poison, if any, could have been employed to obtain that result. He made a long explanation to me, most of which, I must admit, I did not follow, but it amounted to this: That death might have been due to some strong vegetable alkaloid.

"The idea I had was this: Supposing the taint of insanity was in Geoffrey Denman's blood also, might he not have made away with himself? He had, at one period of his life, studied medicine, and he would have a good knowledge of poisons and their effects.

"I didn't think it sounded very likely, but it was the only thing I could think of. And I was nearly at my wit's end, I can tell you. Now, I dare say you modern young people will laugh, but when I am in really bad trouble I always say a little prayer to myself—anywhere, when I am walking along the street, or at a bazaar. And I always get an answer. It may be some trifling thing, apparently quite unconnected with the subject, but there it is. I had that text pinned over my bed when I was a little girl: *Ask and you shall receive.* On the morning that I am telling you about, I was walking along the High Street, and I was praying hard. I shut my eyes, and when I opened them, what do you think was the first thing that I saw?"

Five faces with varying degrees of interest were turned to Miss Marple. It may be safely assumed, however, that no one would have guessed the answer to the question right.

"I saw," said Miss Marple impressively, "the window of the fishmonger's shop. There was only one thing in it, a fresh haddock."

She looked round triumphantly.

"Oh, my God!" said Raymond West. "An answer to prayer—a fresh haddock!"

"Yes, Raymond," said Miss Marple severely, "and there is no need to be profane about it. The hand of God is everywhere. The first thing I saw were the black spots—the marks of St. Peter's thumb. That is the legend, you know. St. Peter's thumb. And that brought things home to me. I needed faith, the ever-true faith of St. Peter. I connected the two things together, faith—and fish."

Sir Henry blew his nose rather hurriedly. Joyce bit her lip.

"Now what did that bring to my mind? Of course, both the cook and the house-parlourmaid mentioned fish as being one of the things spoken of by the dying man. I was convinced, absolutely convinced, that there was some solution of the mystery to be found in these words. I went home determined to get to the bottom of the matter."

She paused.

"Has it ever occurred to you," the old lady went on, "how much we go by what is called, I believe, the context? There is a place on Dartmoor called Grey Wethers. If you were talking to a farmer there and mentioned Grey Wethers, he would probably conclude that you were speaking of these stone circles, yet it is possible that you might be speaking of the atmosphere; and in the same way, if you were meaning the stone circles, an outsider, hearing a fragment of the conversation, might think you meant the weather. So when we repeat a conversation, we don't, as a rule, repeat the actual words; we put in some other words that seem to us to mean exactly the same thing.

"I saw both the cook and Dorothy separately. I asked the cook if she was quite sure that her master had really mentioned a heap of fish. She said she was quite sure.

" 'Were these his exact words,' I asked, 'or did he mention some particular kind of fish?'

" 'That's it,' said the cook, 'it was some particular kind of fish, but I can't remember what now. A heap of—now what was it? Not any of the fish you send to table. Would it be a perch now—or pike? No. It didn't begin with a P.'

"Dorothy also recalled that her master had mentioned some special kind of fish. 'Some outlandish kind of fish it was,' she said.

" 'A pile of—now what was it?'

" 'Did he say heap or pile?' I asked.

" 'I think he said pile. But there, I really can't be sure— it's so hard to remember the actual words, isn't it, miss, especially when they don't seem to make sense. But now I come to think of it, I am pretty sure that it was a pile and the fish began with C; but it wasn't a cod or a crayfish.'

"The next part is where I am really proud of myself," said Miss Marple, "because, of course, I don't know anything about drugs—nasty, dangerous things I call them. I have got an old recipe of my grandmother's for tansy tea that is worth any amount of your drugs. But I knew that there were several medical volumes in the house, and in one of them there was an index of drugs. You see, my idea was that Geoffrey had taken some particular poison and was trying to say the name of it.

"Well, I looked down the list of H's, beginning He. Nothing there that sounded likely. Then I began on the P's, and almost at once I came to—what do you think?"

She looked round, postponing her moment of triumph.

"Pilocarpine. Can't you understand a man who could hardly speak trying to drag that word out? What would that sound like to a cook who had never heard the word? Wouldn't it convey the impression 'pile of carp?' "

"By Jove!" said Sir Henry.

"I should never have hit upon that," said Dr. Pender.

"Most interesting," said Mr. Petherick. "Really most interesting."

"I turned quickly to the page indicated in the index. I read about pilocarpine and its effect on the eyes and other things that didn't seem to have any bearing on the case, but at last I came to a most significant phrase: Has been tried with success as an antidote for atropine poisoning.

"I can't tell you the light that dawned upon me then. I never had thought it likely that Geoffrey Denman would commit suicide. No, this new solution was not only possible, but I was absolutely sure it was the correct one, because all the pieces fitted in logically."

"I am not going to try to guess," said Raymond. "Go on, Aunt Jane, and tell us what was so startlingly clear to you."

"I don't know anything about medicine, of course," said Miss Marple, "but I did happen to know this, that when my eyesight was failing, the doctor ordered me drops with atropine sulphate in them. I went straight upstairs to old Mr. Denman's room. I didn't beat about the bush.

" 'Mr. Denman,' I said, 'I know everything. Why did you poison your son?'

"He looked at me for a minute or two—rather a handsome old man he was, in his way—and then he burst out laughing. It was one of the most vicious laughs I have ever heard. I can assure you it made my flesh creep. I had only heard anything like it once before, when poor Mrs. Jones went off her head.

" 'Yes', he said, 'I got even with Geoffrey. I was too clever for Geoffrey. He was going to put me away, was he? Have me shut up in an asylum? I heard them talking about it. Mabel is a good girl—Mabel stuck up for me, but I knew she wouldn't be able to stand up against Geoffrey. In the end he would have his own way; he always did. But I settled him—I settled my kind, loving son! Ha, ha! I crept down in the night. It was quite easy. Brewster was away. My dear son was asleep. He had a glass of water by the side of his bed; he always woke up in the middle of the night and drank it off. I poured it away—ha, ha!—and I emptied the bottle of eye drops into the glass. He would wake up and swill it down before he knew what it was. There was only a tablespoonful of it—quite enough, quite enough. And so he did! They came to me in the morning and broke it to me very gently. They were afraid it would upset me. Ha! Ha! Ha! Ha! Ha!'

"Well," said Miss Marple, "that is the end of the story. Of course, the poor old man was put in an asylum. He wasn't really responsible for what he had done, and the truth was known, and everyone was sorry for Mabel and could not do enough to make up to her for the unjust suspicions they had had. But if it hadn't been for Geoffrey realizing what the stuff was he had swallowed and trying to get everybody to get hold of the antidote without delay, it might never have been found out. I believe there are very definite symptoms with atropine—dilated pupils of the eyes, and all that; but, of course, as I have said, Dr. Rawlinson was very shortsighted, poor old man. And in the same medical book which I went on reading—and some of it was most interesting—it gave the symptoms of ptomaine poisoning and atropine, and they are not unlike. But I can assure you I have never seen a pile of fresh haddock without thinking of the thumbmark of St. Peter."

There was a very long pause.

"My dear friend," said Mr. Petherick, "my very dear friend, you really are amazing."

"I shall recommend Scotland Yard to come to you for advice," said Sir Henry.

"Well, at all events, Aunt Jane," said Raymond, "there is one thing that you don't know."

"Oh yes I do, dear," said Miss Marple. "It happened just before dinner, didn't it? When you took Joyce out to admire the sunset. It is a very favourite place, that. There by the jasmine hedge. That is where the milkman asked Annie if he could put up the banns."

"Dash it all, Aunt Jane," said Raymond, "Don't spoil all the romance. Joyce and I aren't like the milkman and Annie."

"That is where you make a mistake, dear," said Miss Marple. "Everybody is very much alike, really. But fortunately, perhaps, they don't realize it."

THE BLOODSTAINED PAVEMENT

"It's curious," said Joyce Lemprière, "but I hardly like telling you my story. It happened a long time ago—five years ago to be exact—but it's sort of haunted me ever since. The smiling, bright, top part of it—and the hidden gruesomeness underneath. And the queer thing is that the sketch I painted at the time has become tinged with the same atmosphere. When you look at it first it is just a rough sketch of a little steep Cornish street with the sunlight on it. But if you look long enough at it, something sinister creeps in. I have never sold it, but I never look at it. It lives in the studio in a corner with its face to the wall.

"The name of the place was Rathole. It is a queer little Cornish fishing village, very picturesque—too picturesque perhaps. There is rather too much of the atmosphere of 'Ye Olde Cornish Tea House' about it. It has shops with bobbed-headed girls in smocks doing hand-illuminated mottoes on parchment. It is pretty and it is quaint, but it is very self-consciously so."

"Don't I know," said Raymond West, groaning. "The curse of the tourist bus, I suppose. No matter how narrow the lanes leading down to them, no picturesque village is safe."

Joyce nodded.

"There are narrow lanes that lead down to Rathole and very steep, like the side of a house. Well, to get on with my story. I had come to Cornwall for a fortnight, to sketch. There is an old inn in Rathole, the Polharwith Arms. It was supposed to be the only house left standing by the Spaniards when they shelled the place in fifteen hundred and something."

"Not shelled," said Raymond West, frowning. "Do try to be historically accurate, Joyce."

"Well, at all events they landed guns somewhere along the coast and they fired them and the houses fell down. Anyway, that is not the point. The inn was a wonderful old place with a kind of porch in front built on four pillars. I was just settling down to work when a car came creeping and twisting down the hill. Of course, it would stop before the inn—just where it was most awkward for me. The people got out—a man and a woman—I didn't notice them particularly. She had a kind of mauve linen dress on and a mauve hat.

"Presently the man came out again and, to my great thankfulness, drove the car down to the quay and left it there. He strolled back past me toward the inn. Just at that moment another beastly car came twisting down, and a woman got out of it, dressed in the brightest chintz frock I have ever seen, scarlet poinsettias, I think they were, and she had on one of these big native straw hats—Cuban, aren't they?—in very bright scarlet.

"This woman didn't stop in front of the inn but drove the car farther down the street toward the other one. Then she got out and the man, seeing her, gave an astonished shout. 'Carol,' he cried, 'in the name of all that is wonderful. Fancy meeting you in this out-of-the-way spot. I haven't seen you for years. Hello, there's Margery—my wife, you know. You must come and meet her.'

"They went up the street toward the inn side by side, and I saw the other woman had just come out of the door and was moving down toward them. I had had just a glimpse of the woman called Carol as she passed by me. Just enough to see a very white powdered chin and a flaming scarlet mouth, and I wondered—I just wondered—if Margery would be so very pleased to meet her. I hadn't seen Margery near to, but in the distance she looked dowdy and extra prim and proper.

"Well, of course, it was not any of my business, but you get very queer little glimpses of life sometimes, and you can't help speculating about them. From where they were standing I could just catch fragments of their conversation that floated down to me. They were talking about bathing. The husband, whose name seemed to be Denis, wanted to take a boat and row around the coast. There was a famous cave well worth seeing, so he said, about a mile long. Carol wanted to see the cave, too, but she suggested walking along the cliffs and seeing it from the land side. She said she hated boats. In the end, they fixed it that way. Carol was to go along the cliff path and to meet them at the cave, and Denis and Margery would take a boat and row round.

"Hearing them talk about bathing made me want to bathe too. It was a very hot morning and I wasn't doing particularly good work. Also, I fancied that the afternoon sunlight would be far more attractive in effect. So I packed up my things and went off to a little beach that I knew of —it was quite the opposite direction from the cave and was rather a discovery of mine. I had a ripping swim there and I lunched off a tinned tongue and two tomatoes, and I came back in the afternoon full of confidence and enthusiasm to get on with my sketch.

"The whole of Rathole seemed to be asleep. I had been right about the afternoon sunlight—the shadows were far more telling. The Polharwith Arms was the principal note of my sketch. A ray of sunlight came slanting obliquely down and hit the ground in front of it and had rather a curious effect. I gathered that the bathing party had returned safely, because two bathing dresses, a scarlet one and a dark-blue one, were hanging from the balcony, drying in the sun.

"Something had gone a bit wrong with one corner of my sketch and I bent over it for some moments, doing something to put it right. When I looked up again there was a figure leaning against one of the pillars of the Polharwith Arms, who seemed to have appeared there by magic. He was dressed in seafaring clothes and was, I suppose, a fisherman. But he had a long dark beard, and if I had been looking for a model for a wicked Spanish captain, I couldn't have imagined anyone better. I got to work with feverish haste before he should move away, though from his attitude he looked as though he was perfectly prepared to prop up the pillars through all eternity.

"He did move, however, but luckily not until I had got what I wanted. He came over to me and he began to talk. Oh, how that man talked.

"'Rathole,' he said, 'was a very interesting place.'

"I knew that already, but although I said so that didn't save me. I had the whole history of the shelling—I mean the destroying—of the village and how the landlord of the Polharwith Arms was the last man to be killed. Run through on his own threshold by a Spanish captain's sword, and of how his blood spurted out on the pavement and no one could wash out the stain for a hundred years.

"It all fitted in very well with the languorous, drowsy feeling of the afternoon. The man's voice was very suave and yet at the same time there was an undercurrent in it of something rather frightening. He was very obsequious in his manner, yet I felt underneath he was cruel. He made me understand the Inquisition and the terrors of all the things the Spaniards did better than I have ever done before.

"All the time he was talking to me I went on painting, and suddenly I realized that in the excitement of listening to his story I had painted in something that was not there. On that white square of pavement where the sun fell before the door of the Polharwith Arms, I had painted in bloodstains. It seemed extraordinary that the mind could play such tricks with the hand, but as I looked over toward the inn again I got a second shock. My hand had only painted in what my eyes saw—drops of blood on the white pavement.

"I stared for a minute or two. Then I shut my eyes, said to myself, 'Don't be so stupid, there's nothing there, really,' then I opened them again, but the bloodstains were still there.

"I suddenly felt I couldn't stand it. I interrupted the fisherman's flood of language.

" 'Tell me,' I said. 'My eyesight is not very good. Are those bloodstains on that pavement over there?'

"He looked at me indulgently and kindly.

" 'No bloodstains in these days, lady. What I am telling you about is nearly five hundred years ago.'

" 'Yes,' I said, 'but now—on the pavement . . .' The words died away in my throat. I knew—I knew that he wouldn't see what I was seeing. I got up and with shaking hands began to put my things together. As I did so the young man who had come in the car that morning came out of the inn door. He looked up and down the street perplexedly. On the balcony above his wife came out and collected the bathing things. He walked down toward the car but suddenly swerved and came across the road toward the fisherman.

" 'Tell me, my man,' he said, 'you don't know whether that lady who came in that second car there has got back yet?'

" 'Lady in a dress with flowers all over it? No, sir, I haven't seen her. She went along the cliff toward the cave this morning.'

" 'I know, I know. We all bathed there together, and then she left us to walk home and I have not seen her since. It can't have taken her all this time. The cliffs round here are not dangerous, are they?'

" 'It depends, sir, on the way you go. The best way is to take a man what knows the place with you.'

"He very clearly meant himself and was beginning to enlarge on the theme, but the young man cut him short unceremoniously and ran back toward the inn, calling up to his wife on the balcony.

" 'I say, Margery, Carol hasn't come back yet. Odd, isn't it?'

"I didn't hear Margery's reply, but her husband went on. 'Well, we can't wait any longer. We have got to push on to Penrithar. Are you ready? I will turn the car.'

"He did as he had said, and presently the two of them drove off together. Meanwhile, I had deliberately been nerving myself to prove how ridiculous my fancies were. When the car had gone I went over to the inn and examined the pavement closely. Of course there were no bloodstains there. No, all along it had been the result of my distorted imagination. Yet, somehow, it seemed to make the thing more frightening. It was while I was standing there that I heard the fisherman's voice.

"He was looking at me curiously. 'You thought you saw bloodstains here, eh, lady?'

"I nodded.

" 'That is very curious, that is very curious. We have got a superstition here, lady. If anyone sees those bloodstains—'

"He paused.

" 'Well?' I said.

"He went on in his soft voice, Cornish in intonation, but unconsciously smooth and well-bred in its pronunciation, and completely free from Cornish turns of speech.

"'They do say, lady, that if anyone sees those blood-stains, there will be a death within twenty-four hours.'

"Creepy! It gave me a nasty feeling all down my spine.

"He went on persuasively. 'There is a very interesting tablet in the church, lady, about a death—'

"'No, thanks,' I said decisively, and I turned sharply on my heel and walked up the street toward the cottage where I was lodging. Just as I got there I saw in the distance the woman called Carol coming along the cliff path. She was hurrying. Against the grey of the rocks she looked like some poisonous scarlet flower. Her hat was the colour of blood. . . .

"I shook myself. Really, I had blood on the brain.

"Later I heard the sound of her car. I wondered whether she, too, was going to Penrithar, but she took the road to the left in the opposite direction. I watched the car crawl up the hill and disappear, and I breathed somehow more easily. Rathole seemed its quiet sleepy self once more."

"If that is all," said Raymond West as Joyce came to a stop, "I will give my verdict at once. Indigestion, spots before the eyes after meals."

"It isn't all," said Joyce. "You have got to hear the sequel. I read it in the paper two days later, under the heading of 'Sea Bathing Fatality.' It told how Mrs. Dacre, the wife of Captain Denis Dacre, was unfortunately drowned at Landeer Cove, just a little farther along the coast. She and her husband were staying at the time at the hotel there and had declared their intention of bathing, but a cold wind sprang up. Captain Dacre had declared it was too cold, so he and some other people in the hotel had gone off to the golf links near by. Mrs. Dacre, however, had said it was not too cold for her and she went off alone down to the cove. As she didn't return, her husband became alarmed and in company with his friends went down to the beach. They found her clothes lying beside a rock but no trace of the unfortunate lady. Her body was not found until nearly a week later, when it was washed ashore at a point some distance down the coast. There was a bad blow on her head which had occurred before death, and the theory was that she must have dived into the sea and hit her head on a rock. As far as I could make out, her death would have occurred just twenty-four hours after the time I saw the bloodstains.

"I protest," said Sir Henry. "This is not a problem—this is a ghost story. Miss Lemprière is evidently a medium."

Mr. Petherick gave his usual cough.

"One point strikes me," he said, "that blow on the head. We must not, I think, exclude the possibility of foul play. But I do not see that we have any data to go upon. Miss Lemprière's hallucination, or vision, is interesting, certainly, but I do not see clearly the point on which she wishes us to pronounce."

"Indigestion and coincidence," said Raymond, "and anyway, you can't be sure that they were the same people. Besides, the curse, or whatever it was, would only apply to actual inhabitants of Rathole."

"I feel," said Sir Henry, "that the sinister seafaring man has something to do with this tale. But I agree with Mr. Petherick, Miss Lemprière has given us very little data."

Joyce turned to Dr. Pender, who smilingly shook his head.

"It is a most interesting story," he said, "but I am afraid I agree with Sir Henry and Mr. Petherick that there is very little data to go upon."

Joyce then looked curiously at Miss Marple, who smiled back at her.

"I too think you are just a little unfair, Joyce dear," she said. "Of course, it is different for me. I mean, we, being women, appreciate the point about clothes. I don't think it is a fair problem to put to a man. It must have meant a lot of rapid changing. What a wicked woman! And a still more wicked man."

Joyce stared at her.

"Aunt Jane," she said. "Miss Marple, I mean, I believe —I do really believe you know the truth."

"Well, dear," said Miss Marple, "it is much easier for me sitting here quietly than it was for you—and being an artist, you are so susceptible to atmosphere, aren't you? Sitting here with one's knitting, one just sees the facts. Bloodstains dropped on the pavement from the bathing dress hanging above, and being a red bathing dress, of course, the criminals themselves did not realize it was bloodstained. Poor thing, poor young thing!"

"Excuse me, Miss Marple," said Sir Henry, "but do you know that I am entirely in the dark still. You and Miss Lemprière seem to know what you are talking about, but we mere men are still in utter darkness."

"I will tell you the end of the story now," said Joyce. "It was a year later. I was at a little east-coast seaside resort, and I was sketching, when suddenly I had that queer feeling one has of something having happened before. There were two people, a man and a woman, on the pavement in front of me, and they were greeting a third person, a woman dressed in a scarlet poinsettia chintz dress. 'Carol, by all that is wonderful! Fancy meeting you after all these years. You don't know my wife? Joan, this is an old friend of mine, Miss Harding.'

"I recognized the man at once. It was the same Denis I had seen in Rathole. The wife was different—that is, she was a Joan instead of a Margery; but she was the same type, young and rather dowdy and very inconspicuous. I thought for a minute I was going mad. They began to talk of going bathing. I will tell you what I did. I marched straight then and there to the police station. I thought they would probably think I was off my head, but I didn't care. And, as it happened, everything was quite all right. There was a man from Scotland Yard there, and he had come down just about this very thing. It seems—oh, it's horrible to talk about—that the police had got suspicious of Denis Dacre. That wasn't his real name—he took different names on different occasions. He got to know girls, usually quiet, inconspicuous girls without many relatives or friends; he married them and insured their lives for large sums, and then—oh, it's horrible! The woman called Carol was his real wife, and they always carried out the same plan. That is really how they came to catch him. The insurance companies became suspicious. He would come to some quiet seaside place with his new wife. Then the other woman would turn up and they would all go bathing together. Then the wife would be murdered and Carol would put on her clothes and go back in the boat with him. Then they would leave the place, wherever it was, after inquiring for the supposed Carol, and when they got outside the village

Carol would hastily change back into her own flamboyant clothes and her vivid make-up and would go back there and drive off in her own car. They would find out which way the current was flowing and the supposed death would take place at the next bathing place along the coast that way. Carol would play the part of the wife and would go down to some lonely beach and would leave the wife's clothes there by a rock and depart in her flowery chintz dress to wait quietly until her husband could rejoin her.

"I suppose when they killed poor Margery some of the blood must have spurted over Carol's bathing suit, and being a red one, they didn't notice it, as Miss Marple says. But when they hung it over the balcony it dripped. Ugh!" She gave a shiver. "I can see it still."

"Of course," said Sir Henry, "I remember very well now. Davis was the man's real name. It had quite slipped my memory that one of his many aliases was Dacre. They were an extraordinarily cunning pair. It always seemed so amazing to me that no one spotted the change of identity. I suppose, as Miss Marple says, clothes are more easily identified than faces; but it was a very clever scheme, for although we suspected Davis, it was not easy to bring the crime home to him as he always seemed to have an unimpeachable alibi."

"Aunt Jane," said Raymond, looking at her curiously, "how do you do it? You have lived such a peaceful life and yet nothing seems to surprise you."

"I always find one thing very like another in this world," said Miss Marple. "There was Mrs. Green, you know. She buried five children—and every one of them insured. Well, naturally, one began to get suspicious."

She shook her head.

"There is a great deal of wickedness in village life. I hope you dear young people will never realize how very wicked the world is."

THE HERB OF DEATH

"Now then Mrs. B.," said Sir Henry Clithering encouragingly.

Mrs. Bantry, his hostess, looked at him in cold reproof.

"I've told you before that I will not be called Mrs. B. It's not dignified."

"Scheherazade, then."

"And even less am I Sche— What's her name? I never can tell a story properly; ask Arthur if you don't believe me."

"You're quite good at the facts, Dolly," said Colonel Bantry, "but poor at the embroidery."

"That's just it," said Mrs. Bantry. She flapped the bulb catalogue she was holding on the table in front of her. "I've been listening to you all and I don't know how you do it. 'He said, she said, you wondered, they thought, everyone implied'—well, I just couldn't, and here it is! And besides, I don't know anything to tell a story about."

"We can't believe that, Mrs. Bantry," said Dr. Lloyd. He shook his grey head in mocking disbelief.

Old Miss Marple said in her gentle voice, "Surely, dear—"

Mrs. Bantry continued obstinately to shake her head.

"You don't know how banal my life is. What with the servants and the difficulties of getting scullery maids, and just going to town for clothes, and dentists, and Ascot, which Arthur hates, and then the garden—"

"Ah!" said Dr. Lloyd. "The garden. We all know where your heart lies, Mrs. Bantry."

"It must be nice to have a garden," said Jane Helier, the beautiful young actress. "That is, if you hadn't got to dig or to get your hands messed up. I'm ever so fond of flowers."

"The garden," said Sir Henry. "Can't we take that as a starting point? Come, Mrs. B. The poisoned bulb, the deadly daffodils, the herb of death!"

"Now it's odd your saying that," said Mrs. Bantry. "You've just reminded me. Arthur, do you remember that business at Clodderham Court? You know, old Sir Ambrose Bercy. Do you remember what a courtly charming old man we thought him?"

"Why, of course. Yes, that was a strange business. Go ahead, Dolly."

"You'd better tell it, dear."

"Nonsense. Go ahead. Must paddle your own canoe. I did my bit just now."

Mrs. Bantry drew a deep breath. She clasped her hands and her face registered complete mental anguish. She spoke rapidly and fluently.

"Well, there's really not much to tell. The Herb of Death —that's what put it into my head, though in my own mind I call it sage and onions."

"Sage and onions?" asked Dr. Lloyd.

Mrs. Bantry nodded.

"That was how it happened, you see," she explained. "We were staying, Arthur and I, with Sir Ambrose Bercy at Clodderham Court, and one day, by mistake (though very stupidly, I've always thought), a lot of foxglove leaves were picked with the sage. The ducks for dinner that night were stuffed with it and everyone was very ill, and one poor girl—Sir Ambrose's ward—died of it."

She stopped.

"Dear, dear," said Miss Marple, "how very tragic."

"Wasn't it?"

"Well," said Sir Henry, "what next?"

"There isn't any next," said Mrs. Bantry. "That's all."

Everyone gasped. Though warned beforehand, they had not expected quite such brevity as this.

"But, my dear lady," remonstrated Sir Henry, "it can't be all. What you have related is a tragic occurrence but not in any sense of the word a problem."

"Well, of course there's some more," said Mrs. Bantry. "But if I were to tell you, you'd know what it was."

She looked defiantly round the assembly and said plaintively:

"I told you I couldn't dress things up and make it sound properly like a story ought to do."

"Ah ha!" said Sir Henry. He sat up in his chair and adjusted an eyeglass. "Really, you know, Scheherazade, this is most refreshing. Our ingenuity is challenged. I'm not so sure you haven't done it on purpose—to stimulate our curiosity. A few brisk rounds of 'Twenty Questions' is indicated, I think. Miss Marple, will you begin?"

"I'd like to know something about the cook," said Miss Marple. "She must have been a very stupid woman, or else very inexperienced."

"She was just very stupid," said Mrs. Bantry. "She cried a great deal afterward and said the leaves had been picked and brought into her as sage, and how was she to know?"

"Not one who thought for herself," said Miss Marple. "Probably an elderly woman and, I daresay, a very good cook?"

"Oh, excellent," said Mrs. Bantry.

"Your turn, Miss Helier," said Sir Henry.

"Oh! You mean—to ask a question?" There was a pause while Jane pondered. Finally she said helplessly, "Really— I don't know what to ask."

Her beautiful eyes looked appealingly at Sir Henry.

"Why not dramatis personae, Miss Helier?" he suggested, smiling.

Jane still looked puzzled.

"Characters in order of their appearance," said Sir Henry gently.

"Oh, yes," said Jane. "That's a good idea."

Mrs. Bantry began briskly to tick people off on her fingers.

"Sir Ambrose—Sylvia Keene (that's the girl who died) —a friend of hers who was staying there, Maud Wye, one of those dark ugly girls who manage to make an effect somehow—I never know how they do it. Then there was a Mr. Curle who had come down to discuss books with Sir Ambrose—you know, rare books—queer old things in Latin—all musty parchment. There was Jerry Lorimer—he was a kind of next-door neighbour. His place, Fairlies, joined Sir Ambrose's estate. And there was Mrs. Carpenter, one of those middle-aged pussies who always seem to manage to dig themselves in comfortably somewhere. She was by way of being *dame de compagnie* to Sylvia, I suppose."

"If it is my turn," said Sir Henry, "and I suppose it is, as I'm sitting next to Miss Helier, I want a good deal. I want a short verbal portrait, please, Mrs. Bantry, of all the foregoing."

"Oh!" Mrs. Bantry hesitated.

"Sir Ambrose now," continued Sir Henry. "Start with him. What was he like?"

"Oh, he was a very distinguished-looking old man—and not so very old really—not more than sixty, I suppose. But he was very delicate—he had a weak heart, could never go upstairs—had had to have a lift put in, and so that made him seem older than he was. Very charming manners—courtly—that's the word that describes him best. You never saw him ruffled or upset. He had beautiful white hair and a particularly charming voice."

"Good," said Sir Henry. "I see Sir Ambrose. Now the girl Sylvia—what did you say her name was?"

"Sylvia Keene. She was pretty—really very pretty. Fairhaired, you know, and a lovely skin. Not, perhaps, very clever. In fact, rather stupid."

"Oh, come, Dolly," protested her husband.

"Arthur, of course, wouldn't think so," said Mrs. Bantry dryly. "But she was stupid—she really never said anything worth listening to."

"One of the most graceful creatures I ever saw," said Colonel Bantry warmly. "See her playing tennis—charming, simply charming. And she was full of fun—most amusing little thing. And such a pretty way with her. I bet the young fellows all thought so."

"That's just where you're wrong," said Mrs. Bantry. "Youth, as such, has no charms for young men nowadays. It's only old duffers like you, Arthur, who sit maundering on about young girls."

"Being young's no good," said Jane. "You've got to have S.A."

"What," said Miss Marple, "is S.A.?"

"Sex appeal," said Jane.

"Ah yes," said Miss Marple. "What in my day they used to call 'having the come hither in your eye.' "

"Not a bad description," said Sir Henry. "The *dame de compagnie* you described, I think, as a pussy, Mrs. Bantry?"

"I didn't mean a cat you know," said Mrs. Bantry. "It's quite different. Just a big soft white purry person. Always very sweet. That's what Adelaide Carpenter was like."

"What sort of aged woman?"

"Oh! I should say fortyish. She'd been there some time —ever since Sylvia was eleven, I believe. A very tactful person. One of those widows left in unfortunate circumstances, with plenty of aristocratic relations, but no ready cash. I didn't like her myself—but then I never do like people with very white long hands. And I don't like pussies."

"Mr. Curle?"

"Oh, one of those elderly stooping men. There are so many of them about, you'd hardly know one from the other. He showed enthusiasm when talking about his musty books, but not at any other time. I don't think Sir Ambrose knew him very well."

"And Jerry next door?"

"A really charming boy. He was engaged to Sylvia. That's what made it so sad."

"Now I wonder—" began Miss Marple, and then stopped.

"What?"

"Nothing, dear."

Sir Henry looked at the old lady curiously. Then he said thoughtfully:

"So this young couple were engaged. Had they been engaged long?"

"About a year. Sir Ambrose had opposed the engagement on the plea that Sylvia was too young. But after a year's engagement he had given in and the marriage was to have taken place quite soon."

"Ah! Had the young lady any property?"

"Next to nothing—a bare hundred or two a year."

"No rat in that hole, Clithering," said Colonel Bantry, and laughed.

"It's the doctor's turn to ask a question," said Sir Henry. "I stand down."

"My curiosity is mainly professional," said Dr. Lloyd. "I

should like to know what medical evidence was given at the inquest—that is, if our hostess remembers, or, indeed, if she knows."

"I know roughly," said Mrs. Bantry. "It was poisoning by digitalin—is that right?"

Dr. Lloyd nodded.

"The active principle of the foxglove—digitalis—acts on the heart. Indeed, it is a very valuable drug in some forms of heart trouble. A very curious case altogether. I would never have believed that eating a preparation of foxglove leaves could possibly result fatally. These ideas of eating poisonous leaves and berries are very much exaggerated. Very few people realize that the vital principle, or alkaloid, has to be extracted with much care and preparation."

"Mrs. MacArthur sent some special bulbs round to Mrs. Toomie the other day," said Miss Marple. "And Mrs. Toomie's cook mistook them for onions, and all the Toomies were very ill indeed."

"But they didn't die of it," said Dr. Lloyd.

"No, they didn't die of it," admitted Miss Marple.

"A girl I knew died of ptomaine poisoning," said Jane Helier.

"We must get on with investigating the crime," said Sir Henry.

"Crime?" said Jane, startled. "I thought it was an accident."

"If it were an accident," said Sir Henry gently, "I do not think Mrs. Bantry would have told us this story. No, as I read it, this was an accident only in appearance—behind it is something more sinister. I remember a case—various guests in a house party were chatting after dinner. The walls were adorned with all kinds of old-fashioned weapons. Entirely as a joke, one of the party seized an ancient horse pistol and pointed it at another man, pretending to fire it. The pistol was loaded and went off, killing the man. We had to ascertain in that case, first who had secretly prepared and loaded that pistol, and secondly, who had so led and directed the conversation that that final bit of horseplay resulted—for the man who had fired the pistol was entirely innocent!

"It seems to me we have much the same problem here. Those digitalin leaves were deliberately mixed with the sage, knowing what the result would be. Since we exonerate the cook—we do exonerate the cook, don't we?—the question arises: Who picked the leaves and delivered them to the kitchen?"

"That's easily answered," said Mrs. Bantry. "At least the last part of it is. It was Sylvia herself who took the leaves to the kitchen. It was part of her daily job to gather things like salad or herbs, bunches of young carrots—all the sort of things that gardeners never pick right. They hate giving you anything young and tender—they wait for them to be fine specimens. Sylvia and Mrs. Carpenter used to see to a lot of these things themselves. And there was foxglove actually growing all among the sage in one corner, so the mistake was quite natural."

"But did Sylvia actually pick them herself?"

"That nobody ever knew. It was assumed so."

"Assumptions," said Sir Henry, "are dangerous things."

"But I do know that Mrs. Carpenter didn't pick them," said Mrs. Bantry. "Because, as it happened, she was walking with me on the terrace that morning. We went out there after breakfast. It was unusually nice and warm for early spring. Sylvia went alone down into the garden, but later I saw her walking arm in arm with Maud Wye."

"So they were great friends, were they?" asked Miss Marple.

"Yes," said Mrs. Bantry. She seemed as though about to say something but did not do so.

"Had she been staying there long?" asked Miss Marple.

"About a fortnight," said Mrs. Bantry.

There was a note of trouble in her voice.

"You didn't like Miss Wye?" suggested Sir Henry.

"I did. That's just it. I did."

The trouble in her voice had grown to distress.

"You're keeping something back, Mrs. Bantry," said Sir Henry accusingly.

"I wondered just now," said Miss Marple, "but I didn't like to go on."

"When did you wonder?"

"When you said that the young people were engaged. You said that that was what made it so sad. But, if you know what I mean, your voice didn't sound right when you said it—not convincing, you know."

"What a dreadful person you are," said Mrs. Bantry. "You always seem to know. Yes, I was thinking of something. But I don't really know whether I ought to say it or not."

"You must say it," said Sir Henry. "Whatever your scruples, it mustn't be kept back."

"Well, it was just this," said Mrs. Bantry. "One evening —in fact the very evening before the tragedy—I happened to go out on the terrace before dinner. The window in the drawing room was open. And as it chanced I saw Jerry Lorimer and Maud Wye. He was—well—kissing her. Of course I didn't know whether it was just a sort of chance affair, or whether—well, I mean, one can't tell. I knew Sir Ambrose never had really liked Jerry Lorimer—so perhaps he knew he was that kind of young man. But one thing I am sure of: that girl, Maud Wye, was really fond of him. You'd only to see her looking at him when she was off guard. And I think, too, they were really better suited than he and Sylvia were."

"I am going to ask a question quickly, before Miss Marple can," said Sir Henry. "I want to know whether, after the tragedy, Jerry Lorimer married Maud Wye?"

"Yes," said Mrs. Bantry. "He did. Six months afterward."

"Oh! Scheherazade, Scheherazade," said Sir Henry. "To think of the way you told us this story at first! Bare bones indeed—and to think of the amount of flesh we're finding on them now."

"Don't speak so ghoulishly," said Mrs. Bantry. "And don't use the word flesh. Vegetarians always do. They say, 'I never eat flesh,' in a way that puts you right off your nice little beefsteak. Mr. Curle was a vegetarian. He used to eat some peculiar stuff that looked like bran for breakfast. Those elderly stooping men with beards are often faddy. They have patent kinds of underwear too."

"What on earth, Dolly," said her husband, "do you know about Mr. Curle's underwear?"

"Nothing," said Mrs. Bantry with dignity. "I was just making a guess."

"I'll amend my former statement," said Sir Henry. "I'll say instead that the dramatis personae in your problem are very interesting. I'm beginning to see them all—eh, Miss Marple?"

"Human nature is always interesting, Sir Henry. And it's curious to see how certain types always tend to act in exactly the same way."

"Two women and a man," said Sir Henry. "The old eternal human triangle. Is that the base of our problem here? I rather fancy it is."

Dr. Lloyd cleared his throat.

"I've been thinking," he said rather diffidently. "Do you say, Mrs. Bantry, that you yourself were ill?"

"Was I not! So was Arthur! So was everyone!"

"That's just it—everyone," said the doctor. "You see what I mean? I'm saying that whoever planned this thing went about it very curiously, either with a blind belief in chance, or else with an absolutely reckless disregard for human life. I can hardly believe there is a man capable of deliberately poisoning eight people with the object of removing one among them."

"I see your point," said Sir Henry thoughtfully. "I confess I ought to have thought of that."

"And mightn't he have poisoned himself too?" asked Jane.

"Was anyone absent from dinner that night?" asked Miss Marple.

Mrs. Bantry shook her head.

"Everyone was there."

"Except Mr. Lorimer, I suppose, my dear. He wasn't staying in the house, was he?"

"No, but he was dining there that evening," said Mrs. Bantry.

"Oh!" said Miss Marple in a changed voice. "That makes all the difference in the world."

She frowned vexedly to herself.

"I've been very stupid," she murmured. "Very stupid indeed."

"I confess your point worries me, Lloyd," said Sir Henry. "How ensure that the girl, and the girl only, should get a fatal dose?"

"You can't," said the doctor. "That brings me to the point I'm going to make. Supposing the girl was not the intended victim, after all?"

"What?"

"In all cases of food poisoning the result is very uncertain. Several people share a dish. What happens? One or two are slightly ill; two more, say, are seriously indisposed; one dies. That's the way of it—there's no certainty anywhere. But there are cases where another factor might enter in. Digitalin is a drug that acts directly on the heart—as I've told you, it's prescribed in certain cases. Now, there was one person in that house who suffered from a heart complaint. Suppose he was the victim selected? What would not be fatal to the rest would be fatal to him—or so the murderer might reasonably suppose. That the thing turned out differently is only proof of what I was saying just now—the uncertainty and unreliability of the effect of drugs on human beings."

"Sir Ambrose," said Sir Henry, "you think he was the person aimed at? Yes, yes—and the girl's death was a mistake."

"Who got his money after he was dead?" asked Jane.

"A very sound question, Miss Helier. One of the first we always ask in my late profession," said Sir Henry.

"Sir Ambrose had a son," said Mrs. Bantry slowly. "He had quarrelled with him many years previously. The boy was wild, I believe. Still, it was not in Sir Ambrose's power to disinherit him—Clodderham Court was entailed. Martin Bercy succeeded to the title and estate. There was, however, a good deal of other property that Sir Ambrose could leave as he chose, and that he left to his ward Sylvia. I know this because Sir Ambrose died less than a year after the events I am telling you of, and he had not troubled to make a new will after Sylvia's death. I think the money went to the Crown—or perhaps it was to his son as next of kin—I don't really remember."

"So it was only to the interest of a son who wasn't there and the girl who died herself to make away with him," said Sir Henry thoughtfully. "That doesn't seem very promising."

"Didn't the other woman get anything?" asked Jane. "The one Mrs. Bantry calls the Pussy woman."

"She wasn't mentioned in the will," said Mrs. Bantry.

"Miss Marple, you're not listening," said Sir Henry. "You're somewhere far away."

"I was thinking of old Mr. Badger, the chemist," said Miss Marple. "He had a very young housekeeper—young enough to be not only his daughter but his granddaughter. Not a word to anyone, and his family, a lot of nephews and nieces, full of expectations. And when he died, would you believe it, he'd been secretly married to her for two years? Of course, Mr. Badger was a chemist, and a very rude, common old man as well, and Sir Ambrose Bercy was a very courtly gentleman, so Mrs. Bantry says, but for all that human nature is much the same everywhere."

There was a pause. Sir Henry looked very hard at Miss Marple who looked back at him with gentle quizzical blue eyes. Jane Helier broke the silence.

"Was this Mrs. Carpenter good-looking?" she asked.

"Yes, in a very quiet way. Nothing startling."

"She had a very sympathetic voice," said Colonel Bantry.

"Purring—that's what I call it," said Mrs. Bantry. "Purring!"

"You'll be called a cat yourself one of these days, Dolly."

"I like being a cat in my home circle," said Mrs. Bantry. "I don't much like women anyway, and you know it. I like men and flowers."

"Excellent taste," said Sir Henry. "Especially in putting men first."

"That was tact," said Mrs. Bantry. "Well, now, what about my little problem? I've been quite fair, I think. Arthur, don't you think I've been fair?"

"Yes, my dear. I don't think there'll be any inquiry into the running by the stewards of the Jockey Club."

"First boy," said Mrs. Bantry, pointing a finger at Sir Henry.

"I'm going to be long-winded. Because, you see, I haven't really got any feeling of certainty about the matter. First, Sir Ambrose. Well, he wouldn't take such an original method of committing suicide—and on the other hand, he certainly had nothing to gain by the death of his ward. Exit Sir Ambrose. Mr. Curle. No motive for death of girl. If Sir Ambrose was intended victim, he might possibly have purloined a rare manuscript or two that no one else would miss. Very thin, and most unlikely. So I think that, in spite of Mrs. Bantry's suspicions, Mr. Curle is cleared. Miss Wye. Motive for death of Sir Ambrose—none. Motive for death of Sylvia pretty strong. She wanted Sylvia's young man, and wanted him rather badly—from Mrs. Bantry's account. She was with Sylvia that morning in the garden so had opportunity to pick leaves. No, we can't dismiss Miss Wye so easily. Young Lorimer. He's got a motive in either case. If he gets rid of his sweetheart, he can marry the other girl. Still it seems a bit drastic to kill her—what's a broken engagement these days? If Sir Ambrose dies, he will marry a rich girl instead of a poor one. That might be important or not—depends on his financial position. If I find that his estate was heavily mortgaged and that Mrs. Bantry has deliberately withheld that fact from us, I shall claim a foul. Now Mrs. Carpenter. You know, I have suspicions of Mrs. Carpenter. Those white hands, for one thing, and her excellent alibi at the time the herbs were picked—I always distrust alibis. And I've got another reason for suspecting her which I shall keep to myself. Still, on the whole, if I've got to plump, I shall plump for Miss Maud Wye, because there's more evidence against her than anyone else."

"Next boy," said Mrs. Bantry, and pointed at Dr. Lloyd.

"I think you're wrong, Clithering, in sticking to the theory that the girl's death was meant. I am convinced that the murderer intended to do away with Sir Ambrose. I don't think that young Lorimer had the necessary knowledge. I am inclined to believe that Mrs. Carpenter was the guilty party. She had been a long time with the family, knew all about the state of Sir Ambrose's health, and could easily arrange for this girl Sylvia (who, you said yourself, was rather stupid) to pick the right leaves. Motive, I confess, I don't see; but I hazard the guess that Sir Ambrose had at one time made a will in which she was mentioned. That's the best I can do."

Mrs. Bantry's pointing finger went on to Jane Helier.

"I don't know what to say," said Jane, "except this: Why shouldn't the girl herself have done it? She took the leaves into the kitchen after all. And you say Sir Ambrose had been sticking out against her marriage. If he died, she'd get the money and be able to marry at once. She'd know just as much about Sir Ambrose's health as Mrs. Carpenter would."

Mrs. Bantry's finger came slowly round to Miss Marple. "Now then, school marm," she said.

"Sir Henry has put it all very clearly—very clearly indeed," said Miss Marple. "And Dr. Lloyd was so right in what he said. Between them they seem to have made things so very clear. Only I don't think Dr. Lloyd quite realized one aspect of what he said. You see, not being Sir Ambrose's medical adviser, he couldn't know just what kind of heart trouble Sir Ambrose had, could he?"

"I don't quite see what you mean, Miss Marple," said Dr. Lloyd.

"You're assuming—aren't you?—that Sir Ambrose had the kind of heart that digitalin would affect adversely? But there's nothing to prove that that's so. It might be just the other way about."

"The other way about?"

"Yes, you did say that it was often prescribed for heart trouble?"

"Even then, Miss Marple, I don't see what that leads to?"

"Well, it would mean that he would have digitalin in his possession quite naturally—without having to account for it. What I am trying to say (I always express myself so badly) is this: Supposing you wanted to poison anyone with a fatal dose of digitalin. Wouldn't the simplest and easiest way be to arrange for everyone to be poisoned—actually by digitalin leaves? It wouldn't be fatal in anyone else's case, of course, but no one would be surprised at one victim because, as Dr. Lloyd said, these things are so uncertain. No one would be likely to ask whether the girl had actually had a fatal dose of infusion of digitalis or something of that kind. He might have put it in a cocktail or in her coffee or even made her drink it quite simply as a tonic."

"You mean Sir Ambrose poisoned his ward, the charming girl whom he loved?"

"That's just it," said Miss Marple. "Like Mr. Badger and his young housekeeper. Don't tell me it's absurd for a man of sixty to fall in love with a girl of twenty. It happens every day—and I daresay with an old autocrat like Sir Ambrose, it might take him queerly. These things become a madness sometimes. He couldn't bear the thought of her getting married—did his best to oppose it—and failed. His mad jealousy became so great that he preferred killing her to letting her go to young Lorimer. He must have thought of it some time beforehand, because that foxglove seed would have to be sown among the sage. He'd pick it himself when the time came and send her into the kitchen with it. It's horrible to think of, but I suppose we must take as merciful a view of it as we can. Gentlemen of that age are sometimes very peculiar indeed where young girls are concerned. Our last organist—but there, I mustn't talk scandal."

"Mrs. Bantry," said Sir Henry, "is this so?"

Mrs. Bantry nodded.

"Yes. I'd no idea of it—never dreamed of the thing being anything but an accident. Then, after Sir Ambrose's death, I got a letter. He had left directions to send it to me. He told me the truth in it. I don't know why—but he and I always got on very well together."

In the momentary silence she seemed to feel an unspoken criticism and went on hastily:

"You think I'm betraying a confidence—but that isn't so. I've changed all the names. He wasn't really called Sir Ambrose Bercy. Didn't you see how Arthur stared stupidly when I said that name to him? He didn't understand at first. I've changed everything. It's like they say in magazines and in the beginning of books: 'All the characters in this story are purely fictitious.' You'll never know who they really are."